THE PERFECT POSSESSION

RANDOLPH CASEY HORROR THRILLERS
BOOK 2

ROCKWELL SCOTT

THE PERFECT POSSESSION

PROLOGUE

Fear was a foreign thing to Hoby.

He'd been big his whole life, taller and more built than most other people he knew. There was never any reason for him to be afraid of anything.

So why now?

It was nearing midnight, and Hoby strode through the dark halls of the old mansion, doing his final round before he could retire for the evening.

The job that Hoby had been hired for was the same as all his previous jobs. He was needed for only one thing—his size, strength, and protection.

The old man who owned the mansion—Hoby's employer—was paying Hoby handsomely to be a private bodyguard, while also adhering to a few odd requests.

The first was that Hoby had to live inside the mansion.

Second, the lights were to be kept off inside, even at night, forcing Hoby to use a head torch just to see where he was going.

But more important than anything else, the employer was not to be disturbed when he was inside his study.

The evening patrol was all that Hoby's employer required before Hoby could take the rest of the night off. Normally, that would be easy work, but making the rounds of the run-down mansion always made Hoby feel uneasy.

He didn't like the way his heavy footsteps echoed off the grey, empty walls, which made it sound like he was always being followed.

There were random spots in certain rooms that were colder than others for no reason that Hoby could discern.

Even more disconcerting were the times Hoby swore he'd heard voices. He would spring into action and follow the sound to its source, only to find no one. Those instances made him wonder if his imagination was getting the better of him.

In those moments, Hoby would stiffen up and remind himself that he was strong and powerful.

As Hoby treaded through the quiet halls, he couldn't help but wonder why his employer felt he needed protection in the first place.

The house was empty, mostly devoid of furniture and appliances. Even if someone were to break in, there was nothing of value to steal. That, and the old man was loved around town, so it was hard to imagine that he had a single enemy.

But that night, when Hoby approached the old man's study, he found the door slightly ajar, which was unusual. He paused, feeling his curiosity bubble up. His employer had made it clear that he was to *never* be disturbed while he was inside his study.

Hoby decided he would not be doing his due diligence if he didn't at least check to make sure his employer was all right in there. Deep down, though, he knew he was more interested in finding out what the old man was hiding.

He crept toward the open door, switching off his head torch so as not to be noticed. The study was illuminated only by the light of the fire that the old man kept roaring in the hearth every night.

Hoby peeked into the room. The old man was bowing on his knees in front of the fire, speaking in tongues as he prayed to the flames.

Hoby listened for a long time, but none of the words were intelligible to his ear.

I'll leave him be, Hoby thought.

Hoby turned and stepped quietly away from the open door, but then he heard the old man finally say something that he could understand.

"The time has come."

When Hoby looked back into the study, the old man was still on his knees, but now his back was straight as he gazed into the fire.

"We have been waiting a long time for this," the old man said. "It is clear that you have ordained this moment. I will carry this out for you. I will serve you."

The fire swelled in the hearth, bursting and expanding as if someone had thrown gas on the flames.

Hoby leapt back from the door, startled from what he'd seen. The old man had not moved a muscle, unafraid of the sudden burst of fire.

It was like the fire had responded to the old man's promise to serve.

Hoby had seen enough. If he wanted to stay sane in the job, it was best to ignore what the old man did in the privacy of his own study.

Hoby tore himself away from the unusual sight and continued his patrol within the dark corridors of the mansion.

Still, the horrible tension within him remained—his body's way of telling him that something was very wrong.

"Any questions so far?"

Randolph Casey scanned the sparse collection of students. A quick head count gave him twenty-two, which was a decent turnout. The classroom they'd assigned him was still too big, which highlighted that his class was severely under attended.

"Good," he said, turning his remote to the screen and clicking the button. The slide changed to display a single word in a large font.

MIMICRY.

"Today, we'll talk about mimicry. Does anyone know what that means?"

The students stared at him, a few of them nodding.

"To pretend to be something," said Stacy Thompson. She was his constant front row fan. Rand knew she was gunning for a 4.0, and that was why she worked so diligently in his class, not necessarily because she was interested in the subject material. Not that she had to work hard. His tests were the easiest in the entire Religious Studies department.

"Exactly. Its meaning in context to what we're learning today, though, is that mimicry is a common weapon of evil spirits. They use it to gain our trust, confuse and frighten us, and even impersonate."

Rand clicked the remote again and changed the slide.

THE CANTON FAMILY

"I think it was…" Rand looked at the ceiling as he tried to calculate the time in his head, "… maybe four years ago? Yeah, four years ago I met the Cantons. They were a family of five, with three daughters. The mother came to me because they were experiencing strange occurrences in their house. It all began with the youngest child—as it always does." He clicked the remote and Laura's name appeared on the slide. "She was five years old, and at least once a week she would tell her mom she'd seen one of her sisters somewhere in the house when they were really at school. Maybe in the bathroom putting on makeup, or in the bedroom flipping through clothes in the closet. She claimed she'd even spoken to them, and they'd answered her back. But her mother, Frances Canton, told her it was not possible, because the girls were at school, or out visiting a friend. When Frances checked the bedroom or bathroom, there would be nobody there. At first Frances thought her daughter was just confused, or imagining things because she missed her sisters, but then the situation got weird."

Stacy Thompson shifted in her seat. A few of the other students exchanged nervous glances. Rand's past stories often frightened his class. There were, of course, the token skeptics who leaned back in their chairs, amused grins on their faces, waiting to hear whatever nonsense he came up with next.

"The middle child, Ashley, was thirteen at the time, and told her parents one day that she had spotted her mother in the garden. When Frances came back an hour later with shopping bags, Ashley was confused. Frances told her daughter that she had been at the mall, and had not been in the garden all day. Ashley burst into hysterics and swore what she saw was real.

"This all came to a head when Frances became the target. She was a stay-at-home mom, and would spend a lot of time alone in the house. Several times, she heard her husband saying her name, or her daughter Laura calling out for her in the back of the house, or one of the bedrooms, clear as could be. It was unmistakably their voice. She would rush to the room, wondering what they were doing home—especially since she herself had dropped her daughters off at school, or watched her husband drive away to work. She would find no one in the house."

Stacy Thompson cringed, as if watching an unnerving scene in a horror movie.

"That was when she came to me. Sure enough, my team and I sensed a presence in her home, and we were able to remove it before too much damage was done. Usually, people let this supernatural activity go on for too long because they don't believe in it, and then it gets too strong. But Frances was a believer, and luckily she got in touch with me in time."

Stacy Thompson raised her hand and didn't wait to be called on before she said, "What's the point of the spirit mimicking people?"

"To cause confusion and to frighten. Put yourself and your family in the Cantons' shoes. If this kind of activity went on for a long time, you'd think you were crazy, right?" Rand let the question linger and got a few nods in return. "Imagine the arguments it could cause. Your brother or sister insisting you were home, yet you weren't. Or spotting your father in the garage when he was supposed to be out of town. You see someone you know appear in places that don't logically make any sense."

"And it's a spirit pretending to be these people?" Stacy asked.

"Precisely. It causes division in the family by making them argue and doubt each other. Then it's easier for the spirit to take over and destroy them."

Stacy shivered. His skeptics in the back row didn't seem impressed, and likely thought there was no such thing as the Canton family.

But Rand remembered them well. Laura, the youngest, had drawn him a picture after he cleansed their home, and he still kept it in a frame in his home office. That particular spirit had put up a tough fight.

Rand clicked his remote again to move to the next slide.

MIMICRY TO GAIN TRUST

"Not all demons mimic people to scare and divide. There's another tactic I've encountered, where they'll do it to gain your trust. In this instance, the demon will appear to someone and pretend to be a child or a teenager, and make up a tragic story about how they died. The person communicating with the spirit will often want to help the 'lonely ghost' or be his friend. At that point, the demon has gained trust. This happens when people play with spirit boards or do other kinds of séances or rituals to talk to spirits. How many of you in here have ever used a spirit board?" A few hands went up. The class knew well by then how their teacher felt about spirit boards. "I hope you cut that out. People go into it wanting to contact someone specific, like a relative that's passed. What they get is something completely different. And you have no idea who it is you're talking to on the other line."

Rand changed the slide to move on, but Stacy Thompson's hand went up again. "Wait. Do you have any stories of times you dealt with this?"

"Yes, of course," Rand said. "Recently, actually. It was…" He trailed off, flipped the remote around in his palm as he fidgeted, lost his train of thought for a moment. "Um. Yeah, it was a sick teenage girl in the hospital. She saw the ghost of her friend who had died a few months before of the same condition." He looked at the floor between Stacy's feet as he spoke. "But that ghost was not who he said he was. He was impersonating her friend to gain her trust, and it worked. And by the time I was called in to remove it, things had escalated very far."

He swallowed the lump in his throat that came from thinking about Georgia Collins and her case. He hadn't talked to her in a while, but his daughter Libby followed her on social media, and reported she was doing well.

"But you removed it, right?" Stacy asked, eyebrows going up.

"Yes," Rand said.

And when he looked up, someone else had joined his

class, sitting in the chair in the top-most corner of the stadium.

Shindael.

The demon's frame was thin with light blue skin that made him look frozen. His face was smooth, featureless, without a nose and ears, except for small, pure-black eyes.

Rand stared at him for a long time, his mouth going dry and his skin turning to ice.

Stacy Thompson even followed his gaze, but was confused. She saw no one there.

Rand clenched his eyes closed for a few seconds and opened them again.

Shindael was gone.

"Mr. Casey?" Stacy asked.

Rand snapped back to reality. "I think that'll be all for today. You can go."

No one moved. They all stared at him blankly, some of them exchanging nervous glances between each other.

"Go on!" Rand said, louder and snappier than he'd meant to. All his students jumped into motion at once, closing their notebooks, picking up their bags, and streaming out the door.

Rand leaned on the podium, and the remote dropped from his loose grip. A sudden fatigue had taken over him, leaving him winded and weak, as if he'd run a mile with the flu.

That was typical when in close proximity to Shindael. The demon had appeared to Rand many times in the last several weeks. He knew Shindael was making good on his promise to torment him.

Stacy Thompson stayed behind after everyone else left, concern on her face. "Are you okay?"

"Yeah. I'm fine." Although he knew he didn't sound convincing at all.

"It's just… this is the third time you've canceled class in three weeks."

"Really?"

"Yeah. You're normal at the beginning, then you start to look pale and sick. Then you kick us out."

"Nothing to worry about," Rand said. "Just a bit under the weather."

"For three weeks?"

Rand closed his laptop and gathered his books and shoved them into his bag. He slung it over his shoulder. "I'll be all right."

"Just making sure," Stacy said, like she saw right through him.

"I appreciate it," Rand said, walking away from her and up the stairs of the stadium classroom. "Have a good weekend, Stacy."

It wasn't like him to turn his back and run out on a student—or anyone—but he had to get out of that room. It felt tainted by Shindael's momentary presence, closing in on Rand, suffocating him.

2

R and found fresh air outside as he strolled through campus. It was Friday afternoon, and he blended in with the hundreds of students that moved in crowds all around him. A grey sky ahead threatened rain, so all the kids had a certain quickness in their steps that usually wasn't there on sunny days. The grounds were notorious for rapid flooding, even during the shortest of rainfalls.

Rand ran through a mental list of things in his office and decided he had all he needed for the weekend, so he could go straight to his car and beat the afternoon traffic. And save himself from getting caught in the rain.

Although so late in the week, the Student Union was a hive of activity. Tents, trailers, tables, and chairs had already been set up as the tailgaters prepared for tomorrow's home game. It didn't matter to these die-hard fans if the sky opened a torrential downpour on them. Nothing would cramp their football season.

There was a light chill in the air, the first hints of a

coming winter, a reprieve from the hot southern summer. Rand threw on his jacket—one so casual that it clashed with the slacks and the nice shirt he wore to work.

But the tailgaters weren't the only ones out in full force. Apparently, that day was also chosen by the campus's religious zealots that dropped in once a week.

There were about ten of them, and Rand slowed to read their picketing signs.

SALVATION FOR THE SAVED, HELL FOR THE SINNER!

GOD HATES SINNERS!

REPENT NOW! THE END TIMES ARE NEAR!

YOU ARE SINNER SCUM! JESUS IS THE ONLY WAY!

The words were painted in big black and red letters, decorated with what resembled fire and blood. These guys must've spent hours working on their signs and they still looked like bad art projects. Did they really have nothing better to do than come out on campus and yell at everyone?

A tattooed skateboarder zipped by Rand, nearly running over his toes. One picketer spotted him as he went past. "Your body is a temple, and you've desecrated your gift from God with all that trashy ink! Hell is the only thing you have coming!"

The skateboarder glided along as if he didn't hear and disappeared into the crowds.

A little girl, no more than five years old, walked up to Rand and meekly handed him a flyer. Saying nothing, she rejoined her father, whose sign read NO HOPE FOR GAYS AND FORNICATORS.

The flyer was black and had simple instructions for

him written in red text. It declared he was a sinner and bound for hell, and that Jesus was the only one that could save his filthy soul. Then there was a list of Bible verses, all from the book of Romans, that instructed him on what he could do to be saved.

The Romans Road, Rand thought to himself. A series of passages in Romans that laid out the path to salvation. He knew it well, and was surprised these guys recommended it. Usually, they preferred to beat people over the head with threats.

Rand crumpled the flyer in his hand and continued on. But he spotted a man sitting opposite the picketers in a simple folding chair. A second chair was across from him, as if he was waiting for someone to sit with him. In his hands, he held a small, white placard, and on it was a single word.

PRAYER?

Rand saw the zealots every week, but he'd never seen this guy before. Sometimes the more religious-minded students would engage the fire and brimstone guys, getting into loud and passionate debates that went nowhere because no one was changing their minds. But this man... it seemed he wanted to take a more Christ-like approach to combating the insanity.

It was then that Rand realized he'd been caught staring.

"Won't be long before the hellfire gets extinguished." Rand gestured toward the cloudy sky, which now had taken on shades of black. Thunder rolled in the distance.

"It won't stop these guys." The man smiled at him. "Why don't you have a seat?"

"Ah. Not in the market for any prayer at the moment, and I'd hate to take up a spot for someone who needs it."

"You're always in the market for prayer."

Rand figured he was the only person to give this guy any attention all day long. So he dropped his bag and lowered himself into the folding chair.

"Patrick Perryman." He extended his hand.

"Randolph Casey. Friends call me Rand." Rand squeezed Patrick's hand.

Patrick Perryman looked to be about his age. Although sitting, Rand could tell he was short, with sandy brown hair and small, wire-rimmed glasses. His jeans were faded and years old and not from any named brand, and he wore a tan jacket over his plain white t-shirt.

"Are you a teacher, Rand?" Patrick asked.

"Yes."

"Are you saved?"

"You don't like to waste time, do you?"

Patrick only shrugged and smiled. "I know what's important. My priorities are straight."

"Do you get much success out here? With these hooligans shouting and yelling?" Rand pointed his thumb over to the guys with signs.

"It's important that everyone knows our God is a God of love, not hate. Screaming to people that they're going to hell won't help anyone. We're not meant to scare folks into their faith, but demonstrate the love of Jesus to them."

"Right."

"Are you saved?" Patrick asked again.

"I would say so," Rand said.

"That doesn't sound like a confident answer. Maybe you are saved, but have drifted away from God."

Rand started to regret sitting down with Patrick Perryman. After the ordeal with Georgia Collins, and the lingering threat of Shindael, Rand had considered rededicating himself to God. But he still couldn't reconcile how a loving God allowed demons to prowl the earth, terrorizing the innocent and unsuspecting.

A single image of Georgia appeared in Rand's mind, possessed by the demon Karax, and the way those black eyes had stared at him.

Rand clenched his eyes shut and forced the memory away.

"Maybe you're angry at God for something," Patrick said, his smile faltering.

"Things are complicated in that area," Rand told him.

"I understand. My faith was weak my entire life. When I was in college, I didn't believe at all. I smoked dope and drank for three semesters and eventually dropped out. Never could keep a job. Had no direction at all."

"And now?"

"Now I've found my mission. To reach people for Christ."

"Does it pay?"

Patrick chuckled. "Money is of little consequence when we're talking about eternity. Listen, Rand. Maybe you haven't found the right church yet. Maybe you haven't discovered a place that gives you the proper connection you need to get all the way there in your heart."

"I was never a fan of church hopping," Rand said. "I always figured people who did that were looking to make themselves happy rather than have a legitimate religious experience."

"Wise man," Patrick said. "You know what you're talking about. I can tell you've dipped your toes in and out of faith. So for someone like you, I know what you need."

"Assuming I'm interested," Rand said. He wanted to keep a healthy distance from this man he'd just met.

But Rand had stumbled upon Patrick at the same time Rand was considering giving God a second chance. Was that some kind of miracle? Divine intervention? God's timing?

"Of course," Patrick said. "I won't force you to do anything. But I sense you want this on your own and were seeking something before you ever sat down."

Rand did his best to hide his surprised reaction to the correct pseudo-prediction.

Patrick reached into a plastic shopping bag by the side of his chair and pulled out a flyer. He passed it to Rand.

"More flyers," he said, taking it without looking at it. "Just like those guys."

To his right, a college girl walked by, and one of the sign holders caught sight of her short skirt.

"Respect yourself, whore!" he shouted at her. "Fornicating women will spend eternity in hell. Turn to God so he can clean your soul and save you from your life of sin."

The girl only put headphones in her ears and quickened her pace.

"You should already know this is different," Patrick said.

Rand looked at the flyer. It was a brochure for whatever church Patrick attended, although curiously enough, he couldn't find the name. Instead, the advert was all centered on a specific person.

"Pastor Deckard Arcan," Rand read out loud.

"Pastor D," Patrick said, a smile lighting up his face as if Rand had asked him about his father. "That man saved my soul. He put me on the right path and changed my life. Awakened in me a passion to reach people for the Lord who were lost like I was."

"I see."

Pastor Deckard Arcan invites you to his Sunday Service. All are welcome. Come worship and hear divinely inspired teachings and learn what God has in store for you.

Every Sunday at 10:00 AM. Located five miles down Highway 38 in Finnick.

"Join us for our service this weekend," Patrick said. "I think you'll like what you see."

"Finnick is two hours away from here," Rand said. He'd heard of the small town, but had never been.

"It's worth the drive. Trust me."

Rand didn't trust him that it would be worth the commute. But at least the guy felt he was doing something right. Rand stood and folded the flyer into his pocket alongside the one given to him by the little girl.

Patrick rose with him. "Although you didn't ask for prayer, I'll still pray for you. And I hope to see you this Sunday, Rand."

He extended his hand, and Rand took it. "Don't delay the service on my account. Take care, Patrick, and try to keep dry."

Overhead, the blackened clouds edged open and the first raindrops fell among the thunder.

3

Rand drove home through the heaviest downpour in recent memory. He parked in his driveway, which inclined just enough to dump the water into the street. The drains couldn't keep up with the huge amount of rain coming from overhead. Although he ran the short distance to his front door, he was still soaked by the time he made it inside.

His house was uncomfortably cold. He checked the thermostat to make sure he didn't leave the air conditioner running. He hadn't, so he figured it was his wet clothes.

Rand emptied his pockets on the kitchen table—wallet, keys, and the two flyers he'd collected, each suggesting radically different ways to reclaim his faith—and went straight to the bathroom for a shower.

Even after he'd finished, he lingered in the hot water, letting it wash over him for several minutes. He knew after he got dressed, his mind would wander again. Although his house was not large, it still felt that way when he was there alone. The place was always so quiet, and it was in that silence that memories came back to him. Georgia. Karax.

Shindael.

Sometimes he would even spot the bastard in the periphery of his vision. A shadow that peeked at him around corners, disappearing as soon as he looked. Making him feel watched and pursued.

He turned off the water and snatched the towel from the rack. He dried and pulled on a clean pair of underwear. That was when he heard a sound from the front of the house.

He froze and listened, his entire body tensing.

Footsteps. Something being picked up and put back down.

Who's in my house? he thought.

Rand opened the bathroom door, the icy temperature of the bedroom chilling his steamed skin. He crept down the hall, listening for any clue as to who was there.

He rounded the corner into his kitchen to find a figure walking straight toward him.

And leapt back and howled. So did Libby.

She fell backwards, hand on her heart. "Dad, what are you doing sneaking up on me?"

"What are you doing in my house?" he shouted, still numb from the scare they'd given each other.

"I can't come over? Fine, I'll leave."

"No, no. I meant I thought I was here by myself. When I heard you, it freaked me out."

Having Shindael on the mind so often kept Rand on edge.

"Doesn't mean you need to sneak up on me." Libby took a few breaths to steady herself.

"We scared each other, so now we're even."

"Whatever." Libby rolled her eyes. "Why do you never wear pants?"

"I was just in the shower."

"This is weird. Normal people wear pants most of the day."

"It's my house and I'll walk around naked if I want to. I paid for the place."

"In that case, I'll give back my key." Libby picked up one of the flyers from the kitchen table. "I saw this when I came in. Where did you get it?"

Rand walked over to the fridge and pulled a bottle of beer from the door. There were only four left, and he'd recently bought a crate. "Have you been drinking my beer?"

"No, Dad," Libby said. "You've just been drinking a lot lately."

He winced. That was true.

"I asked you a question. Where did you get this?"

Rand used the magnetic bottle opener on the refrigerator to pry off the cap. He took a long swig. "The religious fanatics were out on campus today."

"No, not that. *This*."

Both flyers were black and looked similar, and Rand realized she was talking about the one he'd gotten from Patrick. "There was another guy there. Not with the crazies. I sat down and chatted with him for a few minutes and he asked me to come to his church. Then he gave me that."

"You know Justin goes to this church, right?"

Rand took another sip of beer. Justin was Libby's boyfriend, and Rand had only met him a grand total of one time, briefly. He seemed like a nice enough kid, but Rand still wasn't that impressed. "Really?"

"Yeah. Like, every Sunday."

"I didn't take him for the religious type."

"You don't know anything about his type because you've never gotten to know him."

"You never bring him over."

"I don't bring him over because you'll give him a hard time."

"Then don't be mad at me for not knowing him. And you're wrong, by the way. I don't have to know him to know his type. Guys have *types* and I can peg them coming from a mile away."

Justin was a soft spoken, introverted and introspective musical guy. All girls fell for one of those at some point in their lives, and apparently it was Libby's turn. Rand was glad she was going through it now instead of later. She was getting it over with, like chicken pox.

"Whatever, Dad," she said. "So… are you going to go?"

Rand was taken aback by that. "Seriously?"

"Yeah."

"When have you ever known me to go to church?"

"Whenever you need it."

Rand knew what she meant, and she was right. After fighting head-to-head with a demonic entity, Rand almost always felt the need to recover somewhere holy.

Like what I'm going through now, he thought as he stared at the beer in his hands. *I went through a whole crate in less than a week.* He hadn't even noticed until then.

"Your last case with Georgia took a bigger toll on you than the others," Libby said.

"Yeah."

"Do you still see him?"

Shindael.

"Every day. And in the most random places."

Libby chewed her lip. Rand could see the worry on her face. He hated to put her through this. "Let's go to church this Sunday and see what it's all about," she said. "I'll come too, so I can get Justin off my back. He's been begging me to check it out, and I'd much rather do it if you were there."

Rand sighed and looked away as he considered it. It wouldn't hurt and it could only help. His only plans for Sunday were lying around and finishing the crate of beer if he didn't manage that on Saturday.

"Fine," he said. "But you realize it's a long drive, right? Down by Finnick."

"What's Finnick? Is that a town?"

"You've proved my point."

"It's a date then."

"Must be one hell of a church if your boyfriend will travel two hours there and back just to go."

"He says it's incredible." Libby had never been a church girl. She took after Rand and her mother.

"We'll see."

Then Libby said, "Now can you please put pants on?"

4

After a long and silent drive, Rand edged his Jeep onto the Interstate exit and followed the highway until he came to a crossroads marked by two signs.

Turning right would bring him to Finnick. Going straight would take him to Highway 38.

Highway 38 was paved for only a mile until it turned into a dirt road that was mostly mud. It had rained the entire weekend, and even now the skies were still grey. Rand had checked the weather before leaving, and the weatherman warned that there were more showers left to come.

Libby rode in the passenger seat wearing a black and blue dress she'd bought for fifteen dollars three years ago. She called it her "recycled dress" because she wore it whenever she needed to look presentable, but didn't feel like going all out. Rand had donned a navy suit, shirt unbuttoned at the collar.

Justin Tidwell was in the back, having spent the entire

drive staring out the window into the grey morning and saying nothing. His black hair was overgrown, shaggy, and dangling low into his eyes. Whenever he tossed his head to throw it out of his line of vision, it revealed a garden of zits on his forehead. He'd also pierced his ears, which Rand was dying to comment on, but knew it would only earn him a sharp punch from his daughter, who had grown quite strong in her mere sixteen years.

The zealots that came to campus would have threatened Justin with hell if they'd seen the way he'd desecrated his temple with the small hoops that dangled from his earlobes. That meant this church—and the pastor—were much more liberal and inviting.

When the muddy road turned into a copse of dense magnolias, Rand said, "Are you sure we're going the right way?" His Jeep's tires skidded, and he felt like he was off-roading through a forest.

"Yeah," Justin said, his voice cracking. "Keep going."

There were tire tracks through the mud as they went, so Justin must've known what he was talking about.

When the dense trees gave way to a clearing, Rand found himself in an open field filled with cars and people. Rand pulled up alongside them and killed the engine. When he got down from the driver's seat, though, his nice brown shoes sank into a couple inches of mud, water, and slime.

"Ugh." He'd assumed that the church would have a parking lot like any other building, but apparently not. He'd just shined the damn things, too.

Libby wobbled in her heels as they went, planning each step before making it in order to land on the sturdiest ground. Justin leant her a hand to keep her steady.

The overgrown grass was still wet, leaving dark marks on the bottom of Rand's pants.

As they fell in with the other churchgoers, Rand noticed that he and Libby were way overdressed. These guys looked like they'd come straight from their manual labor jobs, or their lounging clothes, or even their pajamas. One woman had curlers in her hair. Another man, about eighty years old, wore a camouflage getup as if he'd planned to hit the deer stand as soon as church was over. Knowing small town Finnick, he probably was.

Libby had also noticed the motley crowd around them, and she and Rand exchanged a silent, confused look. Justin was not put off at all. Rand would've thought the kid might have mentioned it was a casual church.

"Justin!"

A woman approached them. She wore faded jeans and a plain yellow sweater.

Justin broke into a smile and halted as the woman caught up with him. "Happy Sunday, Chloe."

"Happy Sunday to you, too. How was your week?"

Rand figured Chloe was about his own age, but she looked much older. Her skin was leathery, wrinkled, and sagged. A bandana covered her bald head, and when she rolled up her sleeves, she had purple bruises around her thin veins.

"Chloe, this is my girlfriend, Libby. And her dad, Mr. Rand."

"Hi, nice to meet you," Rand said. When he shook her hand, it trembled involuntarily.

"How are you feeling today?" Justin asked.

"Oh, you know," Chloe said, still smiling. "The doctors say all kinds of things, but what it sums up to is that each day is a blessing from the Lord." She glanced at the sky as if God was listening. "I am thankful for every hour."

They walked together while Justin and Chloe chatted about her treatment, her daughter who'd come to visit, and her cat. Libby eyed her dad and only shrugged.

Justin's more plugged into this place than I assumed, Rand thought. Apparently Libby hadn't known it either.

And then Rand saw what they were walking toward.

A huge tent was erected in the field. It resembled an old circus tent with bright stripes, all colors of the rainbow. Its flamboyance clashed against the grey, stormy sky.

"What in the world…" Rand halted. *It's a tent church.* "Did you know about this?" he asked his daughter.

"No."

"What's wrong?" Justin asked them both. He and Chloe looked concerned.

"Nothing," Rand said. Although these southern, pop-up tent revivalist preachers tended to be far more charismatic than Rand was comfortable with. They spoke in tongues, played with snakes, and the highly emotional congregations loved every minute.

"This isn't for me," Rand whispered to his daughter.

"Come on. We drove for two hours. We can sit through a sermon."

"No one's going to sit through a sermon in a place like this," Rand told her. "Watch. They'll jump around all over the joint, hollering and crying."

Libby jabbed his ribs and pulled him along.

Justin and Chloe only smiled, ignoring his obvious hesitation.

Although the tent was open on all sides, everyone seemed to file into one designated entrance area. And there, greeting people with a warm smile and a "good morning" was Patrick Perryman.

Justin lit up when he saw the man, and he introduced his girlfriend and her father.

"Oh, I know Rand," Patrick said, smiling.

Justin wrinkled his brow. Libby must not have told him about the flyer.

"I knew I'd see you here today," Patrick said. "I prayed all weekend for the Lord to move your heart."

"Yeah, yeah," Rand said. "You should've prayed for the rain to stop while you were at it."

As the procession moved inside the tent, Patrick abandoned his post and walked with Rand. "We have special spots up front for our guests. I'll show you."

"Actually, I'm a back row kind of man," Rand told him.

Patrick smirked. "I could've guessed that. Always the troublemaker in school, huh?"

"Something like that."

"But Mr. Rand," Justin spoke up, "the front is the best. You need to try it." It was perhaps the only time Justin had ever addressed him without being asked a question first.

"I appreciate it, but I'll hang back."

Libby gave him a look. She wouldn't be able to refuse. She and Justin disappeared into the crowd toward the front of the tent. There was a small raised platform that served as a stage, and a single podium on top.

"I'll ask you to take the second to last row," Patrick said when they had gone. "We prefer to save the back for our special needs guests."

"Special needs guests are given the back? Aren't they supposed to be in the front?"

Patrick's cheery demeanor faltered for only a moment

before he recovered it. "Come. I'll show you where you can sit."

Patrick directed Rand there like an usher, despite being capable of finding it on his own. The seats were nothing more than wooden benches, similar to what would be found on picnic tables. He slid in and went all the way down and sat next to a large woman dressed in a baggy white dress. She smiled at him.

Although it was a cool autumn day and the storm clouds made it even colder, it was warm inside the tent now that all the people were crammed together. Rand definitely regretted wearing the suit. He estimated there were about a hundred and fifty people there, maybe two hundred.

Already the bench was uncomfortable. The uneven planks bit into Rand's ass and he rocked back and forth, trying to find a comfortable way to sit. There was nothing to lean on, so a dull ache formed in his lower spine.

Rand checked his watch. By ten o'clock, everyone was seated, and Patrick Perryman walked onto the stage and took the microphone. "Good morning and happy Sunday," he said, his voice projecting through speakers mounted to the thick poles that kept the tent propped up.

"Happy Sunday," the congregation said in unison.

Rand hadn't taken Patrick for a public speaker. It seemed he was a big deal in this church and not just an enthusiast and evangelist.

"How's everyone doing this morning?"

A jumble of murmuring.

"Are you all ready to celebrate life with the Lord?"

That earned him a more hearty response. The woman

next to Rand let out a noise that was a mix of a yelp and a cheer.

"Then let's not waste anymore time. There's a great message in store for y'all today, and it's life changing stuff. So give a round of applause for Pastor D!"

The congregation burst into claps and shouting, and everyone stood. Rand rose with them so he could get a look at the guy.

Pastor D wore a suit—grey, tailored, with the coat buttoned and a fluffy purple tie. Rand guessed the pastor was about sixty-five years old with a head full of silver hair, combed and styled to the side. His eyes shown when he looked out on his flock.

Another tall, broad-shouldered man wearing a black suit took his place at the front of the stage, hands folded gently in front of his body, like a bouncer.

This guy has his own bodyguard? Rand thought.

Pastor D took the microphone from Patrick and surveyed the room. Everyone returned to their seats and quieted down and waited for him to speak.

"What is the will of God?" he asked into the microphone. No one answered his rhetorical question. He held a folded piece of paper that he glanced at. "Is it God's will that we be unhappy?"

"No!" Half the crowd responded.

"Is it God's will that we have nothing?" For an older man, he had a clear and powerful voice.

"No!" More this time.

"Is it God's—"

Pastor D stopped short. He lowered the microphone and scanned the room, letting the tent fill with an awkward silence he seemed to relish. All eyes were on him, all attention was his.

So we're getting a show as well, Rand thought.

Then Deckard Arcan tore his sermon notes in half and let the two pieces float to the floor. A few people murmured in concern, including the lady in the white dress next to Rand. She'd taken a fan out of her purse and fluttered it near her face, and Rand appreciated the residual breeze.

"I'm looking around and I see a lot of new faces today," Pastor D said.

"Praise Jesus!"

"I had a sermon prepared, but I've just received a new word from the Lord."

Oh, here we go, Rand thought.

Deckard let the silence linger, presumably as he listened to a clearer message from God. Rand figured it wouldn't be a proper tent church without a dramatic performance.

"I feel led to give my personal testimony," Deckard said. "I know some of you long-term members have heard it a few times by now, but do you mind if I share it again for the newer folks?"

"Do it, Pastor D!" someone shouted. Others clapped and cheered.

"I won't bore you with all the details, but believe me when I tell you that my whole life, I was a godless sinner. No direction, no love, no hope. If it's listed as a sin, I've done it. But we all know what God can do with sinners, don't we? We know how he can pull them out of their own pits of despair, and in a single day, or a single hour, reset the entire course of their life and turn them into powerful warriors for him."

He jabbed a finger toward the sky, and that elicited several cheers from the crowd. A few people even shot from their chairs and stood, eyes closed as if in prayer as they listened.

"I'm reminded of the Apostle Paul. Do we remember his story? He was first called Saul, and it was his mission to persecute early Christians. We know God is powerful enough to strike down someone like that, but what did God do? God said, 'I have a better idea.' And an angel appeared to Saul, and to demonstrate the mighty power of our Lord, blinded him and changed his name to Paul. Paul was so moved by this that he completely reversed direction and became one of the greatest missionaries of all time. All because God stepped in.

"I was a drug addict. I was forty-five and in and out of prison. The security guards greeted me by name each time I came back. Let me tell you, folks, if there's anything on earth that's close to hell, it's prison.

"About three years ago, I was released from my fourth stint and I was broke, homeless, and alone. What did I do? I decided I needed some heroine to keep me company. It had been so long since the last time I'd gotten high, but I knew exactly who to call and where to go to score.

"But that deal went wrong and things got heated and nasty. I jumped into my buddy's car and we sped away from them, driving a hundred miles per hour. But those guys weren't going to let me go.

"They ran me off the road and the car flipped. I wasn't wearing my seatbelt, of course, and I landed outside with the car on top of my legs." Deckard laid his hands on the tops of his thighs. "Pinned down, all the bones broken. I remember lying underneath that car, destroyed and bloody, and seeing those bad guys walk up and look down at me. They were laughing. I was waiting for one to pull out a gun and finish me off. In fact, at that moment, I wish they had. But they didn't. They just left me for dead.

"I was found by a good Samaritan who was passing by, and he called the police. They rushed me to the hospital where I was told it was a miracle I was still alive. But they also said I would never walk again.

"I had never felt so low. Everything in my life had taken me up to that point, and it was all my fault. As long as I kept on living, the more I would suffer." Deckard's voice turned low and heavy.

"So I called a friend and made a request. He brought a bottle of mixed up pills to my hospital room and I told him goodbye. I swallowed every last one and waited for the end. And as I lay there, waiting to die, a profound change came over me.

"I don't know how to explain it, but at that moment, something overwhelmed me. An inner peace I had never known before. And I knew I needed to live, that I had made a mistake.

"I prayed in that hospital bed. I said, 'God, if you let me survive this, I will dedicate the rest of my life to you. I need a new master, and I don't even care if my legs are gone.'"

"Amen!" someone shouted. Rand assumed they were familiar with the story.

"And folks…" Deckard choked up. The energy with which he spoke escaped him as he remembered the wonder that had supposedly happened in that hospital bed. "Folks, God heard my prayer that night. He accepted me into the kingdom of heaven. And like the Apostle Paul, he sent an angel down for me. Azora came and spoke to me, telling me I was now a servant of God. He even healed my legs."

He beat on his thighs, showing off how sturdy they were, and the crowd around Rand cheered.

Azora? Rand thought. That name didn't ring a bell, not from the Bible or any other Christian tradition he was familiar with.

"And when I walked out of that hospital, the doctors were stunned!" More cheering. "And I wasted no time starting the new mission God had given me. I told those doctors that this was the power of God, stronger than any medicine on earth!"

Now most of the people in the congregation were standing, blocking Deckard from Rand's view. But Deckard's voice grew louder over the microphone.

"And the next day I started this church," Deckard declared. "Back then, I had no idea how to run a church, and I didn't care. All I knew was I wanted to reach others for the Lord. What began with just a few has turned into the congregation you see around you today."

"Amen, Pastor D!"

"And I couldn't do any of this without you. You all keep me strong and balanced. And the Lord reminds me every day why I do what I do."

By this time, the people were cheering for their pastor as if he were a rock star. Rand sat still, mind spinning. Deckard Arcan moved around the stage more lithely than a man half his age, yet he claimed a car had toppled over him and crushed both his legs. Then God had healed him.

Rand's alarm bells were ringing. The most likely situation, he noted, was that Deckard Arcan's testimony was true, but the bit about being crushed by a car was a fabrication. There was no way for anyone in that tent to prove it. All they had to go on was his word. And when a charismatic preacher ratcheted up the emotions in the room, people who didn't have the same shields as Rand were prone to believe anything.

Preachers did it every day all over the world. They used their high emotion sermons to lure a large congregation, usually to take their money. On the other side, the followers left feeling spiritually fulfilled, all sorts of loopholes triggered in their psychology to feel satisfied and ready to come back the following week. To Rand, a spiritual experience with God should be simple, direct, and personal, but to each their own.

For the first time since Pastor D had started talking, Rand stood, but not to join the congregation in their worship. He wanted to get out of there and wait by the car for the service to end. If Justin hadn't been with them, he would have grabbed Libby and pulled her along. He knew his daughter was having the same thoughts as him.

"And that's what brings us to this very important day," Deckard said into the microphone. His high-energy voice lowered. "Everyone, please quiet down."

The audience halted their cheers, and a confused silence filled the tent. Even Rand froze in place. Why work so hard building up the emotion only to kill it in a few seconds?

Deckard Arcan gripped the microphone with both hands. A solemn calm had come over him now. His eyes were closed and his lips were moving, although he spoke no words. Praying.

"Please be seated," he said, almost threateningly.

The congregation obeyed. Rand's curiosity was piqued. He looked at the exit, so near since he was in the back row. But in the end, he returned to his spot on the bench.

This guy's good. He can even get me interested.

"I've been praying about this for a long while," Deckard said. "I never knew when the right moment would come, but I kept my heart open to the instructions of the angel Azora. And I believe today is the day. With so many new people here, it's time we witness the power of the Lord at work."

He closed his eyes again, as if listening to God. The congregation waited in total silence to see what he would do next. Thunder rolled in the distance, the newest wave of the storm coming in quick.

"Is there a man here today named Gerald Roberson?"

5

Deckard Arcan kept his eyes closed. Everyone in the room looked around.

Oh no, Rand thought. Now Deckard was trying to divine something.

"Gerald Roberson," Deckard repeated, louder, as if commanding him to show himself. "I know you are here. I feel your name in my heart."

"Here!" someone shouted, and all heads turned. The person pointed at an elderly man at the back of the tent. He sat in a wheelchair.

"I'm Gerald Roberson," the old man said, raising his hand, nervous.

"Happy Sunday," Deckard said to him. "Please join me up here."

Gerald Roberson hesitated, but eventually, the will of Deckard Arcan won out. Gerald rolled himself down the aisle, the wheels struggling through the grass and mud.

It took time, but no one spoke as he approached the altar. It appeared cruel—Pastor D remaining at the front while forcing the old man with the useless legs to do all the work.

Now Rand understood why the special needs guests were relegated to the back of the tent instead of the front. It was all part of the show. When they were summoned, they had to demonstrate an effort to approach Deckard.

Once the old man was close, Deckard looked down, analyzing Gerald, then stepped off the stage to be closer to the wheelchair.

"The Lord has put your name on my heart this morning," Deckard told the man, speaking into the microphone so everyone could hear. "You and I have never met, is that correct?" He held the microphone out to Gerald's mouth.

"No, sir," Gerald said, his nervous voice projecting from the speakers.

"Then the only way I could know you were here is if God told me. Would you agree?"

Gerald considered, then said, "I suppose so."

"You were fifty-five years old when you had your accident. You are sixty-nine now, so you have not walked for fourteen years. You were on a ladder, cleaning leaves out of your gutter. Your wife Paula begged you to hire someone, but you can be stubborn sometimes. You lost your balance and fell. The broken ribs healed, but the nerve damage in your spine meant you would never walk again."

Deckard held the microphone toward Gerald, but the old man said nothing. He stared at the pastor, at a complete loss for words. Finally, he found some. "How did you know?"

"Because the Lord knows the number of hairs on each of our heads, Gerald. He knows everything about all of us, our pasts and our futures. God showed me you, and he showed me all about you. And..." Deckard softened his voice. "I have seen Paula too. Beautiful woman. Her four years in heaven have been filled with joy and reward, and she can't wait for you to join her."

Gerald Roberson wiped a tear that had fallen from his eye.

Deckard placed a hand on the man's shoulder. "Gerald. Do you believe in God?"

"Yes, sir. Of course."

"But do you *really* believe the creator of the universe, who made you in his own image, loves you and has a plan for you?"

"Yes, sir."

"Do you believe God is without limits and has the power to change our lives?"

"Yes, sir."

"Even to heal us, as he once healed me."

"Yes, sir."

Oh, no, Rand thought. A tight ball of nerves formed in his stomach when he realized what he was about to see.

"Do you believe the Lord can return your ability to walk?" This time, Gerald hesitated. Only his breathing filled the microphone, so Deckard took it back. "You must have *faith*, Gerald. This won't work unless you *do*!" His voice rose, and other members of the congregation called out, cheering Gerald on. "I asked you, Gerald Roberson, if you believe the creator of the universe is powerful enough to make you walk again!"

"Yes!" Gerald shouted into the microphone. The cheers and clapping had grown around him, pushing him over the threshold. His energy spiked, joining with the emotional high of his surroundings.

"Tell us all, Gerald," Deckard shouted at him. "Tell us all what you believe!"

"God can make me walk again."

"Louder!"

"God can make me walk again!"

Deckard removed his hand from Gerald's shoulder and lifted it to the sky, clenching his eyes closed. "Then in the name of the Lord, I command you, Gerald Roberson, to walk again and feel no more pain!"

Deckard's raised hand dropped onto Gerald's shoulder again and he tumbled out of the wheelchair as if pushed by an unseen force. The applauding congregation gasped and rose from their seats as the fragile man fell. Even Rand stood to see what was going on.

Gerald rolled around on the ground, his clothes soaking through with water and mud. He looked like he was having a seizure.

And then Gerald Roberson stood.

He jumped up and down several times, waving his hands in the air. The congregation cheered and hollered and shouted, celebrating along with him. In a fit of overwhelming joy, he ran down the aisle toward the back of the tent, running like a marathon man. Tears streamed from his eyes as he went. "Praise God!" he shouted. "Praise God!"

Amidst all the celebration, Rand felt his own legs give way. He lowered himself onto the bench, drowning in a loud sea of cheering and applause. He'd never seen a miracle healing live before—only on internet videos—and every time, he was sure that there was some catch. It was easy enough for Gerald to be a paid actor, but even then, the sixty-nine-year-old was running around like he was sixteen again. Still hard to believe.

Rand was the only one who was not celebrating. It became too much, so he rose and pushed through the crowd, which was well on its way to becoming a riot. People had abandoned their seats and now engaged in full on worship, thanking God for his healing powers and praising his name. Rand left the tent, the cool autumn air giving him rapid relief from the sweat that had broken out all over his skin.

Once he'd put some distance between himself and the tent, he turned and looked back. The celebration that was going on in there would last quite a while.

Deckard Arcan, he thought. *Who are you? Where did you come from? How did you do it?*

So many questions had to be answered first before Rand could ever concede that the old man had actually been healed by God.

6

On Monday morning, Libby drifted through school, existing only in body, but not in mind.

She found it hard to stay awake during first period Chemistry. She hadn't slept well the night before, tossing and turning over what she'd seen at the church the day before.

History class wasn't much better.

She finally woke up in fourth period, just in time for Math, but instead of focusing, all she could think about was Pastor Deckard Arcan and how that old man had run around the tent.

She and her dad and Justin hadn't spoken much on the drive home. Libby's guess was that they were also very stunned. She'd asked Justin if stuff like that happened every Sunday, and he'd only shaken his head.

Once the celebration of Gerald Roberson's new legs had quieted down, baskets for an offering were passed around, and by the time it came to Libby, a mountain of cash was already there. She'd sent it along without contributing.

After, she'd found her dad outside the tent, and she guessed he'd left after the healing, knowing he probably didn't believe it was true.

And no matter what, Libby knew she didn't believe that the man had been healed. Something tricky was going on. It must have been planned beforehand. Gerald Roberson had to be an actor.

She heard her name.

Libby realized that Mrs. Granger was speaking to her, and that all the other eyes in the classroom were on her, waiting.

"Sorry?"

"I've called on you three times," Mrs. Granger said.

"Oh."

A few snickers from the back of the class.

"What did you get for number seven?"

Libby looked down at her notebook, but it was closed.

"We're going over homework right now."

Libby flipped her notebook open to the work she'd done last week. Number seven was blank, with a giant question mark drawn next to it. "I, uh… didn't know how to figure that one out."

"Steve?" Mrs. Granger said impatiently, looking at Steve Kerry, who sat behind Libby. He rattled off the solution, which was correct.

The sudden attention was not enough to snap Libby back to the present. Instead, she remembered Justin, and that she hadn't heard from him all day. They had no classes together, but usually they would have texted by then.

Libby waited until Mrs. Granger looked to the other side of the classroom, then she slid her cell phone out of her pocket and checked the screen. There were a few Instagram notifications, but that was it. She unlocked her phone and opened her messages, wondering if maybe the notification had failed to go off or if she'd missed it at some point.

Nope. Justin had not texted her. That was unusual.

Now that she thought about it, Justin hadn't messaged yesterday after church, either. Libby hadn't noticed at the time because she'd been busy with her mom, working in the garden behind Bill's house.

She checked again to see if Mrs. Granger was looking, then fired off a message without looking at the screen.

Hey. You all right?

By seventh period English, Justin had not responded. Libby also remembered that she was supposed to drive her boyfriend home after school. She texted him again while Mrs. Collier wasn't looking.

Hey. Am I still bringing you home today?

He waited until the end of class to message her back.

Yes please.

They met in the parking lot, and Libby could already tell that Justin was off. Instead of lighting up when he saw her, as he usually did, he merely walked with a frown, eyes on the ground.

"How was your day?" she attempted as they climbed into her car.

"Fine."

Libby took that as a sign to quit trying. Boys were like that, and she'd learned it from her father. If something was bothering them, even if you wanted to help, just let them come out with it in their own time.

So she drove, and when the silence got too awkward, she turned on the radio, tuning it to one of Justin's rock stations he preferred.

Halfway to his house, during her wandering thoughts, she remembered she'd forgotten her Math textbook at school.

"Crap," she muttered.

"What?"

Really? That got your attention?

"Nothing. Just forgot my Math book and I have homework." She sighed. "After today, Mrs. Granger's going to be mad when I turn up with it not done."

"I have mine in my room," Justin said. "You can come in and borrow it."

"Oh. Thanks."

A solution to her problem *and* Justin had started speaking to her again. Progress.

She parked on the road outside his house and they went inside and upstairs. Libby noticed something about Justin's bedroom was different.

Libby scanned the walls as Justin searched for the textbook underneath the pile of mess on the desk. The room used to be covered with posters of rock bands, but no longer.

"What happened to your posters?" she asked.

Justin found the textbook and handed it to her. "Pastor D gave a sermon two weeks ago about listening to evil music. I figured I should take a break from my usual bands for a while."

"Are you okay?" she asked, unable to hold it in any longer. "You've been acting weird lately."

"How?"

"Quiet. Stand-offish. Maybe a little unhappy. Did I do something wrong?" Even though she already knew she hadn't.

"No," Justin said.

She gave him a few seconds to offer more, and then shrugged. "All right. Well, see you tomorrow, I guess."

She went to leave.

"You never said anything about yesterday."

She stopped with her hand on the doorknob. Apparently, he was ready to talk about it after all.

"What do you mean?" She turned back around, and this time Justin looked truly upset.

"I mean, how could you *not* say anything about what we saw?"

"You didn't say anything about it either."

Justin thought about that for a minute. "We watched a man get healed. Right there in front of our own eyes. He couldn't walk, and then he was running around the tent."

Oh no, Libby thought. *Here we go...*

She looked at the floor, unable to think of what to say.

"You *do* believe he got healed, don't you?"

"I... I don't think so."

Justin seemed to deflate. "What?"

"So you actually think that man was healed?"

"Are you serious? Of course! We were sitting like four feet away from them when it happened."

"But Justin..." She was surprised she had to explain this. "People get caught faking this stuff all the time. They hire actors, and..."

46

"Why would Pastor D have an actor?"

"Because..." She remembered the offering baskets that were passed around, stacked high with cash. "I'm sorry. It's just not something I believe in. But if you do, then that's fine."

"I thought you believed in God."

"I do," she said. How could she not believe after all the horrible things her dad had faced in the past?

"Then if you believe in God, then you believe he healed that old man."

"Not necessarily."

Justin furrowed his brow, seemingly unable to put the two concepts together.

"Look, you've been going to this church for a while now," Libby said, "and that's good if it makes you happy. I don't mind going to church sometimes, but ones like that are a little much for me, you know? I prefer them simple. Sing some nice songs, listen to a sermon, then head somewhere for lunch afterward."

"So you like fake churches."

"Fake churches? What does that even mean?"

"A church where God is not really present. Pastor D has warned us about them."

Pastor D. She hadn't realized how deeply this church and that preacher had gotten under Justin's skin. She glanced again at the empty walls where the band posters used to hang.

"Can we talk about this later?" Libby asked. "I don't want to have a fight right now."

I don't want to have our first fight, was what she could have said. Of all the first fights couples had all over the world, she wondered how many of them were over the validity of a miracle-working preacher.

"Fine," Justin said, turning his back on her.

She left him in the bedroom and went downstairs, textbook tucked under her arm.

"Hey, Libby."

She turned toward the living room and saw Justin's dad on the couch, legs crossed, iPad in hand.

"Oh. Hey, Mr. Tidwell. I didn't see you there."

Mr. Tidwell set the iPad down and stood. "How have you been?"

She shrugged. "All right. School and all that."

"Yeah, I hear you. When I was your and Justin's age, I hated school. Never wanted to go, and I skipped a lot. Almost flunked out my senior year."

"Really?" She didn't know much about what Mr. Tidwell did for a living—something in business—but judging by the family's lifestyle and sizable house, he seemed successful. "You must have turned everything around."

"Yeah, sure did."

His small talk was short and stilted, and Libby shuffled her feet, ready to head home and get started on her homework, but didn't want to be rude. She got the impression there was something specific he wanted to ask.

"How's your dad?" Mr. Tidwell asked.

"He's fine. We all went to church together the other day."

"We should get together sometime. Have dinner."

"Yeah," Libby said, struggling to imagine just how she'd pitch such an occasion to her father. "That would be good."

"How about tomorrow night?"

48

Libby froze. "Oh. That's so soon."

"Yeah, it's short notice, but Janet is planning to cook her salmon. It's her grandmother's recipe, and it's incredible. Besides, I haven't met your dad yet, and I think it would be nice."

"Well. I'll ask him." Libby chewed her lip. "I don't know what his plans are. If tomorrow night doesn't work for him, then maybe another time."

"Sure," Mr. Tidwell said, as if he didn't particularly like that answer.

She lifted the textbook. "Got a lot of homework."

"I understand."

Libby turned and left him, feeling weird about their discussion. She opened the front door, but before she could leave, she heard her name again.

Mr. Tidwell walked toward her and closed the door. He glanced around the room and up the stairs, making sure they were alone.

Libby's stomach sank.

"Listen, Libby," he said, his voice low. He gazed into her eyes, and Libby couldn't help but stare back. "It would mean a lot to me and Janet if we could… meet your father. Preferably tomorrow. If he can't make dinner, then let me know another way to speak with him. Please."

"Is there something specific you need to speak with him about?" Libby asked.

Mr. Tidwell glanced up the stairs one more time, then looked back at Libby. "Yes. I've heard a thing or two about this church that Justin's been going to, and I'm worried. Justin's also told me a bit about what your dad does, and I think he's the perfect person to talk to about this."

Libby swallowed. Apparently, Mr. Tidwell was

concerned about Justin's involvement, and Libby was not surprised. She herself was worried after the conversation she'd just had with her boyfriend.

And Mr. Tidwell was right. When the supernatural was involved, there was only one person in town to call.

"I'll tell him," Libby said.

7

Miller Landingham sat in a chair near his cluttered desk, his considerable weight straining it as he reclined. Rand paced in the small office while he recounted his story, trying not to meet his friend's eyes as he spoke; he knew they were narrowing in skepticism.

Miller worked—and now lived—in a used bookstore downtown. Business had been hard, so the man had moved out of his apartment and into the rear office. A mattress with dirty sheets was shoved in the corner, surrounded by old fast food wrappers and empty soft drink cans. Boxes of books and sales invoices were stacked along the edges of the room, making it feel even smaller than it already was. And Rand did not have the heart to tell his friend that the cave had developed quite an odor.

"So yeah," Rand finished. "The guy just got up and ran around all over the place."

Miller had his hands behind his head. He blinked

several times through thick-rimmed glasses. He was silent as he considered Rand's story. Ever since he'd called Rand in to remove a haunting a long time ago, Miller had committed to helping Rand with his future cases whenever possible. That meant, over the years, Miller had heard some weird stuff.

"Nah, not buying it," Miller finally said. "No way."

"I figured you'd say that."

"You mean you actually think it was real?"

Rand only shrugged. "I guess I *want* it to be real. We've both seen ghosts and demons and the power they have. On the other end of the spectrum is God. God is even more powerful than demons. So something like this could potentially be real, right?"

"The deal is, Rand, that this miracle healing business has been going on since the beginning of time. So many preachers have gotten rich off this kind of thing. They all eventually get busted. Research it and you'll see."

Rand chewed on the pad of his finger. "You're probably right."

"I'm definitely right." Miller leaned forward in his chair. "Look, man, I know you're hurting since your case with the young girl. That one banged you up badly. And you've mentioned before you think it's time to reconcile with the big man upstairs. But don't get caught up in some showman."

"I won't," Rand said. "It was just weird. I've never seen anything like that before."

"What did Libby say about it?"

"Same as you. Absolutely no way, it was all staged, it was a performance, all of that."

"She's always been very clever."

"The problem is her boyfriend is super into that church."

"And what does he think?"

"Not sure. I didn't ask. He didn't say anything on the ride home. I think it blew his mind just as much as mine."

"But you said it was the first time this preacher ever healed someone?"

Rand pulled up a sturdy box of books and sat on it. "The way he talked made it sound like it was the *only* time he'd done it. Saying he'd been waiting for this day, praying for the right moment, stuff like that."

"Ah. Okay."

"But as you said, people have been miracle healing since the beginning of time. I tend to believe in things that have been happening for that long. Like ghostly presences, spirit sightings, demonic possessions. You're saying it is *impossible* that someone could be healed? Isn't that the same as a bunch of people saying it's impossible to be possessed by a demon?"

Miller thought about that for a minute. "I guess since I believe in God, I also have to believe it is possible for God to heal a person through someone else. But it's suspicious when some old man in Finnick, of all places, shows up out of nowhere and does it."

"So a healthy skepticism."

"It's the only way. If you bought into everything you saw, you'd be just like…"

"Everyone inside that tent."

"Yes. And that's not you. Or me."

Rand let that tumble around in his head for a few minutes.

"Are you going to go back?" Miller asked.

"I don't know. If I do, do you want to come with me?"

"Not particularly."

"Figured."

Miller stood from the office chair and it creaked, happy to be free of his weight. "Listen, man. You're fragile right now. It's probably best if you stay away from that place until you get your head back on straight. When people go through these hard times, that's when they're more prone to fall for tricks and scams."

"True."

"Are you still seeing what's his name? That shadowy bastard." Miller lowered his voice as if Shindael could hear him. Truthfully, the demon probably wasn't too far away.

"Every day," Rand said.

"Have you been praying?"

"Every time I see him."

"And he leaves?"

"Yeah."

His phone chimed with a text message from Libby.

Where are you? I need to talk to you about something.

He frowned as he typed back. *Is everything okay?*

Yes, but can you please come home? It's important.

"Pray even when Shindael doesn't show up," Miller said. "Do the usual stuff. Command him to leave in God's name. Take baby steps into the religious world rather than jumping all in with some revival-tent miracle healer."

"Yeah," Rand said. "That makes sense." He sighed. "Even when I command Shindael to leave, he will, but he'll always come back. Karax was strong, and he serves

Shindael, so that can only mean Shindael must be one of the elites in hell."

"That means you're one of the elite on Earth, my friend," Miller said. "You've got those demons trembling. But remember. You are stronger, and God is stronger. There is nothing they can do to you."

Rand appreciated his friend's encouragement, and in a way, Miller was right.

But in other ways, he was wrong. There was a hell of a lot Shindael could do to him, and Rand couldn't help but think the demon was just biding his time, waiting for the perfect moment to strike.

8

Rand got home and parked his Jeep next to Libby's brand-new, sky-blue Mini Cooper. He grimaced every time he saw the thing. Bill, Libby's mother's fiancé, had plucked it off the lot and given it to Libby without any discussion with Rand. That had annoyed him.

"She needs a car, Rand," Tessa had told him.

"It's more than just a car," Rand had told his ex. "It's freedom and expenses and risk."

"You don't trust your daughter? You don't have to worry about the expenses."

The conversation still rattled in his head every time he saw the car, but he pushed it away.

He found Libby at the kitchen table doing homework. "What are you doing here? Monday is your mother's night."

"I told her I was here."

"What's up?"

"You and I were invited to dinner tomorrow evening." She closed her textbook.

"You came all the way here to tell me that? With whom?"

"Justin's family wants to meet you."

Rand groaned. "Absolutely not." It shot out of his mouth before he knew what he was saying.

"What? Why?"

Rand had known this was coming. Libby and that kid had been dating for a while now, and when Justin's parents inevitably heard that Justin had already met him and Tessa, they would get antsy and want to know why they weren't taking part in all the fun.

Honestly, he was surprised he'd gotten away with it for this long. "Because what's the point?"

"The point is he's my boyfriend."

"Yeah, but not for long."

"Give it up. I know you don't hate him and you're just putting on that clichéd dad act you see on TV, but it isn't working anymore."

Rand went to the fridge and grabbed a bottle of water. The remaining beers on the door shelf caught his eye, but he ignored them.

"I was putting on that act before, but I'm serious this time. He's into that crackpot church, which makes me concerned for you."

Libby said nothing for a minute and Rand wondered if he'd upset her with that one. She twisted in her seat and looked at him. "I think they want to meet you *because* of the church."

Rand took a sip of water. "What?"

"Justin told them what happened there yesterday."

"Okay…"

"And… they're worried about him."

"They should be."

"I agree. But the way Mr. Tidwell asked me, I could tell he didn't just want a friendly dinner. He said if you couldn't make tomorrow night, he and Mrs. Janet would meet you wherever."

Rand licked his lips. This was making more sense. "They want me to figure out what's really happening there."

"Yeah. Ever since Justin started going to that church, something's been off. He's been changing. And now, after yesterday, he's totally bought into it."

"So Justin thinks that guy was healed."

"We sort of had a fight about it earlier. He believes it, but I told him I didn't, and that I thought Gerald Roberson was an actor or there was some other trick."

"That's my girl."

"But this is what you do, Dad," Libby said. "You help people who can't understand the supernatural things around them."

Rand said nothing.

"I care about him a lot, and I'd hate to see him tricked or misled. Or hurt. Please consider Justin a client."

And there was that magic word. *Client.* As soon as someone became one of those, Rand would stop at nothing to get to the bottom of their situation.

He had planned to never go back to that church. True miracle or no, it had nothing to do with him, or his renewed search for God. If he was going to get right with the Lord, it would not be with the help of Pastor Deckard Arcan.

But Mr. Tidwell wanted Rand to figure out what was going on with that church, so it looked like he had Sunday plans.

9

Despite all his initial dread, dinner at the Tidwells' turned out to be a pleasant affair.

Rand had finished two portions of salmon, the second one forced on him by Janet, who was a lovely woman. Charles Tidwell was a man that Rand could see himself getting along with. Charles was a bit older, was a successful owner of a chain of tanning salons around town, and had even recently expanded into other nearby cities. He had a clear head on his shoulders, which was why Rand predicted he had such trouble accepting his son's choice to frequent Deckard Arcan's church.

Justin spent much of the dinner in silence. He answered questions, but the rest of the time, his eyes were on his plate. Rand noticed Libby nudging him a few times, but he only grew exasperated. The church never came up in the table conversation.

Mrs. Tidwell served a homemade cheesecake for dessert, and when there was only one slice left on the tray, which everyone was too polite to accept, Charles Tidwell leaned back in his chair and rested his hands on his belly.

"So, Rand," Charles said. "You ready for a second dessert?"

"You mean Janet's made more?"

Charles chuckled. "No, sir. I'm talking about whiskey and a cigar. In my office."

Rand grinned. "You lead the way."

Charles Tidwell's office was a large room at the back of the house, containing a huge mahogany desk and book-filled shelves lining the walls. One portion was like a lounge, with black leather chairs, a table between them, a chalice of whiskey, glasses, and an ice bucket.

"On the rocks or neat?" he asked.

"Neat, please," Rand said, surveying the books on his shelf. Almost all seemed to be nonfiction regarding business, history, and economics.

Charles made two of the same drinks and handed him one. Then he opened his cigar box and trimmed the ends off a pair of thick Cubans.

The men sat and lit their cigars. Rand relished the mouthful of cigar smoke and let it out easy. He followed it with a sip of smooth, aged whiskey, and for the first time in a while, felt totally relaxed. "Been too long since I've had a night like this."

"I'm no doctor, but I recommend it twice a week," Charles said.

"I bet this is good for you and Justin. If I had a son, I'd do this with him as often as possible."

Charles blew out a plume of smoke and sighed. "Justin's more into the heavy metal thing. Which is fine. I just wish he practiced it more. I think it's a phase, anyway."

"These things typically are."

"Yeah, but then it's just a bunch of wasted time. If he followed through with the music, then he could start a band and make something of himself."

"Usually parents prefer their kids to forget that kind of dream. You wouldn't want him to follow in your business footsteps?"

"Not if he doesn't want to," Charles said. "There are plenty of ways to build a life, and my path isn't the only one. I want him to do whatever makes him happy, but I'd also want him to stick with it and not give up on it so fast."

"Wise words," Rand said, taking another sip of whiskey. He'd promised Libby he'd lay off the alcohol for a while, but it would have been rude to decline. She would smell it on him later.

"So Justin's told me about you," Charles said, tapping the ash of his cigar into a tray on the table beside his armrest. "And about what you do."

"As a professor?"

"Yes, that. But also your side gig."

"Not sure what he's told you, but I hope he didn't make me sound crazy."

Charles raised his eyebrows and shook his head, eyeing his whiskey glass. "It makes you sound *fascinating*."

"Are you a believer?" Rand asked.

"In what?"

Rand shrugged. "Anything, I guess. Anything that requires faith."

"No. Never have been."

"Fair enough." Rand crossed his legs.

"Obviously you don't share that opinion."

"I don't. But I understand that you and I have had different experiences, which are both valid."

"True. My disbelief has caused me a lot of trouble in my life." Charles inhaled on his cigar. "My father was a preacher. A very popular one. We lived in a small town not too far from here. He was very strict with me, so of course, I rebelled. You've heard the story a hundred times. I almost flunked out of high school, barely scraped by. Then I went to college, because according to Dad, that was the only way to become something."

"Things must have changed with you soon after that," Rand said. The room they were in, and the whole house, was evidence of his business success.

"One day, when I was walking to my freshman Biology class, I realized how damn cold it was. It was seven in the morning and everyone around me was freezing. I remember thinking about how I wanted hot chocolate. That was when I had my idea. After class was over, I ran down to the store and spent all the money I had buying supplies to make hot chocolate. The next day, instead of going to class, I set up a stand and sold it for fifty cents a cup. I ran out in twenty minutes. The day after that, I bought twice the supplies with the money I made, and again, sold out. I did that until the weather warmed up. I failed freshman Biology, but I made a ton of money.

"After that, I dropped out of school and started a text-book hustle. I would sell people's used textbooks for them and keep a percentage of the money, their fee for not having to deal with it. Then when the weather turned cold again, I paid someone to sell the hot chocolate for me. I made money without even having to be there.

"It wasn't long before I started other businesses. By the time I was twenty-three years old, I was worth more than my father."

"He must've been proud," Rand said.

Charles grunted. "You would think that. He accused me of idolizing money, which according to him, was the root of all evil. But I was actually quite frugal. I never bought nice cars and clothes. We grew up poor, and those money-saving habits were ingrained in me. No matter how much I made, I never forgot the value of a dollar. The one thing I wanted to do with the money I made was give it back to my parents. Get them a nicer house, or give them something to invest for retirement, but Dad refused. Funny how after a lifetime of preaching, he never realized how prideful he was being."

Rand puffed his cigar and eyed the other man as he recounted his story. Charles's eyes lingered on the floor, lost in the memory of the past.

"When I was twenty-six, they found a polyp in Dad's colon. They said it was benign, but it could become cancerous, and they wanted to remove it. Dad refused, saying if it was God's will, then God would heal him."

"Oh," Rand said. "One of those."

Charles nodded. "And so, as you'd expect, within a few years he was dead. Wouldn't accept treatment, and me offering to pay for it just made him even more stubborn."

"Sorry to hear that," Rand said.

"His faith was the only thing he held on to, and it seemed to give him a reason to wake up in the morning. But after all that devotion and commitment, he died from something that could have been prevented with a simple procedure, especially since we caught it in time."

"How about your mother?"

"Mom accepted my financial help after Dad was gone. I moved her into a better place, got some live-in help when the time was right. She passed away about four years ago. She eventually told me she'd lost her faith when she saw how it drove a wedge between Dad and me, but she never admitted it to him."

"It doesn't work for everyone," Rand said. "And it seems like you've done well for yourself without it."

"When I knew there was no God who would bless me and give me stuff just for praying and obeying, it meant I had to go out there and build a life on my own."

"I get it."

"And so I never forced religion on Justin. Never brought him to church, never told him what to do. I answered his questions as best I could when he was eight or nine—that was when all his friends who went to church would tell him he was going to hell if he didn't believe. I would've thought those kids would be too young to hear all that, but apparently their Sunday School teachers didn't waste any time. I figured that age was only about singing songs about Father Abraham and coloring pictures of Jesus."

Rand had known Charles would eventually steer the conversation of church and religion to Justin. As they neared the topic, Charles seemed troubled.

"How do you feel about Justin's involvement with the church now?" Rand asked.

Charles Tidwell took in a deep breath and blew it out through puffed cheeks. The ash on the end of his cigar had built up. "If anything, it keeps him from drinking and drugs and all that nonsense. He's a good kid, you know."

"Sure."

"But… when he came home and told me what he saw on Sunday," Charles met Rand's eyes, "and I could tell that he believed it hook, line, and sinker…" Rand nodded along. "What about you, Rand? You were there. You must've seen it."

"I did."

"What do you think?"

Rand hesitated. He knew what he *wanted* to believe, but he also knew what was probably the truth.

"My tendency is to lean toward a rational explanation," Rand said. "They say the Lord works in mysterious ways, but a tent revival in rural Louisiana seems a bit too mysterious for me."

"My thoughts exactly," Charles said. "I know you're a man who's interested in the unexplainable."

"More than just interested."

"Right." Charles leaned forward. "Janet and I have been talking about having you over for a while now. But I also wanted to pick your brain about whatever's going on at that church."

"I understand."

"I know we just met. But if I asked a favor of you…"

"You want me to find out if it's real."

"I already know it isn't real," Charles said. "But I would like you to find proof. Hard evidence. Justin won't listen to me, but he'll hopefully listen to you, since he knows what it is you do."

"Hard evidence." Rand finished the rest of his whiskey.

"Shouldn't be too difficult. This Deckard Arcan fellow seems clever, but he's no magician."

"Do all your investigations lead to supernatural things?" Charles asked.

"Of course not. Actually, less than half of them do." Rand remembered the person who had come to him claiming to hear scratches on the walls at night. Their dog would also go crazy and bark at something that no one else saw. Those were two common signs of a spiritual presence, but Rand discovered what they actually had was a rat infestation inside the walls.

"Then you're an expert debunker as well as a ghost hunter," Charles said.

"You could say that."

"Look, Rand. My goal is to get my son out of that crazy church. I don't care much about what the other people do, or even if this preacher man keeps going. I just want Justin to know the truth." He peered at Rand with a strong, blue-eyed gaze.

Charles Tidwell wanted Rand to prove that Deckard Arcan was a charlatan and did not, in fact, have supernatural powers. Rand officially had a new case.

"As the Bible says," Rand said, "the truth shall set us free."

10

The week passed and Sunday came.

Instead of dressing in a suit, Rand pulled on a pair of nice jeans, a black V-neck t-shirt, and his usual casual jacket. He packed his satchel full of his standard equipment—recorders, cameras, and crucifixes —just in case. This was a different kind of investigation, but still, he never went investigating the unknown without his gear.

The two-hour drive was nothing but silence as Rand turned over in his head what his plan might be. He needed evidence that Deckard Arcan was a fraud and not gifted with miraculous abilities. He'd have to make sure his eyes and ears were in tune for that kind of thing.

Despite Rand forcing himself to remain rational, a small piece of him still wondered if Deckard Arcan could be for real. Perhaps that was the part of Rand that longed to get back into the embrace of God. Maybe Pastor D was the one God sent to show Rand the way. And here he was, trying to sabotage the work of the Kingdom.

When Rand arrived, the field that served as a parking lot was even fuller than the week before. Although the skies were still grey, the rains had halted, and the trek to the tent was less muddy.

Rand fell in with the people who flocked to the church. There were at least twice as many as before, maybe three times. Word of the miracle healing had apparently gotten around.

"Rand!" He turned and found Chloe, the woman who had known Justin. "Happy Sunday!"

"Happy Sunday, Chloe," Rand said.

She gave him a beaming smile and reached out her hand, which Rand shook. She had barely enough strength to hold it and she trembled even more than the week before.

"I'm so happy you're back," she said as they walked together. "Such divine planning that last week was your first!"

"You can say that again."

"Look at all these people," Chloe said. "Amazing. All of Finnick has heard about Gerald, and now they've come to see Pastor D. When the Lord moves, he *really* moves."

Rand had to slow his pace for Chloe as she limped along. Rand offered her his arm, and she slipped her hand through the crook of his elbow.

"Such a gentleman."

Ahead of them, the multicolored tent came into view. The seats inside were already full, and the excess people were standing on the outside. Church had not even started yet.

"Look at all these people," Chloe said, excited. "So many looking to hear the good word."

"Praise be to God," Rand said flatly.

Chloe squeezed his arm. "I don't know what Pastor D has planned for today, but I've been praying all week that there is more healing. I realize it sounds selfish, but I hope the Lord moves him to choose me." Rand looked down at the frail woman, whose smile had faded. "The doctors say there's nothing more they can do. All that's left is to make sure I'm comfortable and that my affairs are in order. I've been coming here to listen to Pastor D ever since they told me that, and now I'm no longer afraid to die. He has done me a great service already. But... I can't help but be hopeful. After seeing what he did for Gerald... maybe the Lord will lead him to heal me next."

Rand's heart broke for the woman. He felt her helplessness and her desperate hope at the same time. And he'd only come for the sole purpose of poking holes in the one thing that gave Chloe peace.

"Looks like standing room only," Chloe said as they reached the entrance of the tent. "Praise Jesus."

"Come on." Rand pushed through the crowds, pulling Chloe along with him. The sea of people parted for him until he was inside the tent, where he guided Chloe to the bench in the back row. A middle-aged man sat at the end.

"Excuse me," Rand told him. "Good morning, happy Sunday. Would you mind giving up your seat for my friend here? It's hard for her to stand for a long time."

The man took one look at Chloe and beamed. "Absolutely. No problem at all."

He stood, and Chloe struggled to lower herself onto the bench. Once she was down, she looked up at Rand with soft eyes. "Thank you," Chloe said, clasping Rand's hand in both of hers. "You are a good person."

Rand stepped back and merged with the crowd. He checked his watch, and at ten o'clock sharp, Deckard Arcan walked onto the stage to an intense standing ovation. Just like the week before, his bodyguard took his position at the front of the stage.

Deckard stood there, basking in the adoration, making no effort to calm the crowd down. He wore another fine suit, this one navy, with a pink bow tie. It was well-tailored and pressed—the man had an impeccable eye for fashion.

When the congregation settled, Deckard took the microphone and said, "Happy Sunday."

The congregation answered back in unison.

"Well, well. It seems we have a lot of new faces here today." He scanned his audience, eyeing all those who were standing on the outside of the tent, raising onto their tiptoes just to get a glimpse of the miracle healer.

"I know I said the same thing last time, but praise be to God for the new people who have come to hear the good news."

"Amen!" called out a few voices in the crowd.

"Yes, my friends, God moved among us. That really happened. Perhaps some of you have had the chance to speak with Mr. Roberson during the week." A few people cheered. "God made him new, and God can do the same for you. Pray with me, please."

The congregation all bowed their heads in unison, and Deckard closed his eyes.

"Dear Lord, we come before you humbly and ask that you move in this place—"

And then he began speaking in tongues.

Rand glanced around the tent, but no one reacted to

Deckard's rapid, nonsensical words. It must've been something he did often.

Rand knew the spiritual gift of tongues was mentioned in the Bible. Someone praying would be so overcome with the presence of God that they would speak in languages that were not known on Earth, only in heaven. Rand also knew the Bible instructed that if someone were to speak in tongues, it was required to have another person there to interpret for the listeners.

It was a small detail that most churches with tongues missed out on, and this one was no different.

Rand slid his cell phone from his pocket, opened the camera app, and switched it to record. He made a video of the rest of the prayer, the rapid sounds flowing from Deckard Arcan's mouth with no effort.

"Amen," the pastor finished.

Rand stopped recording and texted the video straight to Miller. Once it was gone, he typed out a message.

Preacher man speaking in tongues. Can you verify?

A minute later, Miller sent back a thumbs-up emoticon.

"I sense there is a good portion of you here today because you heard of the miraculous things that occurred here last week," Deckard said, looking over the crowd. "Maybe you've never stepped foot in a church before. Maybe you used to attend church, but your faith has drifted. Maybe you don't believe in God, and you're only here to be entertained. Whatever your motive, whatever your past, you are welcome here. The things that happened last week were done precisely to gather you all together so you can witness the awesome power of the creator of the universe. I have spent the last week in prayer and silence. And I have been spoken to. I have been told that there is more good work to be done today."

The congregation cheered for Deckard. He waited for it to die down again.

Deckard raised the microphone to his mouth again, but before he could speak, someone stood from their bench and called out to him.

"Pastor D! My arthritis!" The man lifted his hands into the air. "It's gotten so bad I can't even drive anymore!"

Then a lady on the other side of the aisle stood. "My doctor told me I can't get pregnant! Can you pray for me?"

Then a man in the back, not too far away from Rand, called out, "They found a mass on my kidney! Please, Pastor, can you make it go away?"

Deckard looked at each one of the people as they called out to him, appearing pained by what they told him.

Two or three people stood at once, shouting at him at the same time. Their complaints drowned each other out.

Deckard held up a hand, and everyone fell silent at once. The people who had stood to request prayer lowered themselves back down, disappearing into the crowd once more.

"A lot of you are experiencing great trial and sickness," he said, speaking low. He looked around, and he genuinely appeared heartbroken. "If I could, I would lay hands on each of you and take away your pain. Perhaps the Lord will permit me to do that one day. But it is up to God who will be spoken to today."

Deckard lowered the microphone, lifted his head, and closed his eyes. "Lord, guide me. Tell me who you wish to bless today," he shouted, loud enough to be heard without his microphone.

The only sound was the tent material flapping in the chilly wind. Rand pulled his jacket tighter around him, shivering. He was waiting on edge just as much as everyone else.

Entire minutes passed in silence. Deckard remained still, as if in a trance. His eyelids fluttered, but never opened. He appeared to listen intently to a voice that only he could hear.

Then he brought the microphone back to his mouth. "There is a man here today named Randolph Casey."

11

R and's mouth went dry.

The silence continued, except now everyone looked around, waiting for the man called to identify himself. Waiting to see if Deckard's prophecy was true.

Rand said nothing.

Deckard opened his eyes and joined everyone else by looking around the room. "Randolph Casey," he said again. "The Lord has laid your name on my heart."

No, he didn't, Rand wanted to say. But in that moment, he wasn't sure *what* to believe.

The silence lingered on. Rand already knew he would not come forward. No amount of curiosity would push him to approach Deckard. Perhaps Deckard would back down. Maybe he'd find another name from God since the first one wasn't interested.

"Randolph Casey," Deckard said again, this time firm, almost angry. "Your God has called you forth. Do not deny him."

"Come on!" someone shouted.

"He's there!"

A man in the front row stood and pointed directly at Rand. It was Patrick Perryman, the guy Rand had met on campus.

Hundreds of heads turned to face him at once. The people next to him took a step away as if he had a disease. But of all the eyes, none of them pierced into him more than those of Deckard Arcan.

"Randolph Casey," Deckard said to him. "Please come forward. You have been called."

Rand struggled to find words in his tight throat. "I'm not sick. Thank you, though."

Someone booed.

"It isn't about being sick, Randolph," Deckard said, his voice soft, almost paternal. "I never said there would be a healing today. I only said the Lord would move. And he will move through you. Please come forward."

Everyone's stares continued to bore into him, and Rand felt surrounded. Even if he tried to turn and leave, he had a feeling the wall of people behind him would not let him through.

So Rand broke from the crowd and walked down the aisle toward Deckard Arcan.

Patrick must have given Deckard my name, he told himself. *He saw me come in, but I didn't see him. He told Deckard about me because of our conversation the other day.*

It made perfect sense to him.

Rand stopped a few paces away from Deckard, and the two men watched each other for a long time. Deckard's gaze went from welcoming to something else—perhaps confusion. It was as if the other man realized he had no tricks to perform with the person he had chosen. Rand felt the tension in the room tighten.

"Last week we saw a healing," Deckard said into the microphone, never taking his eyes off Rand. "That is because God is loving and merciful. He gives generously to his faithful children."

An "amen" rang from somewhere over Rand's shoulder.

Deckard went on. "But the Lord is also powerful and just. As with Israel, his own chosen people, he allowed them to be conquered when they did not obey his commands. There can, and will, be judgment."

Rand felt his insides twist.

"The Lord has told me about you, Randolph," Deckard said. "You are a man who is followed by darkness." Gone was the comforting, welcoming voice of a pastor. Now he spoke as if every word produced a bad taste in his mouth. "You have spent your life dabbling in things that no one has any business touching, and yet you persist. This evil has now attached itself to you and is always a step behind. You know exactly what I'm talking about."

Shindael.

Rand clenched his jaw and met Deckard's hard gaze with his own, refusing to back down.

"That's nice and all," Rand said, "but anyone can say that about anyone. It's called cold reading."

A wave of murmurs coursed through the crowd. Deckard eyed Rand hard. He had a feeling this was the first time the man had ever been challenged. To Rand's surprise, Deckard Arcan did not seem ready to back down.

"Cold reading, huh," Deckard said. "So you do not believe."

"In God? Sure. In you? No."

The murmurs grew into louder conversations.

Deckard raised his hand, and everyone shut up all at once.

"If you think I'm cold reading, then maybe we should dive a little deeper," Deckard said. He took a step closer. "Randolph Franklin Casey. You are forty-one years old. You do not go to church regularly. You only come back to God when you need something from him. You are a sinner. You have fornicated with thirty-two women outside of wedlock, the first when you were only fifteen years old. Two of them got pregnant, one of them miscarried. The daughter who was born has lived a tortured life on account of you and your penchant for dabbling with dark spirits."

Deckard stalked closer to Rand, and he unconsciously took a step back.

"You resist God because you are angry with him, but in reality, you are immature. When you get depressed, you drink heavily. You're going through one of those times right now.

"You were here last week and witnessed a miracle, but still you do not believe. In fact, you came here today for the sole purpose of revealing me as a fraud and a liar."

As Deckard's strong presence pushed Rand farther down the aisle, he felt compelled to back away. Out of the corner of his eye, he spotted Justin sitting on one of the benches, his mouth hanging open in disbelief.

"Just because you have no faith, you think you can steal the faith of others. Well, that is not how it works,

Randolph Casey. God is much too strong for people like you."

Now the crowd grew more animated. Some started shouting at him. Others booed. Rand saw angry faces all around him.

"The Lord will always accept those who repent, but that is between you and God. Acceptance is not something you'll find from me," Deckard said. "Today, you are not welcome here. You are attacking the faith of hundreds, and that cannot stand. Come back when you have forgiven yourself and asked God to forgive you as well."

"Get out!" someone shouted.

"God have mercy on your soul!" cried another.

Everyone in the tent erupted into loud shouting, chastising Rand. It was as if the crowd was one second away from attacking him.

Rand did the only thing he could think to do. He turned and ran. As he forced his way through the crowds, he felt slaps and kicks on his arms, torso, and hips. He tripped and almost went down, but caught himself before straightening and quickening his pace.

He burst through the sea of people outside the tent and sprinted down the path, leaving the shouting mob behind him.

The last thing he heard as he left the church in the distance was Deckard Arcan's voice over the microphone. "Praise Jesus!"

12

Rand slammed the door of his Jeep and locked it. He peered through the windshield, half expecting the angry mob to chase after him.

But there was no one there. Now that the skeptic had been expelled from their midst, Rand assumed they were ready to continue on with church as scheduled.

His chest heaved from the running. He hadn't sprinted like that in a long time. Although it was a cold autumn morning, sweat beaded on his face and chest, staining dark spots on the neck of his t-shirt. He peeled his jacket off and threw it into the backseat.

"Holy shit," he whispered as he caught his breath.

Deckard Arcan had nailed him one hundred percent. That was *not* cold reading. Cold reading was purposely vague, causing the target to twist their mind to find ways the words could apply to them.

No. That man had intimate details of Rand's past and present.

And Deckard had rebuked him for it.

He started the Jeep and drove down Highway 38. Deckard Arcan's cold, steel-blue eyes were still burned into Rand's memory. The way the pastor had looked at Rand—such disgust.

He had known.

Known precisely what Rand had come there to do. And had played him perfectly.

Rand came to the crossroads. One way led him to the Interstate that would take him home, back to the city. The other way would take him to Finnick, the nearest small town, and presumably the home of most of the congregation in Deckard's church.

Rand idled there for a moment, glancing back and forth between both signs.

Home was where he wanted to go. His nerves were still shocked and rattled. His heart still pounded in his chest.

But he remembered Justin. The boy was still back there in the church, soaking up every ounce of whatever Deckard told him. Charles Tidwell had wanted Rand to prove to Justin that Deckard was a sham, but after that little incident, there was no telling how credible Justin now thought Deckard was.

But it was more than Justin. Rand knew that something fishy was going on. Patrick Perryman could have told Deckard to call on Rand, but Patrick could *not* have told Deckard all the details that he'd known.

Rand was going to get to the bottom of it. He always did.

He turned left and drove toward Finnick, foot heavy on the accelerator.

ALTHOUGH THE SERMON elicited strong and favorable reactions, Justin Tidwell could not concentrate on any of it. Pastor D had preached vehemently and with conviction. Deckard and the others seemed to have already forgotten about the heretic that had been expelled from the congregation.

But Justin had not. In fact, Mr. Rand remained on his mind the entire sermon, blocking any of Pastor D's words from entering.

Is Mr. Rand really that sinful of a man?

Justin also wondered if he himself was guilty for associating with such a family. Libby was not the same person as her father, but they were still close. Mr. Rand had the potential to influence her a lot.

The event nagged at Justin too much. He had to know if his relationship with the Caseys would interfere with his walk with the Lord. And there was no better person to ask than Pastor Deckard Arcan himself. After Pastor D's amazing feat the week before, Justin was sure that everything Pastor D had said was true. If God gave Pastor D the ability to heal, then certainly God also gave the man divine knowledge.

So after church was over, Justin hung back while the crowd dispersed and headed toward their cars. Pastor D had disappeared through the rear exit of the tent after his sermon as he usually did—otherwise a mob of adoring fans would rush him. Justin assumed he wasn't welcome to search out Pastor D, but he figured his motives were pure and that Pastor D wouldn't mind.

He walked past the raised platform on which Pastor D

gave his messages and through the tent flap behind it. On the other side was the rest of the field, a few cars, and the man himself.

Pastor D spoke to Patrick Perryman. They stood near a sleek black sedan, where the big bodyguard that always hovered like a statue beside the stage waited to drive Deckard away. Justin was acquainted with Patrick, but didn't know how Patrick had come to be so close with Pastor D.

He walked toward them, the butterflies springing up in his stomach. It was like approaching a celebrity, knowing how they acted in public, but not one on one. The last time he'd felt that way was when he'd initially asked Libby out.

Deckard saw him first, and he ceased his conversation with Patrick as he approached. Patrick followed Deckard's gaze.

"Justin Tidwell. Happy Sunday."

Justin flushed. *How did he know me?* Probably the same way he knew Mr. Rand. Then it occurred to Justin that perhaps Deckard also knew every sinful thing Justin had ever done. He was suddenly a lot more nervous.

"H-h-happy Sunday."

Justin realized he didn't know what he would say. He had no plan. He just needed to speak with Pastor D. He regretted wasting the time of such an important man.

"You seem distressed," Pastor D said, his voice gentle— a completely different tone than the powerful one he'd used to expel Rand from the church.

"A little," Justin admitted.

"You felt the need to tell me about it. Come, then. Do not be afraid. What's on your mind?"

Justin shuffled his feet, considering not saying anything at all. But if he wanted to become a true disciple, then these were the hard conversations he needed to have.

"That man. From earlier. The one you said was evil, that ran away from the church."

Deckard's face hardened. Only a bit, but it was enough that Justin noticed. "Randolph Casey."

"Yes. He's my girlfriend's father."

"Is that so," Deckard said, flat and unimpressed.

Patrick also gave him an incredulous look.

"And what is it you have come to tell me?" Pastor D went on. "That I am wrong? That the things I said about the man were not true?"

"No!" Justin said quickly. "I actually don't know him well at all. I've only met him a few times and have barely talked to him."

"Do you believe they were true, Justin?"

"Yes," he found himself saying. "I've seen the things you do and I believe in you."

"Good. I have heard the truth from the angel Azora, and we should not have such a dark man in our midst. Redemption is possible for all men, and I will pray that Randolph Casey finds his way out of the darkness. He can come to me alone for guidance, as you have done, but being in a crowd of saved people is not the right place for him now."

Justin digested those words. He was glad to hear that there would be a second chance for Mr. Rand. He liked the man, although he always got the feeling that Mr. Rand did not particularly like that he and Libby were dating.

"You have come here to ask if I think it is right or

wrong for you to continue dating the daughter of an evil man," Pastor D said.

Justin was shocked, even though he was starting to realize he shouldn't be. "Yes."

"We each have a responsibility to lead good and clean lives," Pastor D said. "We should flee from any sin and darkness, especially those related to hell and dark magic. This is what Randolph Casey is involved in. How can you be sure that his daughter, your girlfriend, isn't as well?"

That couldn't be possible. He'd been with Libby for a few months now, and surely she was not like that.

But when Justin looked into Pastor D's eyes, he saw a stern, challenging look. One telling him to think and discern for himself. On top of that, Justin got the feeling that Deckard knew something he didn't. Yet another piece of hidden information divined from God. Deckard had been right about Mr. Rand, after all…

"I guess I never considered that…"

"Consider it now," Deckard said. "I won't tell you what to do, but you are a smart young man. You know what you need to do to get your life back into the light. Have a good week, Justin."

With that, Deckard climbed into the backseat of the car. His bodyguard closed the door for him and went around to the driver's side. Patrick Perryman joined Deckard in the rear, but before he got in, cast Justin a quick look of disgust.

That was strange. Justin had known Patrick for a while and thought they were friends. Was the news of him dating the daughter of an evil man something that would make Patrick angry? Shouldn't he respect that Justin was coming to Pastor D for guidance?

The car drove away, leaving him alone. Pastor D had been right—Justin knew what he needed to do. If he wanted to be a true disciple, the best thing would be to end his relationship with Libby. Because who knew if Mr. Rand would ever stop dabbling with evil spirits?

But the idea pained him. He cared about her, and they'd had many good times together. Honestly, he never thought he'd ever date someone like her. She was way out of his league, as his few friends reminded him of often. They were right.

Why does the perfect girl have to have an evil father?

Later, on his drive back to the city, Justin felt tremendous guilt over his conflicting desires. So far, all other sacrifices—his music, his movies, his books—to lead a more faithful and obedient life had been easy. But Libby? He wanted to hold on to her tightly.

If he let her go, he knew he'd feel totally empty.

13

R and had never been to Finnick, Louisiana, before. When he got there, he discovered why.

It was a country, nothing town. At first, he wasn't even sure he had arrived. But when the farmlands gave way to buildings, he slowed down to read a sign and realized he was on Main Street.

It was Sunday afternoon, and only a few people were about. As he cruised through, those he passed craned their neck to stare him down with no consideration of being rude. Surely everyone knew everyone, and no one recognized his orange Jeep.

First things first, he thought. *Gerald Roberson.*

It seemed the best place to start—determining if what had happened to the man was real.

He came out on the other end of Main Street and ended up in farmland again, so he did a U-turn in the middle of the road and headed back into town. About halfway down Main Street, he spotted a bar called the Flat Tire. If he was correct in assuming that everyone knew everyone, then someone there would know where to find Mr. Roberson.

Besides. He needed a drink.

He parked on the street and went inside. It was a small country joint filled with empty tables and a few locals sitting along the bar. There were video poker machines in the corner and a pool table nearby, the balls racked in the shape of a triangle on the table.

Rand pulled up a stool among the others and ordered a whiskey from the bartender, a girl who looked much too young to be working there. She eyed him curiously as she poured it—probably the same look she gave everyone who came in that she didn't recognize.

He downed it in one gulp and asked the girl to refill it. That earned him stares from the others at the bar—old men who most likely went there every day just to get out of the house.

Rand knocked it back, and the bartender passed him a third without waiting.

"Careful, son," said the elderly gentleman next to him. "Whatever she's done to you can't be that bad."

"I wish it was as simple as woman trouble."

"You're not from around here, are you?"

"What gave it away?"

"I've never seen you before."

"I'm looking for an old buddy of mine," Rand said. "Gerald Roberson. Do you know where he lives?"

The other man's smile faltered. "You're not the first person who's been looking for him. Everyone wants to see if it's true. If what happened to him was real."

"And was it?"

"Of course. Gerald couldn't get around town without that wheelchair."

"I'd still like to talk to him."

The old man sneered. "Let him be. He's been through a lot and has finally caught a lucky break. Doesn't need to be bothered by skeptics like you."

Then, a loud crack sounded behind Rand—the noise of someone powerfully breaking the racked pool balls.

He turned. No one was there. The balls lay just as they had been when he'd arrived.

The door to the Flat Tire opened and another man walked in. He looked about fifty, khaki shirt tucked into his matching pants. A shiny silver star was pinned to his front pocket.

He ambled up to the bar, where the young girl met him and gave him a shot of whiskey without even asking him what he wanted.

"Afternoon, Sheriff," said the man Rand had been talking to.

The sheriff, whose name was Jones according to his tag, tossed back the drink and wiped his mouth with his hand.

Gotta love small-town law enforcement, Rand thought.

Jones placed the empty glass on the bar. "How are you, Phil? Didn't see you in church this morning."

Phil only shrugged. "Speaking of church, this fella here's looking for Gerald Roberson."

Rand wished Phil hadn't called him out like that.

Jones fixed his attention on Rand for the first time. His eyes narrowed. "*You* were there earlier. Runnin' your mouth about how you don't believe Gerald was healed."

"Afternoon, Sheriff." Rand put on his best smile.

"I already know you're trouble," Jones said, bringing his face closer. Rand could smell the whiskey on his breath. "I suggest you head back to the city, or wherever it is you came from. We don't need people causing problems for folks like Gerald Roberson. He's a good man."

Another loud crack from the pool table. Rand looked again.

And this time, he saw Shindael. Blue skin like a frozen corpse, black eyes staring right at him. The balls scattered all around the table, each sinking into a pocket until none were left.

Rand's heart pounded.

"Are you listening to me?" Jones said.

Rand turned back to the man. He knew the sheriff could not see Shindael. Demons only revealed themselves to those they wanted to be seen by—even in a crowded room—and usually at the most inopportune moments. Shindael was trying to make Rand seem crazy in front of the sheriff; Rand resolved to keep his cool. "Yes, sir. No trouble from me."

Jones snorted as if he didn't believe it.

He shouldn't believe me, Rand thought. He had every intention of poking around town to get the answers he needed.

The young bartender girl watched their tense conversation. She didn't seem nervous, though. Perhaps she was used to seeing barroom arguments.

"You've been warned." Jones dropped a few bucks on the bar and walked outside. Rand watched through the windows as he got into his cruiser and drove away.

He looked back at the pool table. Shindael was gone, and the balls were racked again.

"You heard the sheriff," said Phil. "Best you head home."

Rand followed suit and put some cash on the bar. He could tell when he wasn't wanted. The sheriff's untimely visit had ensured that he wouldn't get any useful information from the Flat Tire anyway.

He went out into the chilly afternoon and pulled his jacket around his body. The whiskey had done little to warm him, but it had taken off the edge that lingered since the episode at church.

"Excuse me." He turned to see that the bartender had followed him outside. "Eight-seven-five Albert Street."

"Sorry?"

"Gerald Roberson lives at eight-seven-five Albert Street. My grandma was friends with Mrs. Roberson before she passed away."

Rand nodded. "I appreciate it very much."

She pulled out a cigarette and lit it. She looked about Libby's age, maybe younger, and Rand felt a twinge of anger. He remembered Georgia Collins and how much she would give to have normal lungs. And here was this girl, voluntarily destroying her own. "I'm like you. I don't believe he was actually healed. I think everyone has gone crazy over nothing. So hopefully you figure something out and set the record straight." She took a long drag.

"I'll do what I can," Rand said.

"Just be careful," she added. "Sheriff Jones is kind of an asshole. He's arrested my boyfriend like three times."

"Noted," Rand said, although there was likely a decent reason for those arrests.

He returned to his Jeep and punched the address into his GPS.

14

Rand followed the driving instructions and soon found himself at 875 Albert Street.

The house was small, despite being two stories. The white paint was flaking off and the posts on the front porch were cracked and looked ready to collapse. One strong hurricane might be enough to blow the place over.

Rand parked on the road and walked up the driveway, now mostly mud and puddles. The porch floorboards creaked underneath him as he approached the screen door.

He rapped on the screen door's window. The interior door was open, allowing him to see into the dark house.

When no one came, he knocked again. Still, there was no answer.

I'll come back later.

He was walking down the porch when an old red pickup truck turned into the driveway. The tires splashed through the mud, then stopped at the side of the house.

The cab door opened and out came Gerald Roberson. No wheelchair, walking on his own two legs.

"Morning," Rand said.

Gerald did not return the pleasantry. He analyzed Rand as if trying to remember where he'd seen him before.

"You're the man they ran out of the church earlier today," he said.

"Ah. Should have known you'd be there."

"After what God has done for me, I'll be there every Sunday until the day he takes me to heaven."

Rand waited for Gerald to demand that he leave, since Mr. Roberson was likely tired of the gawkers that Sheriff Jones had said had been pestering him.

Gerald walked toward Rand, and as he did, Rand kept his eyes on the man's legs. Not a single hint of a limp or joint ache. They didn't even match his upper body movement—his arms hung rigid and stiff by his side, his back slightly hunched. It was like he was young in his lower half, old in his upper. To Rand, it looked very unnatural.

"You're just like everyone else," Gerald said. "Can't stop looking at my legs. Makes me feel like a supermodel, you know."

"You must understand," Rand said. "People don't see that every day."

"I get it," Gerald said. "So, is what Pastor D said about you true? All that stuff." Rand said nothing. "I imagine so. He got all that information straight from an angel named Azora, you know."

"So he said."

"How else could he have known?"

That's what I'm here to figure out.

93

"Well, we can stand out here and freeze our bottoms off, or you can come inside." Gerald walked up the front porch. "You're maybe the hundredth person who's come in the past week to see if my new legs are real or just some trick. You'd think I'd be tired of it by now. But I understand why the Lord blessed me like this. Not so I can walk, but to be living proof of the Gospel. So come on in. I'll make you some coffee."

Gerald went straight for the kitchen and Rand followed. At the bottom of the stairwell, there was a motorized chair Gerald could use to ride to the top.

"What you looking at?" Gerald asked.

"Nothing." Rand caught up with him in the kitchen. "You live here alone?"

"Yeah. Ever since Paula passed." Gerald filled the pot with water. "It's a quiet life. The kids come by now and then. Heading out to hear Pastor D has given me a lot to look forward to."

"Have you always been a believer?" Rand asked.

"It was Paula who led me to the Lord," Gerald said, putting ground coffee into the top of the machine. "She was big into it and she dragged me along to church. We used to go down the road to that place where old Simon Cole preaches. Mount Grace Church."

"Don't know it. I'm not from here."

"Nice church, but simple. Haven't been back since I found Pastor D. Honestly, a lot of the people who went there now head out to the tent. Not sure if there's anyone left for Simon to preach to. Paula's buried in the cemetery behind the church."

Rand made a mental note of the information. *Simon Cole. Church near the cemetery.*

Gerald served his coffee, smoke rising from the mug.

"I guess you're here because you want to know if the miracle was real," Gerald said, walking into the living room. Rand followed him. There was only a couch and a recliner, beside which was a table stacked high with paperbacks. The seat cushion was very sunken and there were stains in the blue material. Gerald lowered himself in without a hint of struggle.

Rand settled on the couch, though he sank lower than he'd expected. "I guess you could say that."

"I'm glad you came. Yes, the miracle was real. It was all a gift from God."

Rand sipped the coffee. The man had made it very strong, just as Rand liked it. "You'll understand why I struggle to believe it."

"Don't understand it too much," Gerald said, his thick southern accent coming out. "You saw it with your own two eyes. What more do you need?"

Rand chuckled. If only it could always be that simple.

"I know what you're thinking. You think Pastor D hired me as some kind of actor or something. Does this look like I'm an actor?" He gestured around the living room. The inside was even more run down than the outside, years of neglect adding up. "Did he pay the whole town of Finnick to tell people I wasn't able to walk, and now I can? Come on." Gerald sipped at his coffee.

"I suppose you have a point," Rand said.

"There can only be one explanation," Gerald said.

"The Lord," Rand finished for him. *And his angel Azora, supposedly.*

Gerald nodded and smiled. "You got it. I suggest you take Pastor D's advice and get right with God. We do not know the hour of our death, and I would hate for you to have witnessed his power firsthand and still miss out on eternity in heaven."

"I'll consider that," Rand said.

This was a dead end. Gerald was not backing down from his story, and there seemed to be no clues in that barren house as to how the old man was suddenly able to walk again. Rand would have to search elsewhere.

"I think I've taken up enough of your time, Mr. Roberson," Rand said, finishing his coffee and standing.

"You need more convincing," Gerald said, his voice becoming low and grave.

Rand lowered himself back onto the couch. "Sorry?"

"I can't in good conscience let you walk out of this house without all the information. I'd be doing a disservice to God and the way he used me to bring you here."

Now Rand's curiosity was piqued. "Okay. What did you have in mind?"

Gerald eyed him for a long time, pursing his lips in and out as he considered. It seemed as if he was rethinking his offer. Finally, he said, "Come back tonight."

"Tonight?"

"Yeah. Eleven o'clock."

"Okay. Then what?"

Gerald set his coffee cup on the table next to the stack of books. He leaned forward in his chair. "Between you and me, the legs aren't the only thing God has given me." He spoke low, secretively.

"What else has he given you?"

"He has allowed Paula and I to be reunited."

Rand swallowed. A solid lump had formed in his

throat. "You mean your wife who passed away a few years ago?"

He nodded. "She visits me now. Every night at the same time. We chat, and she tells me what it's like to be in heaven. She has the most amazing stories, and now I can't wait to join her there. She'll tell you, too. Then you can know it's all real."

Gerald was smiling, but Rand had a terrible feeling about what he was hearing.

"So you're telling me your wife's spirit visits you every night since you were healed?"

Gerald frowned. "I should've figured you wouldn't believe me. If you don't want to see, then fine."

Rand quickly backpedaled. "No, no. I want to see."

Whenever someone claimed to be visited by a spirit, Rand had an obligation to investigate. But what did Gerald's healing have to do with him being visited by Paula's ghost?

Maybe coming here wasn't a dead end after all.

Gerald scowled at Rand, as if trying to decide whether to rescind the offer. Finally, he said, "Eleven o'clock tonight. Don't be late."

"I'll be here at eleven and not a minute after."

15

Back in the Jeep, Rand used his phone to look up a place to stay for the night. There was a small motel about fifteen minutes away. It had four reviews that averaged a rating of one and a half stars, but it was his only option. So he punched the address into his phone's GPS and drove away from Gerald's house, following the highlighted path to the motel.

The Finnick Inn was a ramshackle joint, looking like it had been built in the '60s or '70s and not updated since. The Jeep rumbled as Rand drove through the potholed parking lot and pulled up to the front office.

The reception area was marred by a nasty shade of yellow-green wallpaper and a similarly colored carpet. A magazine rack was filled with old issues, their covers showing headlines for news stories that were years old.

No one was at the desk, and Rand searched around for a bell. A single voice came from the rear office—someone talking on a telephone.

"Hello?" Rand called.

Whoever was there stopped speaking, then resumed their conversation.

So Rand waited. But it seemed like the guy was happy to have him wait there forever.

"*Hello?*"

"Let me call you back," the man barked into the phone. Then he appeared at the desk, looking agitated. "Help you?"

He was an older man, his skin wrinkled, weathered, and tan. He wore a dirty camouflage cap and a collared red shirt that hung loose on his skinny body. A plastic name tag said he was Keith.

"I was hoping to get a room."

Keith grumbled as he snatched up a key hanging on a rack behind the desk. "Forty-three bucks for the night. Cash only." His southern accent was thick.

"Avoiding the tax man, I see." Rand smirked as he dug into his wallet and found the money. "I like your style, my friend."

Keith did not respond to Rand's quip. There was no register, and Keith instead tossed the money into a drawer and made his change. "Follow me."

Outside, the evening had grown colder and the clouds had darkened, threatening more rain. The storms were far from over.

Keith walked with an arched back and his head forward, like a chicken. He wobbled from side to side, as if he had knee problems. He led Rand to a door that had the number 11 nailed into the wood.

Keith inserted the key and jiggled it a bit, but it was stuck. "Son of a bitch," he muttered as he shook it, rattling the whole door on its hinges. Finally, it gave way. He pulled the key out of the knob and handed it to Rand. "Gets caught sometimes. Wiggle to the left while pulling in, and it'll give, eventually."

One and a half stars seems generous, Rand thought.

"Got it," he said.

Keith spat on the ground. "There's only five minutes of hot water in the tank. Trying to get the repair guy out here to take a look, but he's apparently sick. Something with his prostate. Oh, and the phone don't work. Only calls the front office. You got a cellular, right?"

"Not a problem at all."

"Good." Keith marched off without another word.

Rand chuckled to himself as he watched Keith walk away.

The room was about as basic as he'd expected. There was a single bed, hard as a board when he pressed on the mattress, two flattened pillows, a thin red comforter, and a brown carpet with dark stains. The place smelled of cigarette smoke and the air inside was humid and damp.

"Not exactly home," Rand muttered to himself. He'd stayed in worse places while working on cases before, though.

Rand fiddled with the air conditioner and it roared to life, blowing icy air in his face. It hummed and vibrated as it worked. Sleeping with that on would be like trying to fall asleep next to a running lawn mower.

Rand lay on the bed on top of the bedspread. His mind and body were heavy after everything he'd been through that day.

Right. Quick nap, then meet Gerald Roberson, and find out what's going on...

It wasn't long before his eyes closed and he was fast asleep.

———

RAND WAS awoken by a loud crash. He shot up straight, heart pounding, and looked around the room. It sounded like someone had kicked in the wall.

There was no light shining through the thin curtain. Rand pulled his phone from his pocket and checked the time. Nine-fifteen at night.

How did I sleep for five hours?

The room was freezing now, so he got up and cut off the AC, which plunged the room into silence. He heard the pattering of rain outside.

And what the hell made that noise?

A crash again, startling him. It was coming from the room next to his. The thin wall shook, and the stock artwork rattled and almost fell from its mount.

Rand approached the wall and placed his ear against it. He could make out voices on the other side.

"The hell is the matter with you?"

"I'm sorry!" A woman's.

"No you ain't!"

Then something hit the wall again near where Rand was pressed against it, listening. He leapt backwards. Then the woman started crying.

She's in trouble, Rand thought.

He went outside and approached the room next door —Room 12. Rain dripped off the overhead awning in heavy drops.

Another loud crash came from inside.

"Son of a bitch! I thought I told you not to do that anymore!"

The woman cried louder.

Rand pounded on the door of Room 12. "Hey! Leave her alone!"

He expected the man to shout back at him, or fling open the door and confront him. But neither happened. The man inside only continued to shout while the woman cried and begged.

Rand banged on the door again, this time louder, but that too was ignored. He tried the knob, but it was locked.

I have to help her, he thought. He looked toward the front office on the other side of the rain-slick parking lot. *Keith will have the key.*

Rand hurried across the lot, stamping through puddles that had collected in the potholes. He burst into the office, and once again, the manager was nowhere to be seen.

"Keith!" he called. No answer. "Keith!"

Then Keith appeared, looking alarmed. "What?"

"Something's going on in the room next to mine. Let me borrow the key."

Keith narrowed his eyes at him. "What do you mean?"

"It sounds like there's a fight. There's a man yelling and a woman crying. I need—"

"No there ain't," Keith said. "You're the only one here."

Rand paused for a moment, then said, "How could that be? I know what I heard." But even as he said the words, Rand remembered that his Jeep had been the only car outside.

"Don't bother me again," Keith said. "This reception ain't a twenty-four-hour service desk." He turned and disappeared into the office.

Rand looked at the rack of keys behind the desk. The key to Room 12 dangled from the hook. All the room keys were there, except for 11. He leaned over the desk and snatched the key from its hook.

Rand rushed across the parking lot, but stopped short when he heard the phone ringing on the bedside table in his room. He'd left the door wide open in his urgency.

What the hell?

He glanced at the office. According to Keith, that phone only connected to the front office, but Rand didn't see Keith standing at the phone through the window.

Rand sensed that something was very, very wrong.

Rand went inside and hovered over the phone, watching it for a few seconds. It continued to ring.

He snatched the receiver up and brought it to his ear, but said nothing. The line was garbled and filled with static.

"Dad?" Libby's voice.

"Libby?"

"Dad, where are you? Are you coming home?"

A cold spike pierced Rand's heart. *She doesn't know I'm here. It's impossible for her to call.* He slammed the receiver down and stepped away from the phone.

That voice had sounded like Libby, but it was not his daughter.

He's here, he realized. There was only one who could play such tricks on him. *Shindael.*

Another loud crash on the wall.

And now that Rand realized what was going on, he knew what he'd find inside Room 12.

He went next door, then used the key in the lock.

Empty.

The room was exactly like his, except mirrored. The lights were off, the bed made, and no one was inside.

It was all fake. All mimicry. He's definitely here.

And when Rand turned, he saw a black figure standing on the other side of the parking lot near the road. The figure was under a streetlight, the yellow beam doing nothing to illuminate his dark features. The rain fell all around him as he stared at Rand.

"Shindael, you son of a bitch," Rand whispered to himself.

Then a presence to his left startled him.

"What the hell are you doing?" Keith had appeared. He snatched the key from Rand's hand and slammed the door of Room 12 shut, then locked it. "Are you crazy? I told you no one was in there. You can't steal the keys, you maniac."

Rand glanced toward Shindael. He was closer now, half the distance than before.

"He's coming closer," Rand whispered to himself.

Keith followed Rand's gaze. "What the hell are you looking at?"

Shindael, when he appeared, had always been at a distance—usually across the room. Rand knew from experience that when demons neared, especially after they had always maintained space, it meant they were planning to attack.

"Who's closer?" Keith demanded. "Look at me when I'm talking to you!"

Keith gripped Rand's arm and forced Rand to turn toward him.

And in that split second, Shindael appeared just over Keith's shoulder. Smiling with his jagged, razor-sharp teeth, the demon placed his clawed hand on Keith's shoulder, but Keith gave no indication that he felt it at all. Rand knew Keith wouldn't. Shindael was invisible to the man.

He's threatening him.

"Leave him alone!" Rand shouted at Shindael.

Keith glanced behind him, then looked back at Rand. "You're a crazy son of a bitch. I want you out of my motel."

Shindael had made Keith a hostage right before Rand's eyes. The demon certainly had the power to bring Keith great harm.

"He hasn't done anything to you. Don't hurt him." Rand said.

But Shindael only gave a soundless laugh and then disappeared.

"I'm warning you," Keith said. "If you don't leave…"

Shindael's presence has become much stronger, Rand thought. *I'm getting close to something.*

Something that Shindael did not want Rand to discover. He was certain of it.

"You hear me?" Keith shouted at him. "Get out!"

Rand snapped out of his thoughts. Keith was right—Rand had to leave. Shindael had threatened the man, and as long as Rand was there, Keith would not be safe.

Rand swallowed hard. "Sorry to cause you trouble," he croaked out, unable to think of anything else to say.

"I'm calling the sheriff."

"No need for that," Rand said quickly. He grabbed his stuff from the motel room and went straight for his Jeep.

16

R and could barely keep his Jeep straight as he drove away from the motel. His hands shook too much.

Finally, he pulled over so he could gather himself.

He was so close...

The only time Shindael had been that close to him was the night they'd met, right after Rand had defeated Shindael's servant, Karax.

But ever since then, Shindael had always kept his distance. He would appear at random times—when Rand was teaching, when he was out to lunch with his daughter, or sometimes materializing on the side of the road while driving—but always far away.

But this time, Shindael was close enough to touch.

That horrible face over Keith's shoulder. He'd been rude, but Keith definitely did not deserve to be touched by a demonic entity—he would likely discover some mysterious markings on his shoulder the next day, and have no idea where they'd come from.

I'm getting too close to something, Rand thought. *Shindael may have threatened Keith, but Shindael was actually using him to warn me.*

The clock on the dash read 10:21 PM. Rand was meant to meet Gerald Roberson at eleven, the time his deceased wife's spirit supposedly visited.

Shindael doesn't want me to go there, Rand thought.

Shindael had not appeared close until Rand had made a plan to meet Gerald. If Rand wanted out of the case, to leave it all alone, now was the time. He could heed Shindael's warning and return home.

Rand didn't even pause to consider that option.

He put the Jeep in drive and headed toward Gerald's house.

ALTHOUGH THE HOUSE WAS LARGE, Patrick Perryman had been relegated to a small room on the second floor that served as his bedroom.

It was enough. He did not need much. God warned against the dangers of materialism. All he had was a simple bed, a closet for his tiny wardrobe, and a desktop computer.

It was about nine o'clock at night, and he browsed Facebook. He'd found the profile page a few days ago, and he'd viewed it every night since then.

Libby Casey. The girl who had come with Justin Tidwell to church the previous week. She'd caught his eye instantly, and in that moment, he realized she was something special.

Things were starting to make a lot more sense. The

more faithful he was, the better he had become at noticing God's plan for his life in the little details. The day he'd met Rand, Patrick knew the professor was a hurting man, struggling with his faith.

But since Libby Casey came to church, Patrick understood that God was up to much more.

Patrick navigated to her profile, which he had bookmarked. For the first time since he'd found it, she had updated it with a few new pictures. These were of her and some friends from her volleyball team at practice. Libby and two other girls posed for the camera, arms wrapped over each other's shoulders, smiling brightly. Her blonde hair was tied up and her face was flushed and sweaty, but Patrick thought she was stunning. He allowed his gaze to linger on the tight shorts of their uniforms before forcing his eyes away, reminding himself that it was sinful. Still, he felt a primal urge stirring inside him.

There was nothing else new on the page. Libby didn't seem to get on Facebook as often as he did.

So instead, he concerned himself with going through the pictures he'd already scrolled through every night: she and her friends while they were out for dinner somewhere. He especially liked the one where she wore the black dress. If he had a printer, he would have printed it out. There was another of her and her dad hiking. Then a few with a woman who resembled her, which Patrick took to be her mother. There was another man in the pictures with the mom, and they looked friendly with each other. Patrick surmised that Rand and Libby's mom were not together. Maybe they had never been. That would make sense. Pastor D had said Rand Casey was a sinful man.

He scrolled all the way through, taking in the photos he had memorized by then. His body flushed with desire, and he closed his eyes and tried to pray away the temptation. It didn't always work. He had succumbed last night, and he'd spent the day praying for forgiveness. He knew he would eventually have to confess to Pastor D.

Patrick checked the clock on the computer. It was now 9:16, and his appointment with Pastor D was in fourteen minutes. It was better to be early than late, so he minimized Libby's Facebook profile and left the bedroom.

The old mansion on the outskirts of Finnick had been built fifty years ago by a wealthy businessman, but after he died alone in the house, it was vacant until Pastor D purchased it. Perhaps he was the only man in town who could afford it.

Patrick descended the stairs to the first floor, gripping the handrail so as not to tumble down the steps. Pastor D ordered that the house remain dark after sundown—he did not like any artificial light. He'd never explained the reason, but Patrick knew Pastor D was close to cutting off the power. Patrick had convinced him not to, because if he did that, Patrick would not have his computer.

Patrick turned off the main foyer and toward Pastor D's study, where he spent every evening. The door was ajar, and Patrick peeked into the expansive room beyond.

There, he found Pastor D kneeling in front of a roaring fireplace, on all fours, head to the ground. He was speaking to himself, chanting in a language Patrick did not understand. Pastor D spoke in tongues often, especially when he spent his evenings in prayer. That was when he communicated with Azora, the angel of the Lord that gave him his information and blessings.

Patrick lingered by the door, not wanting to interrupt. Pastor D did not like to be disturbed.

Even though they lived in the same house, Patrick still had to make an appointment to meet with Pastor D during the evenings and nights. That was just how Pastor D needed it to be. He was very particular about his time, since he dedicated most of it to prayer and communicating with Azora.

So Patrick remained in the hallway, watching the man in his nightly ritual. Pastor D straightened from his bowed position and sat upright on his knees, looking at the roof, then into the fire, speaking incoherently.

Patrick had always been envious of the man's spiritual gift for tongues. If he could have chosen, that would have been the one he would have picked. Whenever Pastor D spoke in tongues, he looked like he was enjoying a deep connection with Azora, while Patrick, a spectator off to the side, felt left out.

"I know you're there, Patrick."

Patrick straightened at the sound of his name. Pastor D had not turned around, and he was sure he had been quiet enough to not disturb the man in his prayers.

Nerves suddenly clawed at his stomach.

"You can come in."

Patrick pushed open the door to the study and entered. It was uncomfortably warm inside because of the massive fire. That was another of Pastor D's quirks. He liked it hot, to the point of sweating.

As Patrick approached the center of the room, Pastor D stood and looked at him for the first time. The older man wore nothing but a robe and his chest and face were slick with sweat from the heat.

"Sorry to interrupt," Patrick said. "I didn't think I'd made any noise."

"We had an appointment," Pastor D said.

"But I was early."

"It's okay." Pastor D sat in the plush chair and crossed his legs. He wiped at his face with his hands, but that did little to clear the moisture from his skin. It was the only chair in the mostly empty study, which left Patrick standing like a subject before his king. "What did you want to see me about?"

Patrick swallowed. The heat and his nervousness caused sweat to break out on his forehead and back. He'd rehearsed this over and over in his head many times before, but still, it never seemed to be right.

"I've been thinking a lot lately," Patrick began.

"Thinking or praying?"

"Both."

Pastor D nodded.

"Every night, actually. As you've instructed."

"Good."

Patrick never got on the floor and bowed down to a fire and spoke in tongues like Pastor D did. But Patrick was not privy to the voice of Azora.

"I think the time has come," Patrick said.

"What time is that?"

"The time for a wife."

Pastor D eyed him and said nothing for a long while. The flames created shadows that danced on the side of his face, giving him an eerie glow. Patrick couldn't decide if Pastor D was angry or just thinking it over. He swallowed again.

"How old are you, Patrick?" Pastor D asked.

"Thirty-eight, sir."

"And how much have you prayed about this?"

"Every night for a long time."

"Why didn't you tell me until now?"

"Because I did not want to concern you with something that I was not sure was clear from the Lord," Patrick said, and it was the truth. He always tried to tell Pastor D the truth. "But lately… He has laid it on my heart."

"This is a big decision, as you know. Do you feel you are ready to love another for the rest of your days? Or is this something you want only to satisfy your desires?"

Patrick winced. Pastor D was very wise and could read him like a book. Sometimes he thought Azora told Pastor D precisely what was going on inside Patrick's head and heart. It would not surprise him if that were the case.

"Both," he said, opting for honesty. "My desires cause me to fall into sin sometimes. But I always pray for forgiveness. More than that, though, I know I am prepared to love someone else. To care for them. And I feel the Lord is ready for me to move into the next part of my life."

Pastor D watched Patrick again, saying nothing, and he felt as if the preacher was waiting for him to say more.

"Of course, me being married won't change anything when it comes to you and the church. I'll be just as loyal as before, just as present and dedicated. I plan to allow my marriage to help me grow in my faith and to become a better man."

"This is a big decision," Pastor D said. "Do you really think you can stay committed to the church and your faith after you have a wife?"

"Yes, sir," Patrick said firmly, standing straight. "I do."

His sweat dripped down his cheeks and soaked through his shirt now. As usual, the heat did not seem to bother Pastor D at all, even though he was also drenched.

"And who is this lucky lady?" Pastor D asked. "Do you have anyone in mind?"

The way Pastor D said it, Patrick suspected he already knew, the info given to him by Azora.

"Her name is Libby Casey," Patrick said. "She came to church the other week. Whenever I saw her... I don't know. It's hard to explain. The Lord just spoke and has not stopped since."

"You were filled with lust."

"No!" Patrick shot back. "It's not like that."

"Patrick..."

"Well... maybe a little. But as I said, I avoid temptation as much as I can and pray for forgiveness when I fall." Patrick was committed to the truth, but he feared if he made himself sound too weak in the face of sin, Pastor D would forbid him from seeing Libby Casey.

"She is sixteen years old," Pastor D said.

Patrick knew from her Facebook that she was in high school and had figured she was sixteen or seventeen. What he couldn't figure out, though, was how Pastor D knew. Again, it was probably something from Azora.

"I'm willing to wait a few years."

"We all know the laws of God are greater than the laws of men," Pastor D said, "and if God has willed for this girl to be in your life, then there is no reason to delay any further. I can perform the ceremony and the two of you will be man and wife until the end of your days."

Patrick's heart fluttered. For the first time, Pastor D had given him hope that he would accept his request.

"But I will do my own praying about it," Pastor D said. "I do believe that your commitment to me, the church, and the Lord will not waver because of your marriage, Patrick, but things *will* change. I must find out if the timing is right. I hope you understand. From now on, I promise to include this in my prayers to Azora, and I will let you know what he tells me."

And that was that. There was nothing to argue with. "Thank you, Pastor D." It was just about the best outcome he could have hoped for.

"Now, Patrick, go to sleep," Pastor D said.

Patrick left him in the study, the chilled air of the hallway feeling great against his slick skin. His heart still pounded from the adrenaline rush of their conversation, but his boldness had paid off. Pastor D would pray about it, and that was amazing news. God truly knew what he was doing.

Patrick returned to his bedroom and changed out of his sweaty clothes. Pastor D had told him to sleep, but he was too excited. The buzz of his success was still too fresh in his mind. Patrick Perryman hadn't been successful at much during his thirty-eight years.

He brought Libby's Facebook page back up. He couldn't wait until God revealed to her what his plan for her life was. Likely, she did not know yet, and he was excited for her. All young girls wanted to get married, and he would be the best husband she could ever hope for.

As he perused her pictures, he felt a lustful temptation again. So, he clicked off the page and onto a list of random names around the state. He scrolled through the profiles and chose one of a girl whose profile picture was a selfie that was much too revealing.

Patrick sent her a message.

Cover up! God hates whores.

And he sent it.

He scrolled again and found another girl whose pictures were of her making out with a guy. When he clicked her profile, he saw she was unmarried. He sent her a message as well.

God hates fornicators. Repent and be saved.

Sending out warnings to the lost did a lot to calm his temptation. He had learned that from Pastor D. Whenever one feels cornered by the thought of sin, just do the Lord's work, and everything will be better.

17

R and pulled up in front of Gerald Roberson's house and idled his Jeep. The rain still pattered down, tapping on his rooftop. He stopped the wipers and water began to gather on the windshield.

It was ten minutes until eleven.

The man's house was dark except for a dim light that crept through a window on the first floor. It almost looked like no one was home, but Gerald's truck was in the driveway, obscured by the rainy night.

Rand wasn't completely sure what he'd discover inside, but he had a feeling it wouldn't be good. The man had told him the spirit of his dead wife was visiting him every night. Even worse, the visitations had begun *after* Deckard Arcan had restored Gerald's ability to walk. That couldn't be a coincidence.

Plus, Shindael did not want Rand there, and had tried to warn him away.

Rand killed the engine and grabbed his bag of gear

from the backseat. As he crossed the yard, the damp grass squished underneath his shoes.

The front door opened before he got to the porch and Gerald stepped outside.

"This weather is something else," Gerald said. "Colder than it usually is this time of year, and the rain just won't stop."

"You can say that again."

Rand wiped his dirty shoes on the mat by the door and followed Gerald inside. The house was toasty, a nice feeling compared to the chilly air outside.

There were no lights on, just a fire roaring in the living room fireplace.

"Have a seat," Gerald told him. "I'll get coffee."

The last thing Rand needed was coffee. He was already on edge about whatever spiritual activity was happening inside Gerald's house late at night.

Rand returned to the couch, the same spot he'd sat earlier that day. He dropped his bag on the ground at his feet and removed his jacket, the warmth quickly becoming stifling. Sure, it was cold outside, but Rand wondered why Gerald needed it so blazing hot inside the house.

Gerald was gone for a while, but finally returned with two mugs. He had also changed into a suit and tie, which Rand thought was strange. Gerald handed Rand a mug and Rand sipped it. The coffee sent a jolt of energy through his body.

Gerald sat in his recliner. The sweet scent of his cologne mixed with the smell of coffee.

"Interesting pair of pajamas you have there," Rand said, nodding toward his suit.

"I try to look my best when Paula comes."

"Does she come every night?"

"Yes," he said. "Ever since Pastor D gave me my legs back. At eleven thirty-nine at night, just like clockwork."

"Why is that? Is the time significant to you?"

"It's the time she died," Gerald said, taking a sip.

"Oh." Rand checked his watch. It was 11:23.

"But it's strange. She died at eleven thirty-nine in the morning."

That gave Rand pause. And he suddenly had a very bad feeling about this.

"What?" Gerald said. "You look sick."

"I'm just cautious about spirits that reverse times."

"So, you do believe in something after all," Gerald said. "What's wrong with the time?"

"If your wife passed away at eleven thirty-nine in the morning, why wouldn't she choose that time to come to you? Why does she reverse it and come at the same time, but at night?"

"Beats me. I never asked her." The firelight flickered on the side of his face.

Because it prefers to come in darkness, Rand thought. That was never a good sign.

At 11:37, Gerald finished the rest of his coffee in a single gulp and Rand did the same, then placed the cup aside.

"Won't be long now," Gerald said, straightening his tie.

"What should we do?" Rand asked. He felt as if the man were leading him in a séance. He'd been involved in plenty before, but none like this.

"We wait."

The only sound in the room was the popping and

cracking of the fire. As the silence lingered on, Rand grew nervous.

He kept his left arm on his lap so he could see the seconds tick by on his watch.

When the second hand reached the twelve, his watch froze, as if the battery had died.

Rand sensed a presence behind him. He twisted on the couch and looked, but saw only the wall.

"Paula, sweetheart," Gerald said. He stared into the fire. "Are you there?" Rand waited for a reply, but none came. "There's no need to be afraid, dear. We have a visitor tonight, and he is very excited to meet you. He wants to know about heaven and what eternity is like."

They sat in silence for a minute. Then Rand got the unmistakable sensation of a third presence in their midst.

"I feel something," Rand said.

"She's here," Gerald said, not taking his eyes off the fire. "Watch. I do this sometimes." He cleared his throat. "Paula. Can you give me a sign that you are close?"

Loud thumps boomed from the ceiling overhead, as if someone were jumping up and down.

"That's her sewing room," Gerald said. "She spent every evening in there before she went to bed. Paula loved to sew." A sentimental smile came to his lips.

The thumping stopped. Rand looked to his left and right, and then behind him. He felt surrounded, eyes on him from all directions.

"Don't leave our guest confused, sweetheart," Gerald said. "He's come to meet you."

The room, which was stifling hot, now turned cold—it was as if someone had just opened a window and let the autumn air inside. The flames stirred like a strong gust of wind had blown, even though there was none.

The frozen watch. The unmistakable feeling of eyes on him. The unnatural chill in the air. There were too many classic signs that Rand had experienced time and time again.

A demonic presence was in Gerald's home—one that he mistook for his wife's spirit.

Rand knew that he and Gerald were in danger.

"Gerald," Rand began.

"Shh." He stood from his chair and walked to the center of the room, not looking away from the fire. "Yes, it's cold, but that's normal. Paula always loved keeping the house cold, even in the winter. I was the opposite and liked it warm. So she makes it cold in here when she comes, even though I have a fire."

"Gerald… I don't think Paula is here."

Gerald took his eyes from the fire and pierced him with a hard gaze, as if Rand had insulted him. "You said yourself that you sensed her."

"What I mean is that I don't think you've been talking to Paula." He rose from the couch, looking around him, the feeling that they weren't alone growing stronger.

"What are you talking about?" Gerald said, suddenly angry. "I know my wife. You don't."

Rand saw it.

A shadow shaped like a human. Darker than black. An empty space in reality. It crawled along the ceiling like an insect with long arms and legs. Its head twisted around, and Rand saw glowing red eyes glaring down at him.

There it is, Rand thought, body stiffening in fear. He

had to remain calm and remove the creature that Gerald thought was his wife.

Rand reached for his bag at his feet with a trembling hand, never taking his eyes from the demon overhead. If Rand moved quickly enough, he could remove the evil presence from the house.

Gerald followed his gaze, but did not react. "What are you looking at?" He couldn't see the shadow.

"Don't move," Rand told him.

"What are you talking about?"

Rand's hand went inside his bag and he felt around for the crucifix he always kept there. As soon as his fingertips brushed against it, the demon dropped from the ceiling, deftly turning and landing on his feet right behind Gerald.

The shadow stood a foot taller than Gerald. The red eyes remained on Rand, glaring over Gerald's shoulder. Tendrils of blackness streamed from the shadow's head like long, flowing hair caught in a breeze that was not there.

The demon stood in the same threatening position Rand had seen earlier, mirroring what Shindael had done with Keith. The parallel was not lost on Rand, and his flesh crawled.

"Leave him alone," Rand commanded the demon.

"Who are you talking to?" Gerald said.

The demon twisted his head and brought it close to Gerald's face, as if whispering in his ear.

And Gerald froze. Listened.

"Don't listen to him!" Rand said. He gripped the crucifix and pulled it from his bag, straightening up and holding it out toward the demon.

The shadow reacted instantly, backing away to the far

end of the living room.

"What are you doing?" Gerald said, looking at the cross.

"I'll take care of this," Rand said. "Get behind me."

"No." Gerald's voice was firm and resolute.

Rand looked at him. "You need to trust me, Gerald. There is something dangerous inside your home."

"I know. It's you."

Rand was taken aback.

"I heard Paula's voice," Gerald continued, snarling. "She told me you're a very bad man, and if you don't leave, she'll never come back."

It was a typical demonic lie, one easily believed by someone who already trusted that the entity was who he claimed to be.

"Don't listen to him," Rand said. "He's not your wife. He's something else entirely."

"You need to leave," Gerald said. "Right now."

"Don't do this."

"I *won't* take any chances of losing Paula again."

The demon started moving toward Gerald, red eyes glued to him, hand raised and ready to strike.

Rand saw this and bolted around Gerald, holding the cross out toward the shadow. "In the name of the Lord Jesus Christ, I command you to leave—"

"Stop!" Gerald shouted, gripping Rand's arm. "I'm calling the police—"

Rand pulled out of Gerald's grasp. "You are not welcome here," Rand said to the demon. "Leave this man alone. I command you to return to hell and never come back."

The shadow backed away, moving toward the front

door, cowering underneath the power of the cross. Rand advanced further.

The demon's back pressed against the wall near the door. Then he climbed up the wall and onto the ceiling to get away from Rand and the crucifix. The red eyes bored into Rand, clearly ready to attack as soon as he faltered or let the cross drop, which Rand had no intention of doing.

Rand threw open the front door, a burst of cold wind coming inside.

"I command you to leave this house, demon, in the name of the Lord," Rand shouted. "You are compelled to obey. You are not welcome here. Depart!"

The entity on the ceiling contorted and twitched, the blackness seeming to cave in on itself. He turned into a dark, unshapely mass and drifted to the door. The shadow disappeared into the rainy night outside and Rand slammed the door behind him.

Immediately, the temperature of the room rose, and the tension decreased.

They were alone again. Gerald was safe.

"What have you done?" Gerald whispered, voice trembling. He approached Rand in the foyer near the front door. "I don't feel her anymore. She's gone."

And then Gerald lost his balance. He waved his arms around, flapping them wildly as he fell over.

Rand got to his side just in time, catching him before he hit the ground. "Are you okay?"

Rand lowered Gerald to the floor, where he sat up straight, gripping his thighs. "What is this?" He struggled to stand, but couldn't.

"Hang on," Rand said. "Relax. Take it easy."

"What's going on?" Gerald shouted. "My legs! They

gave out!"

"Just rest for a minute."

But Rand already knew what was happening. That demon was what had given Gerald the ability to walk again.

"You did this to me." Gerald looked up at Rand with a desperate, simmering rage. Tears ran down his cheeks now. "Paula is gone. My legs are gone. Why couldn't you just leave me alone?"

Rand wanted to explain the truth. He even opened his mouth to do so, but only managed a dry croak.

It wasn't your wife. It was a demonic spirit. He mimicked your wife so you would trust him. He used his power to make you walk again so you would be loyal.

But Gerald Roberson would never understand. All he knew was what he wanted to believe.

"I'm sorry," Rand said gently. "If you let me explain—"

"Just get out."

Rand knew that, in that moment, leaving was the best thing he could do. Gerald wouldn't listen to anything Rand had to say.

Rand went to the living room and grabbed his bag. When he returned to the foyer, he was struck by the broken man sitting on the floor, unable to move, probably in shock at losing the blessing Deckard Arcan had given him.

Rand knew removing the demon was the right thing, but in that moment, it was hard to feel like he'd done Gerald any favors.

"Is there anything I can do?"

Gerald lifted his hand and pointed toward the door. "You've done enough."

18

After leaving Gerald's home, Rand climbed into his Jeep, but he did not start the engine. Melancholy fell over him as he watched the rain drip down the windshield.

That was awful...

Rand knew he'd never forget the look on Gerald's face for the rest of his life: the look of a man who'd lost his ability to walk for a second time.

Demonic entities were pure evil, but were not above bestowing positive supernatural gifts on humans to gain their trust and loyalty. Those gifts always came with a price, and sooner or later the debt would be collected. Gerald Roberson would never understand how Rand had helped him. Rand couldn't even convince himself that he'd done the man any lasting good.

But Gerald was only the beginning.

That demon he'd expelled from Gerald's home had to be a servant of Shindael. Shindael had known what Rand would discern once he went to Gerald's house, which was why the demon had warned Rand at the motel.

And where did the new entity inside Gerald's house come from?

Deckard Arcan. It all made sense now. The preacher's supposedly divine knowledge, the ability to heal others— classic signs of someone influenced by supernatural evil.

But that only confused Rand. Deckard Arcan himself showed no symptoms of a diabolically possessed person.

Rand thought back to Georgia Collins, his most recent case of possession. Her skin had become scaly, and her eyes had gone black. Her voice had changed to that of Karax—the demon inside her—and her personality had disappeared. Whenever possession occurred, a person's soul was displaced by the possessing entity.

But Deckard Arcan seemed entirely like himself—a normal man. Yet still, he had the ability to wield demonic power.

Rand had never seen anything like it before. And it terrified him.

I'm dealing with something new.

That meant he needed help.

Rand remembered Gerald mentioning the other church in town, the one everyone attended before Deckard Arcan's tent came along.

What was it? Mount something...

Rand searched it on his phone, and it gave him his result.

Mount Grace Church.

Right. Maybe the pastor there will know more about Deckard. I can talk to him tomorrow.

Rand also felt he could do with some time in a holy

place. He always liked to retreat into the presence of God after an encounter with a demon.

Rand checked his watch. It was well after midnight, and the two-hour drive back home did not appeal to him. He decided to find a place to park and sleep in his Jeep—he surely wasn't welcome back at the Finnick Inn. Rand had never been opposed to sleeping in the car—he'd done it plenty of times when he was younger.

Might even be nostalgic, in a way.

As he drove away, he took one last glance at Gerald Roberson's house and hoped that the man would eventually come to understand.

PATRICK WAS in a deep sleep when he heard a soft pounding from somewhere distant.

At first, he thought it was part of his dream. As he woke, though, he knew it was real.

He lay in bed in the dark room, listening. The noise echoed from the first floor of the mansion.

Someone was at the front door.

He checked the digital clock on the bedside table. It was two o'clock in the morning.

What in the world...

Visitors came by sometimes, sure, but in the middle of the night? Never.

Maybe they'll leave.

The poundings boomed out again, louder than before. They were insistent.

Patrick flung the covers off. He had to get down there before they made more noise. Pastor D was in the midst of his prayers, just as he was every night, and Patrick did not want him to be disturbed.

Patrick descended the stairs. Whoever was on the other side of the door had started shouting.

"Pastor D! Someone help me!"

He didn't recognize the voice, but whoever it was sounded crazed and desperate. They'd have to be to show up in the middle of the night like that.

God, protect me if this person is dangerous, he prayed.

He opened the door to find a man lying on the front porch. As soon as the door was open, the man crawled inside like a soldier pulling himself through a trench.

"Patrick!" shouted the old man.

"Mr. Roberson?"

"Please help me!"

He wore a dark suit, wrinkled and covered in mud. Tears and sweat streaked his face.

"What happened to you?" Patrick knelt down beside him. He glanced back outside and spotted a wheelchair at the bottom of the porch steps, abandoned.

"That man!" Gerald shouted. "He came to my house!"

"What man?"

"That one from the church. The man Pastor D said was a sinner."

It took Patrick a minute to place what Gerald was rambling on about, but then it clicked.

Randolph Casey.

"What is going on in here?" Pastor D appeared from his study, wearing his robe. His voice was loud and stern, and he was clearly angry about the interruption.

"Oh, thank God," Gerald said when he saw him. "Please help me, Pastor D!"

Gerald reached out for him, but Deckard did not return the embrace. He only watched the man critically, as if disgusted by the begging and groveling.

Why is he not concerned? Patrick wondered.

"Explain, Mr. Roberson. What happened to you?"

"That man from the service this morning," Gerald said. "You called him to the front and convicted him of his sin."

"Randolph Casey is his name," Patrick added. Pastor D nodded.

"He came and found me. He wanted to know if the miracle was real or fake. I told him it was real, but he still seemed unsure. I figured this was a perfect opportunity to use my blessing to save another soul, so I invited him to my house to meet with Paula when she visited. But..." The man started to cry. "I don't know what happened. He tried to claim it wasn't Paula, then he did some kind of black magic and now Paula is gone and I cannot walk anymore. Pastor, he reversed your miracle."

Patrick looked over to Pastor D. "We need to help him."

"Take him to one of the spare rooms," Pastor D said. "Lay him down and let him rest."

"Will you heal him again?"

"Do as I say, then come and see me when it's done." He'd never heard Pastor D speak to him, or anyone else, that sharply before.

Pastor D only turned his back and returned to his study.

Patrick retrieved Gerald's wheelchair from outside, helped him into it, and pushed him to the other side of the mansion to a spare room that was rarely used.

"Have faith, brother," Patrick said as he left him. "Pastor D will take care of everything. I am sure of it."

Gerald still sobbed and said nothing. Patrick wanted to say something else to console him, but came up empty.

Patrick imagined himself in Gerald's shoes—the loss of his legs and his wife had both surely been traumatic the first time, but the second...

Randolph. What did you do?

Patrick returned to Pastor D's study as instructed. He was in his chair, watching the fire.

"This man has been sent by the devil," Pastor D said without taking his eyes from the flames.

"When I first met him, he seemed harmless."

"Lucifer is a master deceiver, as you know. His servants come in all forms, shapes, and sizes. He has hurt one of our members, and he needs to be dealt with. Are you willing to help me?"

Patrick wished Pastor D would be clearer about how exactly Randolph Casey should be dealt with. But he knew in that moment there was only one answer. "Yes, sir. Of course."

"Good. Now go to bed. We'll address this in the morning."

Patrick had a hundred more questions. Could Gerald Roberson be healed again? Would Paula Roberson come back? Had Azora already given Pastor D a plan to "deal with" Randolph Casey?

And would these new developments interfere with his desire to marry the man's daughter? He thought the instruction had come straight from the Lord, but why would God direct him to marry the daughter of an evil man?

To save her.

It was the only explanation.

Begrudgingly, Patrick tore himself away from Pastor D and returned to his bedroom as he was told, like an obedient child. Although it was late, he knew he would get no more sleep that night.

19

The atrium of the high school's gymnasium was like a museum of the past. Floor-to-ceiling glass cases displayed the trophies, plaques, and medals won by the various sports teams.

Justin walked by them all and stood at the entrance of the actual gym. The volleyball team was practicing. The sounds of shoes squeaking on the polished floor, balls bouncing hard, and the coach's constant whistling echoed off the high walls.

He spotted Libby behind the net, getting low and waiting to return a serve from her teammate. Justin slung his backpack off and sat in the bleachers.

She was great at the game, and she loved it. He'd seen her play many times, and even as a junior she was better than some seniors. In fact, it was her goal to play in college.

That was one of the main reasons Justin liked Libby. She had goals. Had something to work toward. Justin wished he had things like that in his life. Sure, there was guitar, and he'd always wanted to be in a band, but so far it hadn't worked out. Either he couldn't find other guys to play with, or he didn't feel motivated to write any new songs. Usually, he just got addicted to the latest video game that came out.

Now he had his church, and that had given him a sense of purpose more than anything he'd had prior. And as he watched Libby maneuver around the court, darting and volleying the ball back to the other side, he felt such regret that their lifestyles were completely opposed and that he needed to end things.

The coach blew the final whistle, signaling that practice was over. Libby still hadn't noticed him sitting there. It was her friend who spotted him first, and then whispered to her as she toweled off. She looked over, surprised he was there.

She would be. They hadn't talked much since their discussion in his bedroom about the miracle healing.

The girls filed into the locker room, but Libby crossed the gym and went over to him. He stood up to meet her.

"You look good out there," he said. He'd spent the entire practice trying to think of the right thing to say.

"What are you doing here?"

"I wanted to talk to you."

She tensed up. The last time they had talked, it had been an argument about Gerald Roberson.

"My mind hasn't changed, Justin."

"It isn't about that."

She tucked a loose piece of hair behind her ear. "Okay. Then what is it?"

"It's just that…" Her face was flushed and sweaty, but she still looked beautiful. He'd thought he'd come in with a plan, with the words all mapped out, ready to do what was right. But conversations with girls like her never went by the book.

"It's what?" Libby said, a bit firm, maybe even challenging him. As if daring him to break up with her.

Does that mean she doesn't care? Does she not like me anymore after what happened?

The thoughts came, and Justin knew they shouldn't matter. Ending their relationship was the right to do. But they still made him feel terrible. It reminded him that even though it was morally correct, it was not something he wanted to do.

"Why was your dad at church on Sunday?" he blurted out. He couldn't bring himself to say the words that would break them up, so he went with the question that had been nagging at him.

"What do you mean?"

"Your dad was at church on Sunday. You didn't know?"

Libby shrugged. "No."

"Why not?" He found that strange. Surely it seemed like something Mr. Rand would have told her. *Unless they're in it together, whatever he was up to. She could be lying to me.*

"Because I haven't seen him," Libby said. "You know I live with him only half the time. I've been with my mom."

"Right, but I just thought—"

"I figured you would have liked him to be in church." She crossed her arms.

"Well…"

"What is it really, Justin?" She'd lost her patience. "You've barely spoken or texted me since Sunday and now you're here. What do you need to say?"

He hadn't expected her to turn the tables so quickly. He thought he'd walked into the conversation with all the power. He supposed he'd given that power up when he chickened out at the last minute.

"I just wanted to know why your dad was suddenly so interested in Pastor D and the church. Because before—"

And then a realization struck into his head like lightning. So quick and unbidden that he wondered if it was what Pastor D felt when Azora gave him divine knowledge.

Mr. Rand *had* been uninterested in the church after the first week. But then he'd come for dinner a few nights later and spoken to Justin's father in his office for quite a long time.

"My dad is interested in a lot of things, Justin, and he's all over the place. I can't even begin to keep up with every little thing he does. If you want to know so badly, why don't you ask—"

"My dad put him up to it," he said.

Libby stopped speaking. "What?"

"Yeah. That night y'all were over for dinner. My dad pulled him into the office and they talked about me."

Libby's demeanor changed completely. She went from agitated and impatient to looking like a child who'd been caught doing something naughty.

"I'm right, aren't I?" Justin pressed.

"Justin—"

"And you're in on it."

"No! How could I be? I was with you the whole time my dad and yours were together. How could I have known what was going on in there?"

"I just know you do. I have a feeling."

Libby rolled her eyes. "Whatever. I didn't ask what they talked about. If you're so concerned, then maybe you should talk to your dad, or even mine."

Justin studied her and still felt like she wasn't giving him the whole truth.

"I have to get changed. I'll see you later." She started walking away.

It made too much sense. Justin's father was not a believer. Could it be possible that his dad had enlisted Mr. Rand to expose Pastor D as a fraud?

Good luck with that, Mr. Rand, Justin thought. *Pastor D is definitely the real deal.*

"We need to break up," Justin said toward Libby's back.

She stopped in her tracks, then turned around to face him again. She gave him a stony look. "Did your pastor also tell you to do this?"

How did she know?

"I just... think it's best."

"Whatever, Justin. Do whatever makes you happy." Then she turned and left him.

Justin picked up his backpack and slung it over his shoulder.

I did the right thing. I know I did.

Libby, Mr. Rand, and his own father were in a conspiracy to interfere with his growing faith.

Pastor D was right. Only bad things can come from a relationship like this.

Justin trudged out of the gym. He'd handled things

with Libby, but now he needed to know how to approach his own father. He decided to ask Pastor D for advice on Sunday.

The man was quickly becoming one of the few people Justin could trust.

20

The path was a single dirt road through a field filled with old oak trees. The early morning sunlight barely broke through the thick branches overhead. Rand's Jeep rocked back and forth as he went, the big tires dipping into holes in the earth. The shaking hurt the crick in his neck—he must've slept funny.

Maybe my car-sleeping days are over, he thought.

Regardless, Rand was happy to have skipped the drive home—and his own bed—in favor of getting an early start on the day. The sooner he could figure out what was going on in Finnick, the better.

Rand checked his phone GPS several times, wondering if the thing had crossed signals and was taking him to the wrong place, but it seemed to be working. Apparently Mount Grace Church was dead ahead.

The building was simple and possibly one of the oldest in town. The paint on the wood had long since flaked off the structure and it looked ready to topple over from the next gust of strong wind. A cross on the top was cocked to the side as if it had fallen off and been hastily nailed back on.

Right beside the church was a cemetery more expansive than Rand had expected.

He pulled up to the front and got out of the Jeep. The morning was chilly, and he zipped up his jacket. There were no signs of life around, which made Rand feel eerily alone.

The cemetery was delineated by a rusted metal fence that reached to Rand's waist. A larger structure denoted the entrance, but it was bent, faded, and the gate looked like it no longer closed. The grass was overgrown between the headstones, which went as far back as he could see. Rand figured the people of Finnick were still being buried there.

Movement among the graves caught his eye. A man ambled in the distance, approaching the church. As he neared, Rand saw the man walked with a limp and leaned heavily on a cane.

He was a frail black man dressed in an oversized suit. Thin, gray hair covered his head, and his dark eyes were soft and gentle.

"Morning," Rand said, smiling.

"Good morning," the other man said. He walked through the gates and passed his cane to his left hand as he extended his right. "Simon Cole."

Rand shook Simon's hand. "Randolph Casey. Friends call me Rand."

"You're not from around here," Simon said, eyeing the orange Jeep parked in front of the church.

"That easy to tell?"

"I know everyone in this town," Simon said. "Been here a long time, and I've never seen you."

"You're right."

"What brings you here? Services are on Sunday, and that was yesterday."

"I was in church yesterday," Rand said. "Except I went to the big tent."

Rand watched Simon Cole carefully when he mentioned the other church, and all at once, the friendly expression on the man's face changed. His mouth turned into a frown and his eyes seemed to fill with fear.

"I take it you know what I'm talking about," Rand said.

Simon Cole looked him up and down before answering. "You don't seem like the typical person you'd find there."

"You're right again."

Simon Cole nodded. "Please, let's step inside the church. It's cold out this morning."

Simon led the way into the church's foyer, where the only light was from the open door. A series of random paintings adorned the walls—the only decoration. Another set of doors opened into a simple sanctuary, flanked on both sides by rows of wooden pews. A statue of Jesus oversaw the stage and altar at the front of the room. Simon labored as he walked down the aisle toward the altar.

"I was hoping you could give me some information about the tent church," Rand said.

"There's not much I can tell you about that place," Simon said.

"What about Deckard Arcan?"

Simon looked away, as if the name pained him to hear. "Him either."

"Then what *can* you tell me?"

"That my church was the only one in Finnick until Deckard showed up. I hear his fans call him Pastor D. It was earlier this year when the tent first appeared off Highway 38. Slowly, over time, my meager congregation grew even thinner. They all attend *his* sermons on Sunday, now."

"Competition."

Simon shook his head. "It isn't about competition. As long as people find the Lord, it doesn't matter who leads them there—at least in my opinion. I care only for the souls of those in Finnick. Deckard Arcan's church brings in many more folks than my own. When that started happening, I was okay with it, at first. He was doing the Lord's work. Although he is about my age, he still has strength and vitality. I do not. I figured perhaps the Lord brought him here just in time. I considered maybe my time was coming."

Rand thought that was a bit grim. "You are speaking about before. Do you not believe these things anymore?"

"Over time, my doubts about the man grew."

"I was there when he healed Gerald Roberson," Rand said.

Simon wrung his hands together on top of his cane. "Gerald Roberson has been in that wheelchair ever since he fell off the ladder," he said. "That is well known around town. And now he's walking with no issues."

"What do you think about that?" Rand asked.

Simon shook his head. "The Bible is clear that miracle

healings are real. Peter and the other apostles utilized them in the Book of Acts to spread the early church."

"Can they can still happen today?"

"Anything is possible with the Lord."

"True. But what is your take?"

Simon met Rand's gaze and straightened. "Tell me why you're here."

Rand realized he'd put Simon on the defensive. He had a good feeling about the man—there was more power in the old pastor's voice than Rand had expected, and Simon seemed stronger than his frail body let on. They were both suspicious of Deckard Arcan, so Rand chose transparency. "I came back to town to discover the truth about Gerald Roberson. To see if he was actually healed, or if it was all a trick."

"And what did you learn?"

"More than I thought I would."

"Meaning?"

Rand wasn't sure where to begin. This whole thing went deeper and darker than Simon Cole was probably comfortable with.

"Let me start over," Rand said. "I am a Religious Studies professor. But outside of that, I'm a demonologist and paranormal investigator."

Simon Cole set his jaw and digested the information for a few seconds. Then, he said, "Where were you when I needed you?"

That caught Rand off guard. "What do you mean?"

"It's a long story, but Finnick is no stranger to the demonic."

"Really."

"Oh yes."

"So you believe?"

"How can I not? A demon gave me this." He patted his bum leg. "And another tried to possess a young boy that lives in town. It all came to light when a woman arrived searching for her deceased brother. It was quite the ordeal, but we prevailed."

Rand turned around and lifted his shirt to show Simon the three gashes that had scarred his back years ago.

"A frontline fighter, I see," Simon said, not particularly impressed by the marks. If he'd had encounters before, then he was no doubt familiar with scratches that came in sets of three.

"You can say that," Rand said. "I've been asked by the father of someone caught up in the church to find out the truth and get to the bottom of this."

"And what have you found?"

Rand told the story of the night before. How he'd gone to Gerald's house at the man's request to witness the visitation from his wife, but instead, a demon had appeared. As he spoke, Simon's face fell and his forehead wrinkled, but he listened without interruption.

After Rand finished, Simon stared at the floor as if lost in thought.

Finally, Simon said, "So, whatever Deckard did to Gerald that allowed him to walk again caused Gerald's home to become infested with a demonic presence."

"Yes," Rand said. "And when that presence was gone, Gerald once more lost his ability to walk."

"All of this makes much more sense now," Simon said. "You have brought me the missing piece of the puzzle. Deckard Arcan wields demonic power, and that is how he is able to perform these miracles in the name of God."

The old pastor seemed truly unsettled. Rand didn't blame him.

"There's another missing piece, I'm afraid," Rand said. "There is something more going on, but I can't place my finger on it."

"What do you mean?"

"Deckard shows no outward signs of possession. I'm sure you know what I mean. He has no altered appearance, and no strange or erratic behavior. Everything about the man seems normal, except for his supernatural abilities. It's like he gets all the benefits of possession, but none of the downsides."

As Rand spoke, Simon slowly lowered himself into the nearest pew, as if his body had suddenly lost all its energy. His expression showed he was very distressed about what he was hearing.

"Are you all right?" Rand finally asked.

"It's all so clear," he said, lost in thought. His words were barely audible.

"What do you mean?" Rand asked, stepping closer. "What's clear?"

Simon looked up at him, eyes wide. "It seems we're dealing with a perfect possession."

21

R and blinked. "Beg your pardon?"

"A perfect possession," Simon repeated. "You're not familiar with the term? Ah, I suppose not. You said you've never witnessed anything like what Deckard Arcan is demonstrating."

Rand lowered himself into the pew behind Simon, eyes transfixed on the man, and readied himself for what he was about to hear. It wasn't often that Rand learned something new when the demonic were concerned, but he was not foolish enough to proclaim that he knew everything.

"A perfect possession is when the evil spirit and the soul of the victim are so entwined, so complementary of each other, that the two almost become one," Simon explained.

"Become one? How?"

"Desire and a will to submit." The words dropped heavily from Simon's mouth.

"Like when someone invites the spirit to possess him,"

145

Rand said. But that confused him. He'd had cases before where someone had invited a demon into their body, and they still demonstrated the usual signs.

"Yes and no. From what I've seen, the willingness to submit needs to be there, but there is also something more. The subject has to be... *useful*, for lack of a better term."

"Useful?"

"Useful to the entity."

"Can't demons make use of all humans they possess?" Rand asked.

"When I was younger, and had first begun encountering these types of spirits," Simon explained, "I was involved in a spiritual battle alongside my mentor at the time. The victim was a state senator, and one of his staff had approached my mentor, concerned with the changes that had happened in the man over time. The woman who worked for the senator was a spiritualist, and she sensed the senator's negative energy as it grew. He became cold, mean, and seemed to delight in the intentional mistreatment of his workers.

"When we first met the senator, he seemed like a normal man. But it did not take much provocation from my mentor to get the possessing entity to reveal itself. The spirit was deep inside, and we had to draw it out before we could remove it. The two had been working as one."

Rand stood and paced down the aisle between the pews as he reasoned things out. "I've always compared a possession to a puppet and its master. The master pulls the strings while the victim dances." Rand remembered Georgia, her body no longer her own once Karax had taken over. "But what you're telling me sounds more like two co-pilots in a cockpit."

"You could put it that way, yes."

"Working together in harmony to achieve... what, exactly?"

Simon's face grew grim. "This was a state senator— someone who had influence and authority." Simon now stood, though it obviously took effort, one hand on the back of the pew and the other on his cane. "Think of historical figures like Adolf Hitler. Or serial killers like Ted Bundy. They were fully human, but committed heinous acts that make even the most vicious men shudder. How can someone plunge into such a depth of evil? I've heard it claimed many times, and I'm inclined to believe, that these men were examples of perfect possession."

Rand ran a hand through his hair. "High-profile individuals inviting demonic possession as a means of increasing their power and influence."

Simon nodded.

"A regular person being possessed harms that person only. But a powerful and influential person being possessed could mean death, destruction, and chaos on a much larger scale."

"You've got it," Simon said. "I thought Deckard Arcan was just another revivalist preacher. His congregation grew because of his energy and fervor. After what you've told me, though, I'm afraid for this town."

Rand remembered his first visit to the church when Deckard had given his testimony. He'd claimed he was on the edge of death and an angel of the Lord had offered him a second chance.

That was it. That was the moment he invited the spirit into him. It was a demon disguised as an angel. It was a deal with the devil with the classic fine print.

"Do you think Deckard has realized that it wasn't really an angel?" Rand asked.

"I am certain he has," Simon said. "This spirit spared Deckard's life, and now he continues to use this demon's power to spread darkness into the lives of many, all while Deckard's own influence continues to grow. Gerald Roberson was only the first, and you know how popular these miracle preachers can become."

It wouldn't be long before Deckard's spectacles were filmed and posted on the internet. He would eventually move out of Finnick and into the big cities. His audience would grow, and those that he healed, like Gerald Roberson, would be making their own unintentional deals with the devil.

As Rand considered the growth potential of Deckard Arcan's reach, he understood the gravity of the situation.

"We have to stop him," Rand said, voice barely a whisper.

"You're right," Simon said, eyes boring into him. "Any help you need, I will give you. That poor woman I told you about earlier... after she went through what she did with her brother, I was brought back into this spiritual battle against my will. But I believe it was God's plan to bring me back into the fight. Just as I believe it was God's plan to bring you here today. The Lord knows what's happening in this poor town, and he knows you are the one to end it."

Rand's pulse quickened. Perhaps Simon was right. Maybe God wasn't as silent as he always assumed.

His phone buzzed in his pocket.

Miller.

"Hey," Rand answered, voice cracking.

"Rando. What's up?"

"More than you think." Rand resumed pacing up and down the aisle as he spoke. "Lots of crazy stuff has been happening."

"Where are you?"

"Down in Finnick."

"Still? Anyway, listen. I watched the video you sent me a bunch of times. You know, of that preacher speaking in tongues. It wasn't Latin or backwards English. You remember that happened last time you showed me something? So I sent it straight to the same person who confirmed the last language, and they said the same thing —ancient Sumerian."

"Karax also spoke Sumerian."

This proves the demon within Deckard is another servant of Shindael.

"Miller, have you ever heard of a perfect possession?" Rand asked.

"No. What is it?"

Rand met Simon's eyes and saw the pastor was watching him with interest.

"It's..." But the words caught in Rand's throat. The rush of new information from Simon jumbled in his brain. "Miller, can I call you back?"

"You all right, Rando? You sound... afraid."

"I'll call you back." And Rand hung up.

"You have a team?" Simon asked him.

"In a way. It's always good to have support."

His phone buzzed again in his hand. Rand answered it. "Miller, I need—"

But the voice on the other end of the line was not Miller Landingham. "Hello, Randolph."

It was familiar, though it took Rand a few seconds to place it.

"This is Deckard Arcan."

22

It's like he was listening to us.

Rand cleared his throat and tried to make his voice sound natural despite the fear. "Good morning, Mr. Arcan."

Simon's eyes went wide.

"It turns out I was right about you," Deckard said.

"What are you talking about?" Rand asked.

"Mr. Roberson came to my house last night. I've never seen someone so upset in my entire life. I don't know what you did to reverse his blessing, but I realize now that you are working with the devil."

Although Deckard likely knew a demon had saved him rather than an angel, he was apparently still dedicated to playing the part of a preacher.

"Why are you calling me?" Rand asked. "How did you get this number?"

"I got your number because I prayed for it," Deckard said, sounding impatient. It was another unexplainable occurrence chalked up to God. "Azora provides me with what I need to do his work, and now I believe I have a task bigger than any I've had before."

Azora. The possessing demon—surely it's a false name.

"And what might that be?"

"To save your soul."

The way he said it sounded like a death threat. But Rand knew this could be his opportunity.

"If you want to give it a shot, be my guest," Rand told him.

"Your arrogance is astounding. God always humbles the prideful in his time. And I believe yours is coming soon."

"Okay, then. What should we do about it?"

"Meet me tonight," Deckard said.

"Where?"

"At my church. Come at midnight and come alone."

The words sank into Rand. It sounded like it could be a trap. Almost certainly was. But if he wanted to remove the demon that possessed Deckard, then he needed to see the preacher face to face. And this was his chance.

"I'm looking forward to it, Pastor D," Rand said.

The line went dead.

Simon took a few steps closer to him. "What's going on?"

"He wants to meet me," Rand said. "At midnight at the tent. Alone."

"You can't go alone. I'll come with you."

"Are you sure? There will be trouble."

Simon nodded. "What will you do until then?"

Rand glanced up at the statue of Jesus on the altar. "I originally came here to be in the presence of God after what I experienced last night."

"As you should. Now, it is more important than ever." Simon checked his watch. "It is just after ten. Midnight is fourteen hours away."

"When should we begin preparing?" Rand asked.

Not all of Rand's past cases allowed him time to sufficiently prepare for a spiritual battle. But when he did have the luxury of knowing beforehand that there would be a fight, he liked to take advantage of it.

"We will begin now," Simon said. "A perfectly possessed individual is a whole new challenge. The subjects are valuable to the demon inside, and he won't free his victim easily. It worries me that you are inexperienced in this matter."

Rand frowned. "Still. This is what I do. If not me, then who else do you have?"

"You are correct. That is why we will prepare for this encounter now. I only wish we had more time."

"Fourteen hours?"

Simon fixed Rand with a stern look. "Already you are underestimating this particular servant of the devil."

Rand swallowed hard. He always prepared when he could, but he had never done it for fourteen hours straight.

"Okay. Show me what we have to do."

"First, we begin with personal prayer and confession," Simon explained. "I will retire to my quarters behind the sanctuary, and you will remain in here. Submit yourself before the Lord. Ask God to fill you with his spirit. Confess all ways that you have sinned against him. I will do the same. Only after this can we move on."

Rand had his way of doing things, and did not like being told what to do, especially when religious matters were concerned. However, taking on a perfect possession was new territory for him, so he figured he'd best cooperate.

After Simon left him alone, Rand sat crossed-legged at the foot of the altar and peered up at the statue of Jesus.

It's been a while since I've done this...

Simon's simple instruction felt, in that moment, like a monumental task. All at once, the heavy feelings Rand had been wrestling with lately bubbled to the surface: that God had abandoned him in his mission, that he was only a mere plaything for the devil, and that no matter what he did, his family and loved ones would suffer and die at the hands of Satan's servants.

This is how I feel, Rand prayed. The statue of Jesus on the cross looked down at him. *But I know I am doing your will. I must continue to be faithful. Forgive me for the times when I am not.*

But it was hard to ask for forgiveness. It was hard to accept that after all the work he'd done—the exorcisms, removing evil spirits from homes, ushering lost souls to the afterlife—that God had still been so mysteriously silent and absent in his life.

Next, he confessed. He dug deep, strived to remember all the times he had done wrong in his life: the times he had been unfair to Libby, the times he had been cruel to Tessa, the angry thoughts toward students that tested his patience in class, the women he'd caused pain with his inability to maintain a relationship.

As Rand rattled off these shortcomings, his chest tightened and tears came to his eyes. It was a feeling he hadn't experienced in a very long time—being broken before the Lord. His pride had prevented it. That pride came from his belief that even without God, he could take on the devil. He didn't want it to be that way, but as long as God was silent, then it had to be.

You're silent in my life for a reason, Lord, Rand prayed, the tears growing thicker. It pained him to admit it. *But all I do, I do for you. You have chosen me for this life.*

And as the time passed, Rand found himself going even deeper. *God, I am thankful for meeting Simon Cole, because he forced me to sit down and do this. But I am not doing this only because he told me, or because of what's to come tonight. I'm doing it because I want to change. To be the best I can be for you. To serve you better with this task you appointed me here on earth.*

Rand had no idea how much time he spent in prayer. It did not matter. The reconnection with God was long overdue, and already he felt a lightness in his spirit at finally having faced the baggage that had grown over time.

Simon Cole emerged from the room behind the sanctuary. He carried a box, which he set on the altar near Rand. Simon withdrew several long candles, which he placed on the altar's table and lit them. Rand counted seven.

Without saying a word, Simon limped over to each window on the side of the church and drew the curtain. Each curtain he closed plunged them further into darkness. When he was done, only the smallest slivers of daylight peeked into the room.

Simon returned to the altar and took out two old Bibles, each the size of a tome, their leather covers worn from age. He stacked them on the edge of the table.

Next came a loaf of bread wrapped in a white cloth, an unlabeled bottle, and a chalice. Simon filled the chalice with red wine from the bottle.

Rand had never gone so all-out in his own preparations. He usually only prayed and lingered in a holy place, such as a church. Simon's thoroughness was inspiring.

"What's all this stuff for?" Rand asked.

Simon held the loaf of bread in both his hands. "I trust you know the Lord's prayer."

"Of course." It was a prayer Rand found most effective in removing unclean spirits from haunted places.

"Join me," Simon said.

Together, they recited it.

"Our Father, who art in heaven, hallowed be thy name. Thy kingdom come. Thy will be done, on earth as it is in heaven. Give us this day our daily bread; and forgive us our trespasses, as we forgive those who trespass against us; and lead us not into temptation, but deliver us from evil. For thine is the kingdom and the power and the glory, forever. Amen."

Simon tore a chunk of bread from the loaf and offered it to Rand. Rand cupped both his hands and held them out to receive the bread. Simon placed it in his palms. "The body of Christ given to you."

Rand consumed the bread. Simon then removed a portion for himself and did the same.

He set the bread aside and lifted the chalice of wine. "The blood of Christ shed for you."

Rand sipped it, then Simon.

After that, Simon handed Rand one of the Bibles. It weighed heavy in Rand's hands, and he couldn't remember the last time he'd opened the holy book.

"Do you know the Litany of the Saints?" Simon asked.

Rand exhaled. "It's been a long time."

"Open the cover."

The Bible's spine creaked as Rand opened it. Right behind the cover was a folded-up piece of paper that looked as old as the Bible. Rand unfolded it and found the familiar prayer from his youth handwritten in curvy script.

Rand's father had dragged Rand to church every Sunday when he was young, and if he didn't read aloud with the rest of the congregation, he'd receive a stern, sideways glare from his dad.

"Lord, have mercy," Simon began.

"Lord, have mercy," Rand answered.

"Christ, have mercy."

"Christ, have mercy."

"Lord, have mercy."

"Lord, have mercy."

"Christ, hear us."

"Christ, graciously hear us."

Simon recited the Litany impressively by memory as Rand followed along on the paper, answering the invocations as instructed. It made him feel insufficient—perhaps God was right to be silent in his life.

"Holy Mary," Simon said.

"Pray for us."

"Holy Mother of God."

"Pray for us."

Then Simon recited the Patriarchs and Prophets, then Apostles and Disciples, then the Martyrs.

Simon finished with, "Lord God, you know our weakness. In your mercy grant that the example of your Saints may bring us back to love and serve you through Christ our Lord."

"Amen," Rand said, glad to be finished. It had brought up too many memories of his childhood—ones that weren't as buried as he'd like them to be.

Rand found this preparation a bit too thorough for his taste. He'd done much less in the past and was still victorious over demons. But he knew Simon would not want to hear any protests.

"Now, please turn to the Book of Psalms."

Rand opened the Bible to the halfway point, remembering the approximate location of the book among the others. He ended up in Proverbs and flipped back a few pages to the beginning of the Psalms. The pages gave off a musty scent as he turned them, reminding him of the old hymnals from his father's church.

"Blessed is the man that walketh not in the counsel of the ungodly, nor standeth in the way of sinners, nor sitteth in the seat of the scornful," Simon read aloud. After he finished the first verse, he glanced up at Rand. "Please read with me."

"Oh," Rand said.

Simon continued, "But his delight is in the law of the Lord; and in his law doth he meditate day and night." Rand joined him a few words into the sentence and kept pace with the man's steady reading.

They read aloud from the Book of Psalms for a long time, and Rand quickly realized that Simon intended to read the whole thing.

Really? Rand thought. *Is this necessary?*

As Rand stood, the heavy Bible in his hands, his legs and back grew sore. His mouth became dry and his throat parched. But Simon showed no signs of fatigue, or of ceasing his Bible reading. Rand didn't want to be outdone by a man twice his age, so he strengthened his resolve and kept up.

Rand did not know how long it took them to read the entire Book of Psalms out loud, but he knew they'd been going for multiple hours. Rand had to wonder if reading it silently—and faster—would have been more efficient. Maybe a nap would have been a better use of his time.

When it was done, Simon said, "We will stop for five minutes. There is a restroom behind in the foyer."

Rand was thankful for the bathroom break. After he finished, he sat in a chair in the foyer and rested his aching legs while massaging his thighs.

Rand sighed. They were meant to face a perfectly possessed person—supposedly a formidable foe—and all they were doing was making themselves tired. They'd said the prayers and read aloud from the Bible. How much more was needed? Wasn't there some value in showing up to the fight energized and rested, also?

"Rand," Simon called from the sanctuary. "We must continue."

Groaning, Rand pulled himself off the chair and left the foyer.

He wished he could sit for longer, but he also did not want to delay Simon's process.

Rand found the old man standing where he'd been before, and Rand realized that Simon had only allowed a break for his benefit.

"You didn't have to pee?" Rand asked, joining him. "You deserve a medal for your endurance."

"Please turn to the Gospel according to Matthew," Simon instructed, ignoring his quip.

Rand found it, and just as he expected, Simon began to read aloud. "The book of the generation of Jesus Christ, the son of David, the son of Abraham. Abraham begat Isaac; and Isaac begat Jacob; and Jacob begat Judas and his brethren..."

This is too much, Rand thought. *This is insane.*

After Matthew came Mark, then Luke, and then John. In the rare times Rand glanced up from the pages of the

Bible, he noted the vanishing daylight from around the edges of the curtains.

Despite Rand's physical discomfort, a new sensation started to bloom inside him. It began sometime during the reading of the Sermon on the Mount, in the Book of Matthew.

He felt peace, protected, like his entire body was covered with a shield. Maybe that was what the Bible spoke of when it mentioned the armor of God. The rituals, prayers, and readings stirred a latent zeal in him that seemed from another life entirely. He truly felt like he could do all things through Christ who strengthened him.

The strain of standing and reading for so long slipped from his mind—perhaps because his body was growing numb or because God was giving him strength.

By the time they began the Gospel according to Luke, Rand actually felt strengthened by reading the words of Jesus aloud.

When they reached the end of the Gospel according to John, Rand waited for Simon to begin Acts of the Apostles, but he was met with silence.

Rand looked up at him. The room was darker now that night had fully set in. The candles had burned down to mere stubs of wax with the melted remains filling their holders. Soon, there would be nothing left to support the little flames and they would extinguish.

"How do you feel?" Simon asked.

Rand was pleasantly surprised by the truth. "Strong. Ready. I thought you were crazy, but maybe you do know best how to prepare for spiritual warfare."

Simon closed his Bible gently. "Now we will have rest

and more personal prayer. Again, I will go to my room and you will remain here."

Once Rand was alone again, he began praying, and this time did so from a position of power.

I will remove this demon in your name, Lord. Thank you for Simon and for rejuvenating me with your holy presence.

After some time, Rand's thoughts were interrupted by the lights suddenly coming on in the sanctuary. Simon Cole stood near the door that led to the back. Rand had not heard him come in.

He approached Rand and handed him a bottle of water and two apples, which Rand quickly consumed.

"Thank you for leading us," Rand said after he'd finished eating. "I would have never thought a fourteen-hour marathon ritual would work, but I feel... good. And very ready for what's to come."

"Good," Simon said. "Because it's time."

24

Highway 38 looked much different at night. Rand turned his high beams on, but they barely cut through the darkness. The field that served as a parking lot was empty, so Rand plowed through the footpath that people used to access the church.

The tent was a large monstrosity, a darkened shadow against the light of the full moon. There were no other sources of light, so Rand left his front beams on.

He and Simon got out and approached the tent. Rand had his bag slung over his shoulder, which contained his usual supplies for situations such as this: crosses, sage, holy water, a Bible.

Rand found the place eerie during the night when there weren't several hundred people around.

"Have you ever been here before?" Rand asked.

Simon shook his head. "I preach to the few who remain at my church on Sundays."

Rand dug into his bag and pulled out a flashlight. He

used it to scan the rest of the tent. "I just noticed there are no crosses in here. No religious icons at all."

Simon looked around. "You're right. That's very telling."

A noise came from Rand's left, and the two men whirled to face it. Rand jerked his flashlight in that direction, but only saw trees and bushes on the edge of the church property. The foliage rustled in the wind.

Rand grew nervous, his stomach clenching.

"Good evening."

At the entrance of the tent, Deckard Arcan stood as a darkened shadow, backlit by the Jeep's headlights. He had another man with him—Patrick Perryman.

"Simon Cole," Deckard said, walking toward them. Patrick followed a step behind. "I'm surprised to see you here."

"We have something very important to discuss," Simon said.

"Agreed. To be honest, I'm not trying to purge your church of all its members, but I am interested in saving their lost souls. If they find that in my church instead of yours, then so be it. Surely you understand."

"We are not here to talk about saving souls," Simon said. "We are here to talk about saving you."

Deckard neared them in the aisle. He wore a suit as if it was Sunday morning. He turned his attention to Rand. "I told you to come alone."

"You brought your man." He nodded toward Patrick.

"True. I figured you would do the same. But of all the people you could scrape up, Simon Cole was the last person I would have predicted."

Rand reached his hand into his bag that hung at his

waist. Deckard seemed not to notice—or if he did, he made no mention of it.

"I have asked you here tonight because you have brought harm to a member of my congregation," Deckard said. "I cannot let that stand."

"What harm would that be?" Rand asked, although he had a good idea of what the man was referring to.

"Don't play dumb with me," Deckard said. "You went into the house of Gerald Roberson and did a dark ritual to reverse the blessing brought upon him by God."

"That was no blessing," Rand said.

"I had hope for you. All men are lost at some point in their lives, including me. But almost all can be found. I believed I could reach you, but it seems like you are intent on battling God and pushing your own agenda." Deckard frowned, as if the words pained him to say.

And in the small amount of light that came from Rand's flashlight, Rand could see that Deckard earnestly believed he was being guided by God. He had no clue that the entity that held sway over him was anything but holy.

"You have to listen to me," Rand said. "The spirit speaking to you is not God, nor is it an angel named Azora."

"And what would a sinner like you know about the voice of God?"

"Because I fight those spirits," Rand said. "Let us finally get to know each other. My name is Randolph Casey, and I have removed and cast out countless demons from the lives of ordinary people. I know how they act and how they behave. More than anything, I know how they deceive."

Deckard's face grew grim.

"The miracles you perform. The things you learn in prayer that you can't possibly know. Where does it all come from?"

"From God."

"Are you sure?"

"Who else could reveal these things to me?"

"From a servant of the devil. They are timeless and know all things about all people. They are also masters of deception. That is why you think an angel named Azora is speaking to you. Think back to when you had that near-death experience. Of course you would have accepted help from any supernatural being that offered it. But in that moment, when you were at your most vulnerable, it was a demon that slipped inside and possessed you. I know this is hard for you to hear, but I can prove it."

Deckard only glared at Rand. The pastor was half a head shorter, but he had no problem looking up and meeting Rand's steady gaze.

Behind Deckard, Patrick took a step back, as if the growing tension was too much for him.

"These are the ravings of a sinner," Deckard said. "A shame. I hoped better for you. But as it stands, I cannot allow you to come near my congregation again."

Rand's hand found the crucifix at the bottom of his bag. In one quick motion, he pulled it out and pressed it to Deckard's chest.

With blinding speed, Deckard leapt back and slapped the cross from Rand's grip, sending it flying away with a power greater than any mere human could have.

Rand's hand throbbed.

Deckard looked at his own hand, amazed at his

strength, confused. He touched his chest where the cross had been and rubbed as if trying to ease away the pain.

"What was that?"

"You see what I mean?" Rand said. "You cannot stand to be touched by the cross. The entity that follows you won't allow it."

Deckard considered it for a moment, but he only set his jaw. "Impossible."

"Would you like to try again?"

"No!" he barked back at Rand.

"Why not?" Rand asked. "You're not thinking for yourself, Deckard. Why are you so averse to being touched by a cross?"

"You don't know what you're talking about," Deckard snarled.

A change came over the man. Gone was the formal calmness, the cool and collected nature. The facade was cracking. Even Patrick Perryman seemed afraid of him.

"Look at you," Rand said. "You're losing control."

"No—"

"All over a simple cross. Why are you afraid of the sign of your Lord?"

"Shut up!" Deckard shouted, his voice booming. "You are wrong. You are the one who is possessed! People like you are the reason Azora has given me his blessing. He is the one who gives me the strength to resist you."

"You don't need to resist me," Rand said, taking a step back. Deckard's body tensed, and he looked ready to attack. "I am here to help you. Listen to me, and we can get you on the right path to God."

"I will never listen to you!"

Deckard Arcan gripped the end of a wooden bench.

Rand watched in amazement as the old man lifted it off the ground as if it were nothing more than a stick.

The bench was at least ten feet long, but in Deckard's hands, it looked like it was light as a feather. He brought it over his head.

Rand saw that Deckard's eyes had changed. They glowed blood red.

Deckard swung the bench like he was batting with a tree trunk.

Rand dropped flat and felt the thick wood whoosh over him. Simon and Patrick fell away from Deckard, stumbling far out of his range.

Deckard lifted the bench over his head and hammered it down where Rand lay. But Rand rolled out of the path right before the wood embedded itself in the soft earth.

Rand sprang to his feet. *Here we go. God, give me strength.* He rushed toward Deckard, ready to tackle him.

But it was not Deckard. Those glowing eyes told him he was running straight for the dark entity that held the pastor.

Deckard reached out to him first, shoving both hands into his chest. Rand felt a burst of pain in his ribs, as if he'd been hit by a wrecking ball. The force lifted him off his feet and sent him hurtling backwards through the air and out of the tent. He landed hard on the ground near his Jeep and rolled, the breath knocked from his lungs. His chest throbbed. Was his sternum broken? Caved in?

Superhuman strength was a common symptom of possession. Rand had been struck by these individuals before, but he'd never been hit so powerfully before.

He coughed and sputtered and tried to stand. Deckard approached him quickly, and Rand tried to crawl away.

He's too strong.

Rand felt firm hands on his shoulders, flipping him onto his back. Deckard leaned over him, face inches from his, red eyes glaring into him.

"You've gone too far this time," Deckard said. His voice had changed. It had taken on a rougher, demonic edge. "Shindael has marked you for death, and it will come."

Deckard reached out his hand and grabbed his throat. His grip was a vise. Rand tugged on Deckard's wrist with both his hands, but it was not going anywhere.

Deckard clenched Rand's windpipe closed. He struggled and kicked his legs, but Deckard was a rock, sturdy and powerful.

And Rand realized that despite all the prayer and preparation, God was not there to protect him from the servant of Shindael.

Then a loud siren blared in the distance. Red and blue lights flashed through the night.

The glow from Deckard's eyes faded, and he released Rand's throat. Rand gasped and crawled away, forcing air into his lungs.

"Police!" someone shouted.

Rand coughed and sputtered and rubbed at his neck where the demon had tried to crush it. A few seconds more and he would have lost consciousness.

There was shouting, but Rand was too dazed to make out what any of it was.

All he knew was that someone had come to save him. The cops. They had seen Deckard attacking him and were there to rescue him.

But then he felt strong arms grab his right hand, then

his left, and force them behind his back. Cold metal clasped on his wrists and clicked into place.

"Randolph Casey. You are under arrest."

Rand was yanked to his feet. He was face to face with Jones, the sheriff he'd met when he'd first arrived in town. "What are you doing?" The words only croaked out of his mouth.

"You are under arrest for breaking and entering into Gerald Roberson's house."

Jones grabbed his elbow and forced him toward the police cruiser. Rand turned to look back and saw Deckard Arcan and Patrick Perryman standing together, watching him go. Even further in the distance was Simon Cole, looking on helplessly as Rand was led away.

The sheriff shoved Rand into the back of the car.

"Wait—" Rand began, but Jones only slammed the car door in his face.

It was a setup, he realized.

Deckard Arcan had baited him there and called the police. Gerald Roberson must have gone to Deckard and told him Rand had broken in.

Something happened there, however, that not even Deckard had been prepared for—the demon came out. And Rand realized that by arresting him, Sheriff Jones had inadvertently saved his life.

25

I t was Wednesday morning in math class, and Libby could not leave her phone alone.

The last time she'd heard from her dad was Monday evening. He was knee-deep in a case, so she had resisted the urge to contact him on Tuesday knowing she needed to give him his space.

But now it was Wednesday morning. Two entire nights had passed. Usually, his fights with the supernatural took place over the course of a single night.

Everything okay?

The last message she had sent him lingered in her app, delivered but not answered.

When class let out, she went into the hallway and called her dad. He did not answer.

Next, she called her mother.

"Are you at school?" her mother asked when she answered.

"Yeah."

"What have I told you about using your phone at school? You've gotten in enough trouble for that already."

"Have you heard from Dad?"

Tessa paused. "Since when?"

"Since the weekend."

"No, I haven't."

"Oh. He's doing a case right now."

Tessa huffed. "He's supposed to tell me."

This was about Justin—a case that was more personal and close to home. It had sprung up quicker than most, so her dad probably hadn't thought to tell her mom. But it was true. Rand kept Tessa up to date about these matters. Her mother didn't like to admit it, but she still worried about him.

"I'll try calling him," Tessa said.

"I've already tried. Calling and texting. He hasn't answered for two days."

"Hmm. Well, you know how these... *things* can mess with his phone and electronics. Or whatever."

"Yeah. True."

"I'm sure he's fine," Tessa said. "But if he keeps canceling his classes like this, they're going to fire him."

As far as Libby knew, he'd only canceled his classes on Monday while he poked around in Finnick.

Libby hung up with her mother and moved to her next class, where she resorted to Plan B and texted Justin.

Hey.

Her last message to him had gone unanswered as well, and she'd been too annoyed to try any harder. He'd broken up with her a few days before, presumably because she didn't believe his pastor had healed anybody. That, and Rand was investigating the man as requested by

Justin's dad, so talking to Justin during that time almost felt like a conflict of interest.

But she was getting desperate. Maybe he or Mr. Tidwell had heard from Rand.

The class wore on with Libby barely paying attention, and the bell rang. The next class came and went without a message from anyone.

She ground her teeth and waited for school to let out for the day. She went down to her car in the parking lot and tried calling her dad on the way. Nothing. She called her mom back.

"He hasn't answered for me either," Tessa said. "Do you think we should call—"

"No," Libby said quickly, knowing what her mom was thinking. "You know what dad says. When he's on a case, never get the police involved, no matter what."

If her dad was caught up in something crazy, one of the worst things they could do was call the police. She'd learned that the hard way once when she was younger. As counterintuitive as it was, it was always best to trust her dad and his abilities.

Libby drove to Rand's house. His Jeep was not in the driveway and three newspapers laid near the mailbox. Libby picked them up and threw them in the recycle bin around the side of the house.

She used her copy of the key to let herself in and poked around, noting that everything seemed normal.

Nothing was out of place.

She opened her backpack on the kitchen table. She'd work on some homework while she waited. Although she didn't know what she was waiting for. Anything from her dad.

But within five minutes of opening her books, she knew it would be impossible to concentrate.

The phone rang, a shrill, electronic jingling that caused her to jump.

It was the house phone. She couldn't remember the last time they'd used it. Her dad always gave out his cell number to people.

She crossed the kitchen to where the portable landline rested on its cradle. The green light flashed as it rang.

Libby picked it up and checked the caller ID. Unknown. She pressed the button and brought it to her ear.

"Hello?"

"Libby." It was her dad.

Libby let out a huge breath she hadn't realized she'd been holding. "Dad. What the hell? Where have you been?"

"Libby. I need your help."

Her relief suddenly evaporated. "Are you okay?"

"Yes, I'm fine." He said something else, but the line filled with static, as if he were in a bad reception area.

"I can't hear you. You're breaking up."

The lined cleared. "I said I need your help. Can you help me?"

"Yes, of course. What do you need? Should I call Mom or someone?"

"Come to Finnick," her father said. "I need you here."

"Okay… Why? Is everything—"

"Just come now, please. I'll explain when you get here."

"Fine, all right. But where?" She hoped he wasn't about to say the giant tent church. Even thinking about that place gave her the creeps.

"It's called the Finnick Motel."

"Right. Finnick Motel." That must have been where he was staying this whole time. But why not call and check in earlier if he had been at a motel?

I'll know as soon as I see him and he fills me in.

"Are you coming now?" her father asked.

"Yes. Are you sure everything's okay? Do you need me to bring anything?"

"I'm sure. Everything's fine. Just come now."

Then the line went dead.

Libby hung up the phone. Her dad didn't sound desperate or in danger, so why was he so insistent that she meet him urgently?

Maybe something to do with the case.

Libby packed up her books and slung her backpack over her shoulder. As she walked to the car, she typed "Finnick Motel" into the GPS on her phone and dropped a pin. It would take her just under two hours to get there.

Hopefully, she could get there and back to town before it got too late in the day. And have her dad in tow with her, case complete, and everything resolved.

As she backed out of the driveway, she called her mom. "Hey, just talked to Dad."

"Really? What's going on?"

"Not sure. But he wants me to meet him."

"Meet him where?"

"In Finnick."

Tessa paused. "Why there?"

"That's where he's working."

"Right, but why? Did he say?"

"No. But he told me everything was all right, just that

he needed my help. I'll go meet him and then come back later tonight."

"All right." But her mother still seemed unsure. "You sure he said everything was all right?"

"Yes, Mom. I talked to him."

"Okay. Keep me updated, please."

"I will."

She hung up her phone and laid it in her lap.

Although Libby was relieved to have finally heard from her dad, she now found herself frustrated. *We need a new rule. If cases take multiple days, he should call and let me know everything's okay.*

She planned to give him an earful when she saw him.

Libby cranked the radio and pressed the gas pedal to shave time off her drive.

26

The Finnick Inn was a run down dump if Libby had ever seen one. The sun was just starting to set and an eerie, purple-and-orange light peeked through the storm clouds that had taken root overhead the past week. The sign in front tried to light up, but it only flickered on and off. There were no cars in the cracked and pothole-filled lot, and she got the feeling merely stepping inside any of the rooms would have her walking out with a disease.

So basically, it was the kind of place she'd expect her dad to stay. Hunting ghosts and fighting demons hardly had him rolling in dough.

Libby parked and killed the engine. She picked up her phone and called her dad to tell him that she was there and ask him what room he was staying in.

He did not answer.

She tried texting him.

Hey, I'm here at the motel. Where are you?

She let that linger unanswered for several minutes

before she decided she'd have to go to him. When she found him, she planned to give him a verbal thrashing for being so crappy at communicating.

Libby glanced around the area. No shady or shifty characters from what she could see.

She got out of the car and went to the front office. The man behind the desk was a grubby old dude who looked like he hadn't showered in a week. His name tag read Keith.

Keith stared her down a bit harder than she was comfortable with.

"How can I help you, sweetie?" he said, his smile slimy and sketchy. His eyes scanned her entire body up and down.

Libby wanted to vomit. "I'm looking for my dad."

"No one's staying here at the moment," he said, southern accent thick and rough. "You need a room for the night?"

"No. As I said, I'm looking for my dad. He told me to meet him here, so I assumed he was staying here."

Keith only shrugged. "Just cause he said to meet him here don't mean he's staying here. No one's checked in tonight, and I would know. I'm the manager."

Libby took out her phone and found a picture of her dad in her camera roll.

"This man." She showed it to Keith.

Keith donned a pair of glasses from his pocket and stared at the picture for a few long seconds. "Ah yeah. I do know that guy." He removed his glasses. "Was here…" He rolled his eyes up toward the ceiling as he thought. "Sunday night I think."

That long ago?

"That's it? Just Sunday night."

"Wasn't here for very long," Keith said. "Started acting like a crazy man."

The unsettled feeling returned to Libby's stomach. "What do you mean?"

Keith scrunched up his face as he tried to recall. "Came here and checked in. Everything was fine, then he ran in here telling me there was something going on in the room next door. But there wasn't, because he was the only person staying here that night. Still, he kept saying there was. Stole the key right off my rack and broke into the other room. Lo and behold, nothing there, just like I told him. Man was hearing things, I think. Then he started seeing things, or at least it seemed that way. Kept freaking out and looking around like he was hallucinating. I don't know. I don't need that kind of crap in my business, so I threw him out. Ain't seen him since."

Libby took in the story and swallowed hard. "You don't know where he went?"

"No. Honestly don't care, just as long as he ain't here. What about you? I'll hook you up with a room if you need one, just as long as you ain't crazy like your old man."

"Thanks for you help," Libby said flatly, then turned and left the office.

Sunday night.

That was seventy-two hours ago. Why would her dad ask her to meet him at a motel where he hadn't been in three days?

She took out her phone to call her mom, but hesitated. She considered calling the police first—the one thing her dad asked her to never do when he was on a case.

But something just wasn't sitting right this time.

As her fingers moved over the keys, a beat-up truck pulled into the gravel lot and slowly coasted over. It parked next to her car and the driver switched off the ignition. The door opened and out stepped a man that Libby knew she'd seen before, but couldn't place.

He wore faded jeans and had a clean white t-shirt tucked into them. His straight brown hair was swooped to the side and he gave her a smile as he walked over to her.

"Libby," he said.

"Have we met?" she asked, even though she knew they had, and wished she could remember where.

The man laughed with genuine humor. "In a way. My name is Patrick Perryman, and we bumped into each other at church. I'm friends with Justin." He extended his hand. "Nice to meet you again."

"Yeah," Libby said, taking it weakly.

"Listen, your dad asked me to come," Patrick said.

Libby perked up. "My dad. Where is he?"

"He's with me, at my house. He wanted me to come and get you. Told me you were coming to meet him here."

"Why couldn't he meet me himself?" Libby asked.

"He's been crazy busy," Patrick said.

"Is he okay?" Libby asked.

"Yeah, he's totally fine," Patrick said. "Sorry, I didn't mean to worry you, but yes, everything's okay."

"This is all just a little weird," Libby said. "And not really like him at all."

"I understand," Patrick said. "But you know how these things can be with your dad."

That was true, which made Libby wonder just how much Patrick knew about her father. The man was involved with the church, so it made sense that her dad would have sought him out in the investigation. Maybe Patrick Perryman was just as worried about the place as Justin's dad was.

"I'll take you on over to my house. Rand's waiting for us there."

"I'll take my own car," Libby said.

Patrick only shrugged and smiled. "Okay. You can follow."

The two got into their cars and Patrick pulled out of the motel parking lot, Libby close behind.

Along the way, she tried calling her dad again, but he did not answer.

Why send this guy? Dad, what are you involved in?

Libby called her mom again.

"Did you find him?" Tessa asked.

"Not yet. He sent someone else to meet me."

"Who is it?"

"His name's Patrick. I've met him before, actually. I still don't know what's going on down here, but I think Dad's working with this guy."

"Libby, you should come home," Tessa said.

"I will. I'll find out real quick what's going on with Dad, then I'll come back."

"Are you sure everything is fine? Especially with this guy?"

"He's one of Justin's friends from church."

"Why is Justin's friend working with your dad on a case?"

"Long story." Neither she nor her father had told Tessa the details of Charles Tidwell's request. "I'll fill you in on the whole thing after I talk with him."

"Promise?"

"Yes. I promise."

She hung up just as Patrick's truck left the main part of town and meandered down a side road. The neighborhoods turned into farmlands, and after a few more miles, even the houses dropped away.

They came to a single house that was far from town or any other homes. It was a mansion—the last thing she had expected.

Patrick parked in the yard and Libby pulled up behind him. Patrick got out and signaled for her to turn off the car.

She got out of the car, but left the engine running.

"You live here?" Libby said, raising her eyebrows. Surely Justin would have told her if he had a friend that was super wealthy and lived in a mansion.

"Yes. Come on. Your dad's inside and waiting for you."

Patrick started up the steps of the large porch, but Libby hesitated in the yard.

Patrick turned around. "What's wrong?"

"Sorry, it's just that I don't know you. I don't want to go inside your house."

Patrick looked genuinely confused. "But I'm a friend of Justin's. You and I even met at church." He gave a smile, but it seemed forced.

"Look, can you just go inside and tell my dad to come out? Please. I want to see him first."

Patrick's smile faded. His lips tensed into a thin line, and he glared at her.

That's it. I'm out of here.

Her entire world became dark as something was pulled over her head. She tried to scream and run, but strong arms clasped her body and covered her mouth, stifling her.

Then Libby was lifted several feet in the air and carried effortlessly toward the house. She tried to thrust her arms outward to break from whoever grasped her, but they were too strong. She flailed her legs, kicking her tall captor's thighs as he walked, but it did not stop him.

Libby tried to scream, but a large hand covered her mouth and stifled her.

27

The jail cell was a box of bars that Rand estimated was ten feet by ten feet. It was located in the back of the police station, behind the desks and offices, in the far-off corner by the rear exit of the building.

"Sleep tight," Sheriff Jones told him after locking the cell. "I'll deal with you in the morning."

"You can't just leave me alone in here," Rand called after him as he left.

Jones ignored him. Once he was gone, the entire police station was eerily quiet.

Rand was galled when he realized he was the only soul in there. There wasn't even a deputy to keep an eye on him.

This has got to be against some protocol.

Rand sat on the hard ground with his back against the bars. Illegal or not, he had no choice but to wait until Jones came for him in the morning.

Deckard Arcan had arranged for his lock up, and Rand

was starting to realize there was nothing he could do about it. It was Deckard's word against his, and in a small town like Finnick Deckard's word would always win. Especially since Sheriff Jones was a member of the congregation, and had even witnessed Gerald Roberson's healing.

In the silence, Rand had plenty of time to reflect on what had landed him there. He realized just how short his confrontation with Deckard had been, and how quickly the man had overpowered him—and nearly killed him.

You forsook me again, God, Rand found himself thinking. *After all that prayer and Scripture reading. Was fourteen hours straight not enough for you? How long until you actually back me up?*

Rand pressed his fingers into temples as if trying to physically force the thoughts from his mind. His heart wanted to sustain his faith, but his brain wanted to remind him just what faith was: belief in something without any proof that it was true.

And when he found his eyes tearing up, he realized he was more upset than he'd originally thought. Once again, God had hung him out to dry. On top of his emotional pain, he'd had his ass kicked by a perfectly possessed man. His chest still throbbed where Deckard had hit him.

He was without any way to communicate with the outside world. Jones had taken everything—his bag of supplies, his cell phone, his wallet. No one knew he was there except for Simon Cole.

Come on, Simon. Get me out of here. Surely the old pastor was doing everything he could to get to Rand.

His stomach rumbled and his mouth was dry. The full moon's light spilled through the windows, and Rand spotted a sink next to a vending machine on the other side of the room. That cruel sight exacerbated his hunger and thirst, making him feel like a man in the desert who couldn't quite reach the oasis in front of him.

Just hold on until morning, Rand told himself. They may not release him, but they would surely feed him. *Won't be long now.*

Rand checked his watch. It read 11:43.

That's not right. We met Deckard at midnight. It's way later than that.

The moonlight didn't illuminate much, so Rand clenched his eyes shut, trying to adjust them to the darkness. But he had not misread the time. He held it up to his ear, but it was still ticking. It was not broken.

Then something occurred to him.

He twisted his wrist, making the watch face away from him. Then, a few seconds later, he returned it face up and checked the time.

It now read 2:08.

Oh, no.

Rand turned his watch away again, then back.

7:23.

Time distortion.

People who'd had close encounters with demonic entities reported this phenomenon; Rand himself had experienced it himself a time or two. Demons were not bound by time and space, and therefore could insert themselves into any point in history they wanted—even the past. As such, they had the ability to put humans through a distorted sense of time.

Both Rand and Miller had searched for an explanation for this occurrence, but they had only come up with hypotheses. Some claimed the victim was temporarily brought into a parallel dimension that was close to reality as humans knew it, and that was where the supernatural was active. Others suggested it was literal time travel—forced upon the person by the demon to disorient them and make them further question their own sanity.

It was similar to the experience described by lucid dreamers—people who could control their dreams. They said time did not exist normally in dreams, which was why dreams seeming to last three days could occur during a thirty-minute nap. Further, these folks always claimed that if they looked at a clock in a dream, then immediately looked away and back again, it would read an entirely different time.

Regardless of what was true, Rand knew one thing: he'd be there until Shindael decided to relent.

He had no doubt Shindael was behind this. Rand had figured out that Deckard Arcan was perfectly possessed and confronted him. Gotten too close. And now Shindael had him locked in a box with a jumbled sense of reality.

Rand twisted his wrist back and forth, flashing his watch dozens of times. Each time, the watch hands were in a completely different position.

He dropped his head back against the bars, the metal clanging against his skull. He sighed deeply. "Come on, Shindael," he said out loud. "I know you're close, and I know what you're doing. Just get on with it. Make your point."

But he knew it was useless. Shindael would let the attack go on for as long as he wanted.

Without a reliable watch, Rand had no idea how long he sat in that cell. Eventually, he knew it was long enough that the sun should have started to rise, but it never came. With time distortion, the night would last infinitely, as if the earth had stopped rotating.

The only indication of how much real time was elapsing was the weakening of his body. His hunger compounded, and the roars coming from his stomach filled the silent room. His mouth tasted as if it was stuffed with cotton. A sharp headache snuck into the top of his brain, brought on by dehydration.

He laid down and tried to sleep. He dozed a bit, but never for long.

Eventually, his mind began to wander into horrible places. *What if he keeps me like this for years? Decades?*

He imagined Shindael freeing him, only for him to find that Libby had grown up and gotten married. Like he'd been in a coma that lasted a third of his life.

She would have spent that entire time not knowing what became of her father. All she knew was that one day he'd driven away for a case and never came back. She would resent him for having never given up the supernatural work when he had the chance.

He sobbed as he imagined that scenario. The possibility of it all hurt him worse than anything he currently felt—more than his hunger, more than his thirst, and more than God's betrayal.

Rand tried to make himself stop thinking about it. He knew Shindael was close and could see his thoughts, and he didn't want to give the demon any ideas about how to torture him. Shindael had once assured him that his death was not enough—that release would only come after he'd truly suffered.

Rand's dozing felt like sleeping in the middle seat of an

airplane. Just as real sleep started to come, his head would droop and jolt him awake again. After that happened many times, he opened his eyes to find that someone was standing just outside the bars of his cell.

He blinked many times. His eyes burned and watered and his vision blurred. At first he thought he was hallucinating, but no. Someone was there.

Rand was sprawled on his back, and it took all his strength to push himself into a sitting position.

He lifted his head up to see who was there.

Black eyes looked down at him.

Shindael.

The fear that Rand normally felt when Shindael was near never came. His body simply had nothing left to produce it. Instead, he felt relief. Finally, this could end.

Even if it means he kills me...

Rand struggled to push off the floor. His back popped as he straightened it. Then he stood on wobbly legs. With no strength or energy left, it felt like trying to stand on the surface of a planet that had ten times the gravity of earth.

But regardless of the effort, Rand had just enough mental fortitude left to know he needed to face his nemesis on two feet.

"Now what?" Rand's voice was gravelly and stilted, having not spoken in however long.

Whatever I want. You are my plaything, remember?

Shindael's words were a voice in his head. Telepathic. It was deceptively smooth and gentle, different from the demonic voices Rand was used to hearing.

Rand shuffled forward, the soles of his shoes never fully leaving the ground. When he reached the bars, he leaned against them, having run out of energy to stand. He was inches away from Shindael now, closer than he would have normally put himself, but he needed something to happen.

If you want out, there is a way.

"So we're going to play games?"

No games, Randolph. I'm offering you an escape. Behind you.

Rand slowly turned and looked over his shoulder.

Shindael had caused a noose to materialize. It dangled from the roof, just high enough to give him the room to hang himself. Rand reached out and grasped the cold bars to steady himself. As he stared at that rope, so neatly tied, it occurred to him this may be his most merciful exit.

But then Rand remembered the story of Jesus in the desert when he and Simon had recited the Gospels. Jesus had fasted alone for forty days and has been tempted directly by Satan, but never gave in.

"I won't do it," Rand said.

It's so easy. Just slip it on.

"No."

I'm offering you a deal, Randolph. If you do this for me now, I promise to leave your family alone.

"I don't make deals with monsters like you."

Smart man. You are right. You shouldn't make deals with the ones that work under me. But me, I am different and you know it. If I tell you I'm going to do something, you know I'll do it.

Shindael then vanished and reappeared a split second later inside the cell, even closer to Rand than he had been before. Their faces were inches apart, and Rand's breath caught. He wanted to back away, but did not have the energy. He could feel Shindael's heavy, evil aura radiating off of him.

I have watched you every day since the first time we spoke. Sometimes I allow you to see me, just to remind you that I am close. But it is not just you I keep track of. I watch Libby. I watch Tessa. I watch everyone you care about. I know everything about them. I know how they spend their time, where they sleep, and exactly *what they think about you.*

Rand began to tremble. He didn't know if it was from fear or weakness. But his anger rose at his body betraying his brokenness to Shindael.

I can kill them any time I want. Easily. But I don't. Because it's far better to use their misery to torment you. To make you pay for all the times you have interfered.

"Leave them alone. They've done nothing to you."

You are right. But you have, and that is good enough.

Shindael's dark eyes absorbed him like black holes consuming everything.

I will make you a deal. And I will keep my word. If you give yourself, then I will leave them alone forever. All we care about is you. End it all now, and they will be freed.

Rand looked past Shindael at the noose still dangling from the ceiling.

You understand that there is no hope. If you refuse, then you are only hurting them more than you already have. In the end, you know you will die by my hand. It is inevitable. The only question is when and if you will take your family down with you.

No matter how much Rand tried to deny Shindael's words, he knew the demon spoke the truth. He hated to admit it to himself, because he knew Shindael could hear his thoughts as if he'd spoken them aloud.

He could push and fight as much as he wanted. He could banish every demon in hell three times over, but they would always return to haunt another. The work would never end, never be complete. And after Shindael had had his fun, after his minions had inflicted enough chaos and psychological scars, after Shindael had grown bored with toying with him over the years... only then would the demon end it. And once he was gone, Shindael's servants would be free to attack the earth at will.

So why let it go on? Why not end it now and spare his family? Why not take the deal?

You are finally thinking clearly for the first time in your life, Randolph.

There was just one thing Rand could not get his head around. Never, ever, under any circumstances, should a human make a deal with the devil. No matter how sweet it sounded, there was always a twist, always a lie. Even in his weakened, desperate state, Rand knew this was the absolute truth.

"No."

Shindael almost seemed amused by his refusal. The demon's face didn't reveal much, but Rand thought he could see the hint of a smirk on those thin lips.

It seems you have chosen to play games, Randolph. You'll remember this night for the rest of your life. Every time your actions and resistance hurts you or someone you love, you'll remember the time I tried to help, and you refused the offer. Every misfortune that befalls you now is entirely your fault.

A sound. Rand turned and watched as the cell door unlatched and slowly swung open by itself, the rusty hinges creaking.

Let the games begin, Rand thought. He looked back

toward Shindael, but the demon and the noose had vanished.

He'd rejected the deal. Now, there was only one thing to do. He had to persevere. Pick up where he'd left off. Continue fighting, no matter how weak he felt.

Rand stumbled over to the sink and drank heavily from the stream, dozens of gulps filling his stomach. With each new mouthful that went down, he felt more and more alive.

He had to find out how long he'd been trapped in Shindael's time loop. Had to see if there was a still a chance at stopping Deckard Arcan.

Rand bumbled through the dark police station on rubbery legs, finding the door and bursting out into the cold night.

No phone. No car. Only his determination and the clothes on his back.

His nearest ally was Simon Cole. Rand had to get to him.

28

L ibby sensed she was being carried inside the mansion and up some stairs. It was completely dark inside the bag that covered her head, and the more she screamed, the more the air seemed to grow thin inside of it.

Despite her breathlessness, she kicked and squirmed, looking for any give in the strong arms around her body. But they only seemed to grow tighter, forcing her elbows into her sides and causing stabbing pain.

She was dropped into an uncomfortable chair and her hands were bound together behind the back of the chair. Her ankles were tied to the legs, leaving her completely captive and helpless.

She heard footsteps walking away, a door opening and then slamming behind them.

"Let me out of here!"

Though she could not see, she knew she was alone in the room.

She pulled on her restraints.

Stupid, she thought. How could she have been lured all the way here? Even her mother had tried to tell her something seemed off about the whole thing. She didn't listen. She had been too eager to find her dad.

He's hurt.

Mauled by a mob of angry church people.

He's captured.

Tied up just like she was.

He's dead...

Libby pulled against her restraints, which cut into the soft flesh around her wrists. The ropes around her ankles weren't budging either.

I have to get out of here and help him. Somehow.

The more she struggled, the more tired she became. Her breaths came in short, shallow gasps. The limited air inside the sack over her head made her dizzy.

Her adrenaline finally gave out, and she slumped in the chair. Then the sobs surfaced, though she fought hard to suppress them.

Dad wouldn't cry right now.

Libby had never felt so far away from her father in her life. No one knew where she was. This was what she got for interfering with her dad's case.

How many times had he tried to warn her? Never interfere. Never act. Even if he got himself killed.

This was why.

She had no idea how long she sat in that chair, tied up like a prisoner. But after what seemed like an eternity, she heard the door open again.

Footsteps.

They fell differently than the ones that had left her there—less heavy. Light and hesitant. Still, they circled around her and came to rest right in front of her. Libby felt the presence standing only inches away.

"Please let me go," she said, voice muffled by the sack over her head.

A hand gripped the sack and pulled it off, and she relished the cool air as she took her first proper breath since being captured.

In front of her stood Patrick Perryman.

The bile rose in Libby's throat and her anger flared. She had a vivid image of tearing his oversized head from his puny body. But all that aggressiveness had not helped so far, so she forced herself to remain calm.

"Good evening," Patrick said.

"What is going on?" she said. "Why have you done this to me? Where is my dad?"

"I see you are calmer now," Patrick said. "I'd like to untie you, but you have to give me your word you'll behave."

Libby swallowed all the insults that sprung to her mind, all the things she wanted to say to this creep who insisted she *behave.* Instead, she nodded.

"Good girl." Patrick went around to the back of the chair and began working on the ropes that bound her wrists.

The ropes fell away and Libby rubbed at her scraped wrists. Then she placed her hands in her lap and forced herself to stay still as Patrick got down on his knees and worked on freeing her ankles from the chair legs.

Libby looked around the room. *Is there an easy way out of here?*

She was in a darkened attic with a low, pointed ceiling and wooden walls. There was a bed, a couch, and an empty baby crib on the far side of the room. Despite the furniture, it didn't look like anyone lived up there, but it did seem to be prepared for someone who had yet to arrive.

There was a small, square window in the far wall in front of her—a potential point of escape. She saw no door. *The only one must be behind me.* That's where she'd heard Patrick come from.

Once she was free, Libby tried to stand, but Patrick only put his hands on her shoulders and forced her back down.

"Not so fast. You're tired and hungry and thirsty."

All of those things were true, but none of it compared to her desire to escape.

"Welcome to my home." He smiled.

Welcome? You kidnapped me.

"Technically Pastor D owns it, but he graciously allows me to live here."

Keep him talking. Make him comfortable. Then I can find a way to escape. "That's nice," Libby said, rather unenthusiastically. "Who else lives here? Just you two?"

Patrick only smirked. "Soon you will too."

The casual way he said it made her second guess if she'd heard that right. "What did you say?"

"I said this will be your home soon."

The room was dark, but Patrick was standing uncomfortably close, so Libby could make out the glee on his face.

This guy is crazy.

"And um..." Libby cleared her throat. "Why, exactly, would I want to live here?"

"You will be my wife and bear my children."

Yep, I'm definitely hearing this right.

"Excuse me?"

"You have been chosen by Azora to be among his first women," Patrick said. "This is a high honor, and one that Pastor D and I have been looking forward to for a long time. I have seen you clearly in my prayers ever since that first day you came to church. God spoke to me immediately and told me you were the one. The angel Azora has confirmed this to Pastor D."

Libby didn't know what any of that actually meant, but the bullet points were good enough. "Are you fucking crazy? Are you sick? What the hell is wrong with you?"

Patrick knelt down in front of her, shushing her like she was a child throwing a tantrum. His face drew closer, and she recoiled. "I know it's a lot to take in right now. But please don't worry. We will begin teaching you the ways of Azora soon. Before you know it, you'll realize your purpose. I remember when I first learned—"

"My dad will come for you. People know that I'm here. This isn't going to work."

"Your dad has been dealt with," Patrick said flippantly. "He is no longer a problem."

Dealt with...

Her fists balled up, ready to strike. "What have you done to my dad?"

"After you have been introduced to Azora, you won't even remember Randolph Casey. So there's no point in talking about it now."

His refusal to answer filled her with a rage so hot she felt tears coming to her eyes.

"Try to get some rest," Patrick said. His clammy palm snaked up her thigh, and she tried to shake it off, but he only squeezed her so tight it hurt. "Your first prayers with Azora will begin soon. It won't be long before you realize the truth and joy that he has planned for your life."

He stood and walked toward the attic door at the far end of the room. Before he left, he turned back to her. "And do try to be on your best behavior. Trust me when I say if you try to do anything rash, you won't like what happens to you. I'd hate to have to do this the hard way." He gave her a simple smile.

After he'd gone, Libby heard the door lock behind him.

29

Dealt with.

She couldn't get the words out of her head.

Calm down, Libby. Pull it together. First things first, I need to get out of here.

The attic was larger than what she would have considered normal. But then again, she was inside of a mansion. The room looked like it was used for storage—some furniture stood in the center of the room, covered in a thin layer of dust. The bed and baby crib gave her the creeps. Presumably those were meant for her.

No chance in hell, Patrick.

She tried the door even though she already knew what she'd find. It was locked.

But on the other end of the attic, on the far side of the room, was a single window. The glass was dirty, and when she tried to peer through it she couldn't see anything because it was nighttime outside.

Libby tried to open it, but it was locked. But then she found the latch.

The small window opened and she stuck her head out. The cool air hit her, a stark contrast to the dank attic room, and the wind blew through her hair.

After her eyes adjusted, she could barely make out the mansion's roof that surrounded the window. She leaned out and explored with her hands, finding rough shingles. The slope of the roof was very steep, and the darkness would make climbing on it even more dangerous.

I have no choice. I have to get out of here right now.

The wind rustled the leaves of a nearby oak tree. She could see the movements of the branches from the light of the full moon, one of which scraped against the roof like a giant claw.

If that branch was thick enough, she could use it like a bridge to the tree's trunk, then slide down. She'd have some scrapes and bruises and maybe a hard drop at the end, but at that moment she would have taken a lot worse just to escape.

Libby threw one leg over the edge of the window and planted a foot on the sloped shingles.

Once, when she was younger, she'd insisted on helping her dad clean out his gutters. She'd climbed the ladder and followed him onto the roof, leaning against the slope as he'd instructed, but she still remembered the way the ground had loomed far below her. The feeling had made her light-headed, and she'd chickened out.

That was the last time she'd ever been on a roof. She tried not to think about that now that she was two or three times higher up.

Both feet on the shingles, she leaned heavily to the left to keep her balance. She gripped the windowpane with one hand as she took small steps toward the tree branch.

In order to get there, she'd have to let go of the window and walk without its support. She took several deep, steadying breaths.

You can do this. Come on. Dad needs my help.

And just as she was about to let go, she heard a noise from inside the attic. It sounded like a loud thump, maybe a slammed door. She gasped and looked back through the window, thinking Patrick had returned. But she didn't see anyone.

If he caught her going out the window, then he'd tie her up again for sure. This was her only chance. She had to make a break for the tree branch and get away now.

But when she looked back toward the tree, to her escape, she was not alone. A high-pitch shriek burst from her mouth.

A figure had appeared on the roof, a monstrous shadow that was darker than the night. He stood on all fours and appeared to have long hair that blew in the wind.

And his eyes. They glowed blood red as they glared at her.

Libby froze in his presence, barely remembering to hold on to the edge of the windowpane. Her foot scraped an inch down the roof's slope, sending a nervous jolt through her stomach. She cried out again and found her balance just in time.

The shadow's negative energy bored into her, weighing her down, making her feel like she was being crushed.

Libby knew what she was looking at. Her dad had taught her what kind of creature this was.

The shadow took a step closer, walking on both his hands and feet like some sort of animal.

Then he opened his mouth. At the back of his throat, a ball of bright fire formed. The flames lit up the darkness around her, and Libby felt the blast of heat on her face.

He breathes fire. Like a dragon.

Libby knew if she stood there much longer, she'd be toast. Literally.

As quickly as she could, Libby pulled herself back into the attic and tumbled through the window.

She landed hard on the floor, the back of her head bouncing off the wood, a sharp pain shooting through her skull.

This demon. This is what my dad must have discovered.

The source of all the crazy things that happened at the church.

Trust me when I say if you try to do anything rash, you won't like what happens to you, Patrick had said.

Libby shot up and threw the window closed, then locked it again. She backed away just as the demon's face appeared in front of the glass, the red eyes glaring through at her.

A silent warning to stay put. To not try that again.

All of a sudden, Libby understood what was going on.

This preacher thinks he's speaking with an angel.

But now she'd seen the creature that was really pulling their strings. Her dad must have discovered the same thing.

Where are you, Dad? Libby thought, unable to tear her eyes away from the demon's. Finally, the shadow moved away from the window, leaving her alone. She knew that if she tried to escape again, it would only reappear. The ultimate prison guard.

She sat down on the bed, her rear nearly missing the edge of the mattress.

I'm totally stuck. There's no way I can get around that thing.

Her only hope was that her dad would come for her. And it needed to be soon. She didn't know what kind of "prayers to Azora" Patrick had in mind for her, but she did know she didn't want to find out.

30

Rand trudged down the path that led to Simon's church. His legs were barely able to carry him and wanted to give out now that he'd reached his destination. He stumbled side to side as he forced himself a bit farther. He figured that, from a distance, he looked like a zombie from one of his favorite movies.

The church came into view. His Jeep was parked in front and Rand remembered he'd left the keys in the ignition to keep the headlights on during his meeting with Deckard Arcan. Simon must have driven it back after Rand had gotten arrested.

Rand burst through the doors of the foyer and fell into the dark sanctuary. "Simon!" His voice boomed all around him. "Simon!"

Noises from the back. A door on the side of the sanctuary opened and the old pastor came out, leaning on his cane and looking worried.

"Rand." He flipped a switch on the wall and the dim lights above flared to life. "Where have you been?"

"Simon," Rand said. He tried to walk down the aisle, but he nearly collapsed. He had to catch the edge of a nearby pew to break his fall.

"Whoa," Simon said, limping over to him as quickly as the old man's body would let him. "Easy. You look terrible." Simon slid underneath Rand's left arm and supported him. The old man was surprisingly strong for someone who required a cane. "Come on. Let's get you in the back."

"Water," Rand gasped.

"I've got everything you need. Just work with me here."

Rand allowed Simon to assist him to the room behind the sanctuary.

The back section of the church was a small kitchen, further cementing Rand's suspicion that the old pastor lived there full time.

Rand collapsed into a chair at the meager table, all his limbs feeling as if they each weighed a ton. Simon busied himself at the counter and soon brought Rand a simple sandwich on a white plate and a pitcher of water. Rand drank straight from the pitcher and devoured the sandwich without even tasting it.

"Oh. I'll make you another sandwich."

"I'm fine," Rand said, but Simon ignored him and continued. He brought the plate back, this time having made three more. While Rand ate, Simon refilled the water jug and also brought a blue sports drink. Rand wrenched off the top and downed the entire bottle in a series of unbroken gulps.

"Have you been hiding out somewhere?" Simon asked.

"I've been in prison."

Simon furrowed his brow. All the sandwiches were

gone, and now Rand leaned against the chair as they roiled in his stomach. He'd eaten too fast.

"Yes, but only for half a night."

Rand looked at him. "What?"

"You... escaped."

Rand blinked, trying to figure out what he missed. "Yeah, but... when?"

"Three days ago."

Rand shook his head. "I got out maybe an hour ago."

Simon leaned forward, standing with his cane in the space between his thighs. "After you were arrested, I drove your car to the police station, but no one was there. I woke early in the morning and planned to go back to speak with Sheriff Jones about your release, but Jones came here before I could leave.

"He told me you'd escaped and questioned me about where you'd gone. I honestly didn't know. He searched the entire church up and down, thinking I was hiding you, but found nothing. He came back two days later to look again."

"There was time distortion, Simon," Rand told him. "These past three days were one long night to me. No one ever came to the police station. My only visitor was my little demon friend. He tried to make me kill myself, but I refused. He eventually released me."

"Demon friend?"

"Shindael," Rand said. "My own personal demon who follows me around." He waved his hand. "Long story."

"I'm sorry this all happened to you," Simon said. "You are truly doing the Lord's work."

Rand choked on the water as he drank more. "I don't know about that." He wiped his mouth.

"What will you do now?"

"I have to go back to Deckard. I need to remove the demon that's possessing him before he hurts anyone else."

"You can't go tonight," Simon said.

Rand looked at him. "Why? I have to. If we wait, worse things could happen."

"Think about it. Your demon friend freed you from the jail for a reason. He wants you to rush back in. You'll be playing right into his hands."

Rand thought on that for a moment. The old pastor had a point.

"You're in no shape to battle the demonic," Simon went on. "You know this. State of mind and strength of body is everything and right now, you have neither."

Rand took a deep breath and accepted Simon's reasoning. "Okay. What should I do?"

"You *know* what you should do. Go home. Get some rest. Sleep and pray. Recover. Then return, and we will both be stronger to fight another day. These demons want you weak because they know how powerful you are at full strength."

Rand nodded slowly. He hated leaving a job undone and postponed. "Okay. You're right."

Simon leaned forward and patted Rand's shoulder. "You're a good man, Rand Casey. I wish I'd known you before when I was having my own encounters with these things."

Careful what you wish for. Knowing me doesn't make for an easy life.

"I appreciate it."

He suddenly remembered Libby. "Do you have a phone I can borrow?"

Simon pulled his old flip phone from his pocket and handed it to Rand. He dialed Libby's number from memory. The line only rang a few times before her voicemail picked up.

"I guess it is late," Rand said. His daughter had not heard from him the entire time he was locked up and was surely worried. In the past, he had gone long stretches of time without getting in touch with her when he was involved in cases. It worried her, sure, but she knew it was the nature of the beast. He felt bad putting her through it every time. "I'll just head home and call her tomorrow."

"Are you well enough to drive?"

"Yeah." Although Rand wasn't entirely sure that was true.

"You can sleep here if you want."

"I appreciate it, but I best get home." He'd have to gather his backup spiritual cleansing supplies and get a new phone. The belongings confiscated by the sheriff were likely long gone.

"Just be careful, Rand," Simon said. "This town needs you."

"When the time comes to face Deckard Arcan again, can I count on you?" Rand asked.

Simon seemed offended by the question. "Without a doubt. I know how important these matters are."

"Thank you for the hospitality. And for all your guidance."

Rand left him there and passed through the sanctuary on his way out of the church. In the sanctuary, the statue of Jesus on the cross caught his eye and gave him pause.

"Where were you when I was locked up?" he whispered. "Why did you allow a demon to come instead?"

Am I just a sacrifice? Like you were?

Was his entire mission to fight the demonic just a hopeless mess? Destined to end in doom and failure for him, his family, and everyone he tried to help. If Shindael was to be believed, it was.

But it sure would help if God spoke to him even half as clearly as the devil did.

31

For the first time in a long time, Patrick actually felt cooped up.

His bedroom was small, sure, but he did not need much. Pastor D had been very generous with allowing him to live in the mansion at all. He'd never felt ungrateful, or that it was too little, or not what he needed.

But that night, he felt the walls were closing in on him. That he couldn't breathe. That he couldn't focus on his prayers to Azora.

It was probably because his beloved was now in the house. She was up one flight of stairs, on the third floor. Waiting to be introduced to Azora. Soon after that, she would become his wife.

The prospect excited him. Made him giddy. He was thrilled that Azora had willed this girl into his life, and he could not wait to get started on his new path with her.

Hopefully, Pastor D would allow him a larger room once they became man and wife. There was a spare bedroom on the first floor that he'd been scoping out for a while, one that was large and empty, never used.

Patrick walked into the hallway, feeling stuffy in his own bedroom. The air was clearer in the hall and immediately started to ease his senses. It was night, and as usual, the house was still and silent. He wondered what Libby was doing upstairs.

He adjusted his glasses and smoothed his hair. Every bit of him wanted to go upstairs and see her, but Pastor D had warned him about spending too much time with her before she had been properly taught about Azora. She would only lead to sin and temptation, he had said, more than she already had.

Patrick knew Pastor D was right. But still, his body squirmed with anticipation. He took a deep, steadying breath and tried to remind himself that their marriage, and subsequent consummation, was near. If he could only be strong for a little while longer, then Azora would bless him.

He went downstairs into the large foyer of the mansion. He peeked in on Pastor D's study and found the man in prayer before the fireplace, huge flames roaring and creating an uncomfortable heat inside. Patrick left him there and headed toward the front door. He needed fresh air.

Although the night was dark, Patrick froze when he saw a figure lying on the steps of the porch, as if both legs were broken and they'd been trying to crawl up the steps before their body had simply given out.

"Help me," came a woman's voice, barely audible.

Patrick rushed to the figure and crouched down. Once he was closer, he saw who it was.

"Chloe?"

Patrick knew about Chloe's advanced cancer and poor condition, but the woman had always walked into church on her own two feet, ready to give her all to the Lord. Now she was unable to even stand.

Did she crawl all the way here?

The sickly woman looked up at him, barely able to keep her eyes open. Her lids fluttered. She appeared as if she'd been trying to cross a desert and had run out of water. "Oh, Patrick. You're here. Thank the Lord."

"Chloe, are you okay? What are you doing here?"

"I'm dying, Patrick," she said, smiling. "And I need healing."

"Come on," Patrick said. He scooped her up, arms under her legs and neck, and carried her inside. She threw her arms around his neck and held onto him feebly, looking up at him as if he were saving her from a burning building.

Once inside, he kicked the door closed behind him, then gingerly laid her on the floor, unable to hold her longer.

"Please," she said, "I want to see Pastor D."

Patrick glanced uncertainly toward the study door. "He's... busy." But it felt terrible to say to a woman in Chloe's condition.

"Please," she said again. "I've come all this way."

Pastor D had always instructed Patrick to never interrupt him during his nightly prayers. Patrick didn't know how angry Pastor D would be because Patrick had never done it. But surely Pastor D wouldn't mind being interrupted when one of his congregation came to him in the middle of the night.

He'd come out to meet Gerald Roberson. Why wouldn't Chloe be the same?

"Wait here," Patrick said, touching Chloe's cheek. It was slick with sweat. "I'll bring him."

"Thank you so much." She smiled as best she could.

Patrick rushed to the study and hesitated at the door. It was cracked open, as it always was, but that did not mean people were welcome inside. He waited there for a few minutes, watching Pastor D on his hands and knees before the fire, as if worshipping it. Sometimes Pastor D was able to divine his presence. In those cases, Patrick did not feel like he was interrupting. But this time, Pastor D continued on, chanting in an unknown language that only he knew, oblivious to Patrick being there.

Patrick heard Chloe cough and groan in pain from the foyer.

He raised his hand and knocked lightly on the door. Pastor D's head snapped up then slowly turned to the side. "Who is it?"

"Patrick."

"What do you want? I'm praying."

Patrick cleared his throat. "It's Chloe. She's here."

"Bring her to one of the spare bedrooms and let her stay the night."

"It's more than that, sir. She's very sick. She's requesting to see you."

Pastor D was silent for several long moments as he considered.

Surely he would not turn away one of his flock, Patrick thought.

Pastor D rose to his feet and fastened his robe around

his waist. He left the study, brushing by Patrick without a word. Patrick followed him back to the main foyer.

"Oh!" Chloe cried when she saw the pastor. She still lay on the ground, her arms reaching out to him like he was a vision sent from heaven.

Pastor D crouched over her, the stern expression Patrick had received having melted into one of genuine love and concern. "Chloe. What are you doing here at this time of night? Is everything all right?"

It struck Patrick how quickly Pastor D could switch gears. The demeanor he'd had with Patrick and the one he now showed Chloe was completely different. It even frightened Patrick a bit.

"Something is wrong," Chloe said, gripping both of Pastor D's hands. Her own looked like the shriveled claws of a vulture. "It's finally happening. I'm dying."

Pastor D put a hand to her cheek and supported her head off the floor. "Then why did you not go to a hospital?"

Chloe only smiled. "Because my faith is stronger than that. I know that God's power can allow you to heal better than any doctor in the world."

Pastor D smiled. "You have a great faith, Chloe. And you will be rewarded for that."

Chloe began to sob. The woman, although dying, appeared so happy.

Pastor D stood and looked down at her, saying nothing for a long while. Patrick realized he was holding his breath, waiting to see what the man would do next. Would he pray over her? If so, would she be healed? Would she get up and walk out of the house just as Gerald had risen from his wheelchair in the tent?

Instead, he only turned to Patrick. "Take her to the attic."

"I'm sorry?"

"Take her upstairs. I will be with her shortly. I need time to prepare."

Patrick wondered how much more preparation he needed—Pastor D had been in the study all night, just as he had been every night.

"But…" Patrick was no doctor, yet just by looking at Chloe he knew the woman didn't have much time left.

"Do as I say, Patrick." He walked away from them and disappeared down the hallway and back into his study.

Chloe still cried tears of gratitude. "He's going to help me. I'm finally going to be free."

"Come on, dear," Patrick said, scooping her up the same way he had when he'd found her on the front porch steps. "Let's bring you upstairs so you can rest. You can wait for Pastor D up there."

Hopefully he comes in time.

***

LIBBY WOKE to the sound of the attic door opening.

It was Patrick Perryman, and he carried someone in his arms.

"Move!" he barked.

Libby shot up from the bed just before Patrick dumped the limp form right where she had been laying.

She recognized the woman, but it took Libby a few moments to place her—Chloe, from the church. She knew Justin.

Her illness had been evident before, but now she

looked even worse. Libby wasn't sure she'd ever seen someone so frail.

"What's going on?" Libby asked.

"She's very sick," Patrick told her. "She will wait here until Pastor D heals her."

Libby stared at him in disbelief, although she wasn't sure why she'd expected anything sane to happen anymore. "Are you serious? Look at her. She needs a hospital!"

"She needs prayer," Patrick said. "She will stay up here with you. Try not to disturb her too much. Pastor D will see her soon."

Then he left, locking the door behind him.

Libby knelt down at the bedside. Chloe's eyes wandered, but finally seem to find Libby. Recognition dawned.

"I remember you from last week. At church. It was your first time. Libby, was it?"

"Yes, ma'am. What's wrong? Are you in pain?"

"Just my cancer," Chloe said. "But soon enough, it will be gone. I have faith in God and Azora and Pastor D."

"We need to get you to a doctor," Libby told her. But Libby was trapped there, helpless.

"No doctor, dear," Chloe said, resting a bony hand on Libby's arm. "I came here by choice."

Libby could not fathom the level of belief the woman had in Deckard Arcan. But then again, after seeing him make that man walk—or so they all believed—perhaps some people were willing to believe that he could do anything.

It made tears well up in her eyes. Deckard had

deceived Chloe, and she'd bought in. Preying on the diminishing hopes of a dying woman.

Libby stood and pulled the comforter up to Chloe's chin and tucked her in. Chloe gave her a wan smile. "Thank you, dear." Then she closed her eyes and fell asleep.

Libby paced around the room, wracking her brain for some way to call for help. Not just for herself, but to get Chloe the medical care she needed.

The night passed and no one came, not even Pastor D. As the sun rose and the light of dawn shone through the single attic window, Libby eyed the sleeping woman in the bed. For the first time since she'd arrived, she appeared truly at peace and not in pain.

Libby pressed two shaky fingers to Chloe's throat. She waited in silence, trying to feel for a pulse.

Nothing.

She'd passed in the night.

32

The dawn had come, chilly and grey, by the time Rand made it home.

When he got there, Tessa's blue SUV was parked in the driveway. She was out of the car and pacing around the lawn, phone to her ear, while Bill looked on.

When she spotted his Jeep, she immediately hung up.

Rand got a sinking feeling in the pit of his stomach.

He parked and threw open the Jeep's door. "What's going on?"

"Where the hell is our daughter?" Tessa shrieked at him.

"What?"

"Our daughter!" Her face was hysterical, and she shoved his chest. "She said she was going to meet you and I haven't heard from her! Or you! Where is she?"

Rand's mind raced as he tried to find words. "I don't know."

Tessa's eyes slowly went wide when she realized what

he'd just said. "You don't know? What do you mean you *don't know?*"

"I haven't spoken to her since Sunday."

"Yes, you have! She called and told me she talked to you and that you told her to meet you in Finnick!"

Rand's mouth went dry. He looked back and forth between her and Bill. "It... wasn't me."

"Then who was it? She said it was you!"

Anxiety coursed through Rand's entire body. It slowly turned to panic as he put together the pieces of what was going on.

The demon mimicked me.

Rand knew it in his gut.

"Where the hell have you been?" Tessa demanded.

"On a case—"

"What the fuck does that have to do with our daughter? Why is she involved?" Tessa gripped his shirt, shaking him back and forth. A seam in the collar ripped.

Bill stepped in and tried to pull Tessa away, but she resisted.

"Tessa—" Rand began.

"Why is she caught up in this? What does she have to do with all these freaks and weirdos you deal with?"

"If you—"

"Why do you keep doing this?" Tessa continued to scream at him. Bill was not strong enough to restrain her. She beat on his chest, his face, his shoulders, and Rand stood there and took it. "Can't you see it doesn't affect only you? It's ruined your entire family!"

Shindael's words came through Tessa's mouth. He deserved every bit of beating she gave him.

Finally, when he'd had enough, he caught her wrists

in his hands and gripped them tight, subduing her. She tried to pull out of his grasp, but eventually she exhausted all her energy. Her face was streaked with tears.

"How long ago did she say she was going to meet me?"

"Wednesday."

Rand looked at Bill. The man had tried to be calm and impartial during the whole thing, but he still looked sick with worry.

"She said I told her to meet me in Finnick, right?"

"Yes!" Tessa shouted. "Where the hell have you been? Why don't you have a phone?"

"Okay." Rand released Tessa's wrists, and she finally started to calm down. "I'm going to get her."

"You don't even know where she is!"

"I will find her. Trust me."

"I *don't* trust you, Rand!" Tessa shouted. "I can never trust anything you do or say when you're doing a case because of all the weird stuff that happens! I'm sick of it, and this time you've gone too far. Libby has been *missing* for three days!"

"Tessa—"

"I was one minute away from calling the police. I don't give a shit about your 'no police' rule! If you want to go and get possessed by demons or abducted by aliens or whatever the fuck it is you do, then fine! But you have no right to keep involving Libby."

He's behind this, Rand thought. And as he pictured Deckard Arcan luring his daughter to him, the same rage that filled Tessa consumed him as well.

He walked away from Tessa and toward the front door of his house.

"Where are you going?" she shrieked. "Are you listening to me?"

Rand unlocked the door and rushed to his bedroom, where he threw open his closet, shuffled some clothes aside, and found the empty shoebox that he knew was there. He threw off the lid, revealing his small black handgun. He grabbed it, tucked it into the back of his waistband, and lowered his jacket over it.

It was something he never would have brought on a case. Never had before.

But Deckard Arcan had crossed the line. Rand wasn't going to take any chances.

Rand returned to the driveway. Then, he climbed into the Jeep and started the ignition. "I'm going to get her. If you don't hear from me by tomorrow morning, then you can call the police. But until then, don't get them involved."

Calling the police whenever the supernatural was involved *always* made things worse. He'd learned that lesson the hard way.

He closed the door and rolled down the window.

Tessa only stared at him in disbelief, her face completely streaked with tears. "Sometimes I think you are the worst thing that's ever happened to me, Randolph."

"Give me your phone," Rand said, sticking his palm out the window.

"What?"

"I need a phone because I lost mine. Give me yours so I can keep in touch."

"Here," Bill said, digging his own phone out of his

pocket and handing it to Rand. "Take mine and call us as soon as you find Libby. The passcode is Tessa's birthday."

Rand reversed out of the driveway and tore off down the road. Although his body was still weak and fatigued, new energy crashed through him, and he knew it would not subside until he found his daughter.

Deckard Arcan, he thought as he quickly exceeded the speed limit. *You've gone too far with this one.*

33

Rand drove furiously through the roads of Finnick, remembering only at the last second to slow down. If he were pulled over, there would be trouble. Surely the sheriff was on the lookout for him after his miraculous escape from the prison cell.

He had not slept. There was nothing left in the fuel tank of his body. He was driven only by adrenaline, anxiety, and anger.

That man has my daughter. I know it.

There was no time. He could not afford to stop. He had to press on. Had to find her before it was too late.

He found the dirt road that would bring him to Mount Grace Church. He gunned the gas as his big tires threatened to get caught in the mud that still lingered from all the heavy rainstorms.

When he pulled up in front of the church, Simon Cole came outside the front doors of the foyer, giving him a curious look.

Rand dropped out of Jeep and hurried over to him.

"Rand," Simon said as he approached. "Why are you back so soon?"

"I need your help," he said, the words spilling out of him faster and more desperately than he'd intended. But it was how he felt.

"Rand…"

"They have Libby. My daughter." When he was near enough, Rand grabbed the older man by the elbows, and thought he saw a hint of fear in Simon's eyes behind the concern.

"Please, Rand," Simon said, voice gentle as always. "You need to sleep and rest."

"No!" he snapped. "I can't! There's no time. Deckard has taken my daughter."

Simon pulled out of his grasp with surprising strength. "I'm not going anywhere until you calm down." He spoke firmly, as if scolding Rand.

And although Rand knew he was desperate and acting like it, he realized that if anything would get done, he needed to settle down. Usually he remembered this, but when his daughter was concerned…

"You know I will help you," Simon said, speaking gentler now. "But we need to do this correctly. Please come inside."

Simon kept a comforting hand on Rand's back as they walked together into the church. It was toasty in the sanctuary, a stark contrast to the chilled air of the early morning.

He was pretty sure he stank of body odor. His hair was matted and greasy, and his eyes were heavy and dry in his skull. He hadn't changed clothes in days. Simon Cole didn't know him—the man had every right to consider him an insane vagabond and toss him out.

"You're okay," Simon said, rubbing his back and guiding him to sit in the pew. Rand went down, his body thanking him for allowing it to rest.

But Rand's mind snapped into overdrive. "I'm sorry, Simon, but we don't have time. They have Libby."

"How do you know?"

"Because when I got home, her mother told me she came here looking for me, that she'd gotten a phone call from me to meet me in Finnick. But I was locked up for days."

Simon's face turned grim as he listened. "Mimicry."

"Exactly. Whatever demon has taken Deckard has lured Libby here."

"Right," Simon said. He was quiet while he thought it over. "I do not think they mean to harm her."

"I don't either," Rand said. "They only want to get to me. It worked." He stood, no longer feeling comfortable sitting and talking. He was ready for action.

"What are you intending to do?" Simon asked, giving him a strange look—as if afraid of the answer.

"Do you know where Deckard lives? Can you take me there?"

"He won't be at home," Simon said.

"Why?"

"Because it's Sunday morning."

Rand digested that information for a few moments. *I've been at this for an entire week already? That time in the jail...*

He'd have a lot of explaining to do to his boss as well. He'd missed work for cases before, but never for this long.

"Fine. We'll confront him at the tent. Will you come with me?" Without waiting for an answer, Rand started walking toward the door.

"Rand."

He stopped and turned. Simon had not moved to follow him. "What did I feel in your waistband?"

Simon's eyes bored into him, and Rand knew it was a rhetorical question. He'd almost forgotten it was back there. Simon must have felt it when he was comforting him.

He reached behind and withdrew the handgun, showing it to the old pastor.

Simon looked worried, and Rand did not blame him. Still, the man kept his composure. "A curious thing to bring to a spiritual fight."

"I'm well aware, but this has crossed a line. They have my daughter. I'll do whatever it takes to get her back."

"If we go to the church right now, who will you shoot?"

"No one."

"Then why do you have it?"

Rand and Simon stared at each other for several long, silent moments. He had no good answer. He'd grabbed the gun in a wave of desperation and confusion and unclear thinking. He'd been highly emotional—and still was—but Simon was calming him down.

But he already knew he would bring it with him. And brandish it in Deckard's face if he had to.

"I'm going now, Simon," Rand said. "You're either coming with me or you're not."

"Promise me you won't do anything rash."

"It depends on what Deckard does first."

Rand turned and walked out of the church. He was almost to his Jeep when he realized that Simon was actually following him.

"Give me your keys," Simon said. "If you're going, you can't just walk right up to the tent. Not after everything that's happened."

"You know a better way?" Rand asked.

"A side entrance." Simon held out his hand.

Rand considered it for a few moments before dropping his key into the man's palm.

Simon drove the Jeep while Rand sat in the passenger seat. The gun was tucked back into his waistband, covered by his jacket and poking into his spine.

"You don't want to confront Deckard when the entire congregation is around," Simon said. "This matter with your daughter is a private and personal one."

Quite personal, Rand thought.

He still did not know what he would do when they got there. He already figured he'd feel like rushing in and tearing the man's head off his shoulders, but that was why Simon was there—to keep him from doing anything too brazen.

Simon parked in the lot of an old thrift store.

Rand looked around. "Where are we?"

"Finnick is such a small town. I'm surprised you still haven't learned your way."

"I haven't been focused on the geography."

"Follow me."

Simon led him across the lot and behind the store into a thick copse of trees. They trudged over the foliage, sticks cracking and leaves crunching underfoot. Rand pushed low-hanging branches out of his face, and the rough bark caught onto the sleeves of his jacket, as if the trees were trying to physically keep him from proceeding.

Rand remembered the area surrounding the tent church and already knew where they would come out.

When they arrived at the edge of woods, he saw the clearing. They were to the right of the tent, and since all sides were open Rand could see the gathered Sunday-morning crowd sitting on the benches and standing in the back and along the edges, everyone eagerly waiting for their pastor.

The two men stayed hidden behind the trees. Rand checked his watch, but the hands were still stuck at an incorrect time.

He scanned the crowds, although he could not make out much from where he crouched in their hiding place. "I don't see Libby."

"If she's not here, then she might be at Deckard's home," Simon said.

Rand shuddered to think what that could mean. Was she tied up? Drugged? Worse?

"Good morning and happy Sunday." the voice sounded through the microphone. Patrick Perryman stood on the stage.

Rand ground his teeth. *That little runt. I wonder if he had anything to do with this.*

"Happy Sunday." The congregation responded in unison.

Rand noticed there was a table on the back of the raised platform with something on top, covered by a sheet. Rand strained his eyes to see, but his fatigue made his vision blurry, and his desperate situation was probably causing his imagination to run wild.

It looks like a covered body.

He stared at it, trying to convince himself that wasn't true. Surely it was like seeing a shape in the clouds—you saw only what your brain was already thinking about on some level.

He refused to entertain the thought that Libby was under there. Even a millisecond of consideration was inappropriate.

But still. Whatever was under that sheet resembled a body.

"I won't stay up here long," Patrick went on. "This is a very exciting morning, one that Pastor D has been praying about for a while. I say that every Sunday, but this time it's serious." The crowd chuckled. "No, seriously. You all know what to expect from Pastor D and Azora by now, and today you're going to get even more of it."

There was a round of applause, and Patrick placed the microphone back on the stand and left.

Then, Deckard Arcan came. He wore a light blue tailored suit, silver hair combed and perfectly in place, beard trimmed, and a beaming smile. The congregation erupted into cheers when he took the stage. He stood for several minutes, basking in the standing ovation, before signaling everyone to calm down and listen up.

"Good morning and happy Sunday," he said into the microphone.

"Happy Sunday," the crowd intoned back, louder than the rendition they'd given Patrick.

"Patrick was right," Deckard said. "This is a *very* special Sunday. I have spent many nights in prayers with Azora, and I have always known deep in my heart that this day would come. And now today is that day."

Another round of cheers.

"Pastor D!" someone shouted and stood from their seat. The man waved to get Deckard's attention. "My gout has gotten to be too much. I can barely do my work, and I could lose my job."

Deckard held out his hand, and the man quieted. "I hear your pain, brother. But I assure you that you are thinking too small. Today is different. It's a day where you will all witness and remember the true power of Azora."

What is he talking about? Rand thought. The last time he'd promised that, the fiasco with Gerald Roberson had happened. What did he have up his sleeve?

Once Deckard had the congregation silent again, he said, "Brothers and sisters, I have some bad news and some good news. First, the bad. Our sister Chloe Baker has passed away." Murmurs through the crowd. Deckard spoke over them. "For those of you who didn't know, Chloe was a member of this church since the beginning. She was diagnosed with pancreatic cancer, and it only got worse over time. Still, she remained faithful, and her dedication will pay off."

"You could have healed her!" someone shouted at him. It was the first form of heckling Rand had ever heard toward Deckard Arcan.

Deckard rounded on that man. "Where is your faith in the plan of Azora? Have you spent *your* nights speaking with him? I think not. Now listen."

The scolded man shut up.

Deckard let the congregation linger in silence for a few moments before he said, "Patrick and Hoby. Bring her."

Hoby was apparently the name of the big bodyguard

that never seemed far from Deckard. He and Patrick returned to the stage and each gripped an end of the table and lifted it like two men moving furniture. It tipped toward Patrick as he struggled with the weight. The pair brought the table to the forefront of the raised platform, the object on top of it remaining covered the whole time. Once the table was lowered, they disappeared on either side of the stage.

The congregation remained silent as they waited, as did Rand. His nerves twisted violently in his stomach. Whatever was on that table looked like a sacrifice on an altar.

Simon seemed ill as he watched what was happening.

"You are all very fortunate to be here this morning," Deckard said as he went to stand behind the table. He faced the audience. "You will be the first to witness the true power of Azora. This is something that hasn't been seen since Biblical times."

That was the moment that Rand thought the crowd would have cheered, but no one made a sound. He figured that, to them, perhaps the shape underneath the sheet also looked like a body.

"Only the angel Azora can give life back when it has been taken away," Deckard continued. "I have heard this in my prayers, and I have seen it in my dreams and in my visions. Today, it shall be."

Nervous murmuring in the congregation.

Deckard raised his hands and spread them, similar to that of Jesus on the cross. "Azora!" he called, his voice booming. "Come down and join us here. We are ready to be witnesses to your awesome power."

"This can't happen," Rand said. "She's under there. Chloe."

"What is he doing?" It sounded like Simon knew what Deckard had planned, but just didn't want to believe it.

Rand had witnessed a lot of crazy stuff in his life, and most of it would never be believed by anyone who sat and listened to his tales. But this... this was something completely different. He had never seen this attempted before, not even by the craziest of people who had gone down the occult rabbit hole.

"Rand, what is he doing?" Simon asked again.

"Necromancy."

34

Simon shook his head. "It can't be. It won't work." He looked at Rand, his eyes wide and afraid. "Will it?"

"I've never seen it happen, nor have I known anyone to ever try it."

"What do we do?" Simon asked.

Then Deckard's voice changed. He spoke in a different tongue, a language that Rand did not recognize at all. The man's mouth moved, vomiting incoherent words over Chloe's body. His eyes were closed, lost in a trance. It seemed he believed whole-heartedly that what he was doing would be successful.

"We have to stop this," Rand said.

"There's no way this will actually happen," Simon said, placing a hand on Rand's arm and squeezing. "Right? That lady will not come back to life."

"Remember Gerald Roberson?"

"But…"

"We can't just sit here and insist that it isn't going to

work," Rand said. "We have to do something. These people can't see this."

The words spilling from Deckard's mouth affected Rand in a way he couldn't pinpoint. Merely hearing them made him feel sickened, afraid, and like he wanted to turn and run. The people in the congregation must have felt the same—those who stood took several steps back. The ones sitting looked away, as if they could not bear to watch.

And Rand knew he was hearing a voice from hell. Whatever demon that had entered Deckard spoke through him. Rand had already seen the power the entity lent to the preacher, and if he let this go on, then Chloe was going to come back to life.

The sheet moved. As if the body underneath it gave a short twitch with its hand. The crowd gasped in unison. Some stood, ready to flee.

"Hold strong and do not be afraid," Deckard commanded his audience. "Azora is here. It is almost complete." Deckard looked down at the covered body in front of him. "Chloe Baker. Return to us. Your time was ended too soon by a disease you did not deserve. Return and live out the rest of your natural life in the light of Azora."

The sheet moved again, stronger, like a leg kicking back to life.

More shocked cries came from the crowd.

"Rand," Simon said, desperate.

"I'm stopping this." Rand rose from where he crouched and started walking toward the tent.

He knew these people couldn't witness a body raised from the dead by a demonic ritual. If they did, they would believe in Deckard forever and be cemented into his cult. At the moment, he only had one idea of how to break up this madness.

He pulled the gun from his waistband. He clicked off the safety, pointed it toward the sky, and fired a single shot.

35

The gunshot cracked, echoing off the trees on the edge of the clearing.

The entire place erupted into chaos. The crowd screamed and ducked, dropping low and putting their hands over their heads.

Deckard's presentation ceased and he recoiled backwards. Rand watched as Hoby leapt to Deckard's side and tried to pull him off the stage, but Deckard resisted.

Rand fired again, another shot that somehow seemed louder than the first. The people of the congregation scattered in every direction. In only a few moments, the tent was empty.

Only Deckard and Hoby remained. Deckard was on the raised platform, glaring at Rand.

Rand met Deckard's gaze as he walked to the tent's opening. The two men stood off, waiting for the crowds to finish scattering.

About a minute later, the clearing was quiet. Everyone had fled.

"Randolph Casey," Deckard said, stepping down from the stage, never taking his eyes off Rand. "You have gone too far this time."

Libby.

Rand raised the gun and leveled it at Deckard. Deckard stopped advancing, although he did not seem afraid.

Rand had never pointed a gun at anyone before—ever. But as he faced Deckard then, he saw a man who threatened his family, and it was the only thing he knew to do.

"What are you planning?" Deckard said. "You want to shoot me? Go ahead. I'll be a martyr for Azora. I have faith the angel will make quick work of you after you ruined the greatest miracle he's ever done."

"I'm here for my daughter, Deckard," Rand said. "Give her back."

There was movement over Deckard's shoulder, but it did not distract him. Patrick Perryman appeared from behind the raised platform where he'd probably been hiding.

"You heard me," Rand said. "Libby. Now."

"Your daughter came to us willingly," Deckard said. "She was interested in the teachings of Azora, and—"

"*Deckard!*"

The man fell silent, snarling at Rand. Then he finally spoke. "You want the girl? Fine. You can have her."

Behind him, Patrick Perryman looked shocked. Maybe even a little upset.

"Where is she?"

"She's at my home. Not far from here. I'll give her to you, but only on one condition."

"And that is?"

"That you take her place."

What is this, a hostage negotiation?

"You don't make the terms. I'm the one with the gun."

"And I'm the one with Azora. You remember what happened last time you tried to attack me, don't you?" Deckard smirked. "If you want to try again, then go ahead and shoot me. I have all the faith in the world that Azora will protect me."

Rand had already fallen victim to the incredible strength the demon gave to Deckard. It very well could be that a bullet would not hurt him. Also, it was possible that the demon would do nothing, and the shot would kill Deckard, making Rand a murderer. Rand definitely could not shoot him. And Deckard knew it.

The gun had been helpful in disrupting Deckard's demonic ritual, but it was useless against a perfectly possessed man.

"You understand now that this is ridiculous," Deckard said. "And surely you realize that I don't care about your daughter—only you. So put the gun down, and let's sort this out like the gentlemen we are."

Just as Rand figured. They were using Libby to get to him. And it had worked. *Of course it had.*

Rand lowered his weapon.

"That's the right move. Good. Go ahead, Hoby." The big man advanced on him. Hoby gripped Rand's wrist and confiscated the gun from his hand. Hoby tucked it into his inside coat pocket, then spun Rand around to frisk him for any more weapons. Finding none, Hoby grabbed Rand's shoulder, squeezing it hard enough to hurt him, and pushed him forward, forcing him to walk ahead. The man was so strong that Rand couldn't have broken out of the grip, even if he wanted to.

"Hoby will drive you to my house," Deckard said. "He will let your daughter go. Then you will remain behind."

As they walked, Rand caught Patrick's eye. The man looked frightened and confused.

Forget him, Rand thought. *All that matters now is getting Libby back.* And he prayed Deckard would keep his word.

36

Justin heard the shots at the same time as everyone else. His first instinct was to duck low, hands over this head. Everyone around him did the same. Then, in the next split second, everyone scattered. He followed suit almost involuntarily.

In the ensuing chaos, he bumped into people running in every direction. They almost knocked him off his feet. Justin flailed his arms, nearly spilling to the ground.

Pastor D.

The shooter had come to assassinate him. *But why?* He ventured a quick glance over this shoulder and saw that Pastor D was with his big bodyguard, still standing, but Justin did not wait around—he only kept running.

Then he caught a glimpse of the shooter.

Mr. Rand.

Libby's father held a pistol upright, having fired into the air instead of the crowd.

What in the world is going on?

He slowed his run, then stopped. He ducked behind the trunk of a thick tree, hidden from view.

Justin thought of all those shootings he'd read about online. At the time, they'd all seemed so far away, like something that couldn't possibly happen to him.

Within seconds, the entire tent and the surrounding clearing were empty of all people. Everyone except for Mr. Rand and Pastor D and his bodyguard.

Justin knew he should have kept running, but it was Mr. Rand with the gun. Surely he didn't intend to hurt anyone.

He was trying to scatter everyone. He didn't want them to see the rest of the resurrection.

Justin watched as Mr. Rand and Pastor D had a conversation, although it looked more like a stand-off.

On the raised platform, Chloe's body was at rest. It no longer moved like it had before.

The stand-off ended. The big bodyguard approached Mr. Rand, took his gun, and then led him away like he was being arrested.

What in the world is going on? Something is very wrong with all this.

Justin ducked back behind the tree and lowered himself onto the hard roots. He wiped at his forehead, rustled his hair, trying hard to make sense of everything he'd seen.

Especially what he saw a few minutes ago—when Pastor D was moments away from making a dead corpse live again.

He felt ill. Giving Gerald Roberson back his ability to walk was one thing. But what was the point of raising people from the dead? Weren't people supposed to die eventually? Wasn't Chloe in heaven, happy and healthy? Why bring her back?

The power of Azora.

But there had to be a line. A limit. Why use the power of Azora to do things that were not good?

Mr. Rand must have understood that. That must have been why he broke up the crowd, even by doing something as reckless as shooting a gun. And then, because of it, he was taken away on Pastor D's orders. The man that Justin thought he trusted. What if he planned to hurt Mr. Rand?

This is because of me.

The realization dawned on Justin like it was one of Pastor D's divinations. His father had told Mr. Rand to prove that Pastor D was a fraud. Justin had no idea what Mr. Rand had discovered, but all of this had started because of Justin.

He'd been misled. He didn't know the half of what was truly going on. Because whatever it was, it had caused Mr. Rand to get taken.

He pulled out his phone and called Libby. They had not spoken since their conversation in the gym and, unsurprisingly, she did not answer. She was probably frustrated with him, and for good reason, but it was a terrible time for her to not pick up the phone.

Your dad is in danger, he thought.

Something had to happen, and soon.

Before he knew what he was doing, Justin was up and running toward his car. There were several cars left in the area, abandoned by people who had chosen to escape on foot.

He fired up the ignition and pulled out. He was

heading toward Pastor D's house. Mr. Rand was in trouble, and it was all Justin's fault. He had to help the man.

37

At the rear of the tent was a sleek black car, brand new. Hoby pushed Rand toward it, then bent him over the hood of the car, smashing his face into the metal.

"Ow! Easy, man," Rand said.

Hoby ignored him. He yanked Rand's wrists behind his back, as if arresting him. Rand felt them bound by something hard, then cinched up tight.

A zip-tie.

Hoby grabbed Rand by the neck of his jacket and straightened him.

"Really? You just have those on your person? How many people do you kidnap in a week?"

Hoby spun Rand around, glaring at him. He was a good foot and a half taller than Rand. "It would be wise to shut your mouth." His voice was a deep baritone.

After letting the message sink in, Hoby opened the car door and shoved Rand in. He tumbled sideways, hands bound behind his back, causing him to fall awkwardly and then struggle to get up. Hoby got into the driver's seat and soon they were on their way.

"Why do you let those guys boss you around?" Rand asked as they drove. "I mean, look at you. You're a big dude. No one should tell you what to do, right?"

Hoby kept his eyes on the road, not letting on that he'd heard a word.

"How about this," Rand went on. "Free me and my daughter, and I'll help you out. How much are these guys paying you? I can't pay you that, but I can get you a real job. My favorite bar is always looking for bouncers, and you're a perfect fit."

The big man remained focused ahead, hands at ten and two on the wheel as he drove slowly through town.

"Surprises me you'd be in with people who hurt young girls. You seem better than that. Whenever we get to where we're going, I expect my daughter to not have a single scratch on her. If she does, I don't care how big you are—I'll rip your fucking head off."

Hoby finally acknowledged him, glancing in the rearview mirror before turning back to the road.

They turned off the main drag and onto a dirt driveway that led to an old mansion. It looked like a miniature plantation home and, from what Rand could tell, was the only house in the vicinity.

"Putting the tithe money to good use, I see," Rand said.

There was no real driveway since the house was so old, so Hoby parked in the front yard and went around to yank Rand out of the backseat. The big man squeezed Rand's arm extra hard, probably for the head-ripping-off threat.

He dragged Rand across the yard and made him stand a few paces from the porch, then he released him.

"Stay," he said, his voice deep, commanding Rand like a dog.

Then the big man turned, climbed the porch steps, and disappeared inside the house, leaving Rand outside by himself.

There was not another soul in sight. He was unsupervised and could easily escape. But he refused to go anywhere without Libby.

He waited in the chilly morning for several minutes before the door opened again.

"Libby!"

"*Dad!*"

She bolted down the steps and plowed into him, throwing her arms around his neck and almost knocking him off his feet. "Oh my God, oh my God, what the hell is this place? What's going on? These people are insane!"

"Libby," Rand said. He wished his hands were free so he could hug her back. But he knew he only had seconds.

"What is this?" Libby said, noticing his bound wrists. "Why are your hands tied?"

"Libby, listen to me."

She whirled around to face Hoby. "Hey, let him go, you son of a bitch!"

"Libby, listen!"

Hoby closed the distance and seized Rand again by the arm. Hoby pulled him toward the house.

"I said let him go!" Libby struck the big man on the chest, but it didn't faze him at all.

"*Libby!* Mount Grace Church in town," Rand blurted out. He was powerless to resist Hoby's strength pulling him to the front door. "Find Pastor Simon Cole. He can help you."

"I'm not leaving you here, Dad."

"Do what I say! Find Simon Cole!"

She looked ready to cry. It was that look he'd seen before, many times—one of helpless frustration.

He tripped on the porch steps and went down. Hoby pulled him back to his feet, half dragging him up the stairs. "And Miller. Call Miller!"

"Dad—"

"I'll be fine. And remember, no police! Never the police!"

Then he was inside the mansion and Hoby slammed the heavy door shut.

ALTHOUGH IT WAS MIDMORNING, the inside of the mansion was shrouded in darkness. The windows were covered with sheets to block out the light. A musty smell dominated the air, and the lack of furniture made the main foyer look even more expansive than it was.

Hoby dragged Rand to a nearby room, one devoid of anything except for a large armchair and a fireplace. He shoved Rand to the ground and he landed hard, the wind knocked from his lungs.

"Easy," he said, rolling onto his side.

Hoby stood over Rand, studying him with a stony expression.

"She looked all right," Rand said. "Looks like I don't have to tear your fucking head off after all."

Hoby was unamused. Without a word, he turned his

back on Rand and left him there, closing the door behind him.

Rand lay there in the dim room, relief flooding over him. Libby was okay, and now she was free. She would find Simon and round up Miller and, hopefully, between the three of them, they could get him out of here.

Not that Rand was in any rush to leave. He and Deckard Arcan had unfinished business. Specifically regarding the demon he'd allowed to cause chaos in Finnick.

Deckard kept his word. No trickery, no bluffing. It was a straight exchange—Libby for himself. Honestly, that scared him. The man was confident, and he had a plan. Rand had taken the bait.

Not like I had a choice.

Luring Libby there had been the perfect trap.

He tightened his abs and crunched his way up to a sitting position, then stood. He scurried around the room, looking for something he could use to cut the zip-tie from his wrists. He was in a study or library, lined with book-shelves, but there was not a single book on them. Or anything else. There was only a plush, red armchair in front of the fireplace.

Deckard's lair sure is bleak. He wondered if this was where he received all his visions from "Azora" that he loved to brag about.

Just for the sake of completion, Rand tried to open the door. It was locked.

No problem. I can wait.

He was certain it was only a matter of time before Deckard Arcan came for him.

38

L ibby stood frozen as she watched her father dragged off by the big man into the mansion. The door slammed, leaving her alone in the front yard.

She sniffled and wiped at her eyes. She hated feeling helpless, and at that moment, she felt like there was nothing she could do.

Her first instinct was to run back to the door, pound on it until her fists were bloody, and hope someone let her in so she could rescue her dad. But he had traded places with her, and that would only be a waste of his sacrifice.

Simon Cole. Mount Grace Church.

She figured she could trust that her dad knew what he was talking about and decided to find the man he'd told her to look for.

A noise came from behind her—the sound of tires on the dirt path.

Oh no. I need to—

She looked left and right for somewhere to hide. Anyone driving up to the mansion could not be friendly.

Her dad's bright orange Jeep came into view from around the curve in the road, and she relaxed. "Who is this?" she muttered to herself.

The Jeep ambled up, and when it neared, the driver's window lowered. An elderly black man was behind the wheel.

"You must be Libby," he said. "You have Rand's eyes."

"Who are you?"

"My name is Simon Cole."

"Why do you have my dad's car?" But the thoughts darted from her mind and she jabbed her finger toward the mansion. "They took my dad inside. We have to help him."

Simon looked ahead at the house, completely calm and lacking urgency.

"Hell-o, did you hear me?"

"He traded himself for you. I figured they'd bring him here, and it looks like I was right."

"I know," Libby said. "But I don't think he realizes what kind of danger he's in. I've seen the demon. It's..." She trailed off as the thoughts of her escape attempt a few nights before came back to her. How that black creature had blocked her path, glaring at her with blood-red eyes.

"We cannot do anything for him now," Simon said. "We have to prepare before we encounter the demonic entity inside Deckard Arcan."

Libby stared at the man for a few seconds. It was something her own dad would say. "Are you a believer?"

"We can't rush in," Simon said, ignoring her question.

"We'll go to my church and I'll ready myself for the fight. Then we'll return tonight and get your dad out of there."

It was more of a plan than Libby had, so she got into the passenger seat of the car. Although, she didn't like how they would have to wait until nighttime to come back for her father. That was hours away, and anything could happen in that time.

As they drove, Simon told her how Rand had shown up at his church the week before and filled her in on all that had happened.

"In jail for three days?" Libby said, aghast. "How…"

He'd been a prisoner too, just as she had been.

"The entity possessing Deckard Arcan is very power-ful. Through him, it has influence over many people in this town, including the sheriff."

"Ugh. I don't think my dad has ever dealt with some-thing this big before."

Then Libby remembered the other part of her father's instructions to her. *Miller.* "Do you have a phone?"

Simon leaned to the side and dug into his pocket as he drove. He handed her a flip phone that must have been at least ten years old.

"Who are you calling?" Simon asked.

"One of my dad's friends," she said as she dialed Miller Landingham's number. The man was an annexed family member at that point, and she'd had his digits memorized for a while. "He should be able to help."

"Hello?" Miller answered after the fifth ring. His voice was low and suspicious. Libby figured it was because he didn't recognize the caller.

"Miller, it's Libby."

"Libby? Did you get a new phone? I almost didn't answer because I thought you were a bill collector."

"Listen, my dad's in trouble."

"When is he not?"

"He's been kidnapped and being held inside a house down here in Finnick."

"By that preacher?"

"Yes. That preacher is being controlled by a demon."

"Your dad started telling me about it the last time we spoke. Something about a perfect possession, but he couldn't give me more info."

"I can," Libby said. "I've seen it."

There was silence on the other end for a while. Even Simon looked over at her, concern filling his eyes. They turned off the main road and onto a smaller one, passing a sign that read MOUNT GRACE CHURCH.

"Tell me everything," Miller said.

"Completely black," Libby said. "Very large body, darker than a shadow, as usual. But this had... I don't know, black things that came off his head, like long hair. His eyes were red and..."

"And what?" Miller prodded.

"Fire," Libby said. "It can breathe fire, like a dragon." She remembered how the demon had threatened her as she'd tried to escape. There was no doubt in her mind that if she had persisted, she'd have been burned alive.

There was a scratching over the other end of the line—Miller writing what she told him.

"Okay. These are good details. I'll look into this and see if I find anything."

"Miller," Libby said, but the man didn't respond. He

probably knew what she was going to ask him. "Can you come?"

"Umm."

"I know, Miller, you only work behind the scenes. But this is different. I don't know if my dad will be able to get out of this one on his own. Can you please come to Finnick and help?"

There was a long silence on the other end of the phone. "Okay. I'll research what you've told me and then drive down." He sounded terrified, and Libby hated to ask him to do this, but she was out of options. She knew Miller would come for her and her dad if they were truly in trouble.

"Where are you?" he asked.

"A church called Mount Grace." Beside her, Simon nodded. They pulled up in front of the church—a dilapidated building that had seen better days. The adjacent graveyard looked like it was hundreds of years old.

"I'll look up directions online," Miller said. "Are you safe?"

"For now. I'm with the church's pastor. But my dad isn't safe, and we need to help him as quickly as possible."

"Okay. I'll see you soon, Libby."

"Thank you, Miller."

They hung up and Libby handed the phone back to Simon as they got out of the Jeep. She followed him inside the church. The old pastor walked slowly and leaned on a cane as he limped.

"I'll spend time in prayer," he said to her. "We can return to Deckard's home once your friend gets here."

Libby didn't want to say it, but she wondered how long Simon could withstand a fight with the demonic when he was already so frail. She'd heard her dad's stories about him being thrown around the room by these monsters, sustaining some terrible bangs, cuts, and bruises. How could Simon tolerate the same?

But right now, Simon Cole was the best she had.

The church was dim and warm inside, and smelled a little funky because of its age. Simon wobbled down the aisle toward the altar, overlooked by a hanging statue of Jesus on the cross.

"What should I do?" Libby asked.

"You should do the same as I am," Simon told her. "Pray. Prepare. Ask God to equip us with his blessing and protection. The monster you described is a formidable enemy. I've already seen what he can do."

With that, Simon disappeared into the back of the church, leaving her alone.

Libby chewed her lip and looked again at Jesus. She didn't pray often, but if she was ever going to, then this would be the occasion.

Please hurry, Miller. I don't think we have much time.

39

J ustin arrived at the dirt road he remembered would take him to Pastor D's mansion. He'd been there one time, early on when he had first started attending the church. It had been a special Sunday where Pastor D had invited the entire congregation to his home for the service instead of meeting at the tent.

He figured he shouldn't drive up the dirt path, since he could be spotted. So, he parked on the side of the road and went on foot, walking through the trees that lined the path.

When he came to the mansion, everything was silent and still. Not a sign of life. But Mr. Rand was somewhere inside.

Justin crept around, surveying and looking for a way in. All the windows, even the ones on the second floor, had bars over them.

He went along the side of the house and into the back-yard. There, at the edge of the woods that lined the property, he spotted something shrouded by the trees. And as he drew nearer, he got a better look.

Libby's blue Mini Cooper.

Oh my God...

It looked like someone had tried to hide it, but hadn't cared enough to put it completely out of sight.

Is she here too?

Was Libby also held captive? Was that why he hadn't heard from her in days? A newfound resolution to get inside bloomed in him.

But there seemed to be no way in besides knocking on the front door, which he knew wouldn't do any good.

On the side of the house, though, he noticed a third-floor window that did not have bars. It was the only one.

But how in the world am I going to get up there?

He used his imagination to trace a path. There was a steep, shingled roof that surrounded the window. Along the edge, an overgrown oak tree had branches that scraped against the side of the house. One of those branches looked sturdy enough to support his weight. Justin followed the oak down to its roots, noticing the strong limbs that were within reach of each other.

I can climb.

He hadn't climbed a tree since he was a kid, but that didn't stop him. Perhaps it was his desperation to get into the house that drove him. The rough bark bit into his soft palms, but he only tightened his grip and maneuvered from branch to branch, getting farther and farther away from the ground as he went.

When he reached the mansion's roof, he made the mistake of looking down. His stomach turned over when he saw the drop below him. One wrong move and he'd have a broken bone for sure.

He inched himself along the branch that extended to the roof. It bent underneath his weight and wasn't as sturdy as it had looked from the ground. Still, he pushed forward, his body and shirt scraping against the bark. He focused on keeping his balance, not wanting to lean too far to either side. Doing so might send him toppling down.

He reached out and laid his hands on the black shingles, transitioning from branch to roof as carefully as he could. He leaned into the roof's slope as he shuffled along, easing to the window.

When he made it, he peered through the glass, but it was dirty and smudged, and the room on the other side was dark. There was nothing he could see.

He tried the latch, but it wouldn't move. He pushed and pulled, but it was either stuck or locked.

I didn't come all the way up here just to go back down.

He would have to break it. But the thing was, he would have to shatter the glass in his first attempt. If he didn't, the force of bouncing off the window would send him rolling down the roof and tumbling to the ground.

The image of him sprawled in the grass, broken and bloody, came to his mind, sending waves of fear through him. Justin shook it away, though. He had to do this for Libby and her dad.

He positioned himself and drew back with his left hand, mustering all the strength he could. He clenched his teeth. *This is going to hurt.*

Then he punched forward, crashing his fist through the glass. It broke, and he snaked his arm in and grabbed hold of the other side of the window to keep himself from falling.

Cuts burned his forearm. A wetness dribbled down toward his hand. He fished around inside and found the latch, which he turned. The window opened.

He crawled into a darkened attic, a room that looked like it hadn't been used in a long time. The shards of glass crunched underneath his shoes. He tried to inspect the wounds on his arm as best he could in the dim light. Red lines ran down his skin where the glass had cut him, and the deepest one was dripping blood.

A bed and baby crib were against the wall near the window, which Justin thought was odd. There were also a few other pieces of neglected furniture. He spotted a door on the other side, and as he walked toward it, he passed a box of old bed linen. He took a pillowcase and wrapped his bloody arm as tightly as he could.

Justin reached for the doorknob, and just as he was about to touch it, someone started unlocking it from the other side.

He gasped, but reacted quickly. He dove to his left and dropped behind a dusty chest of drawers just before the door opened.

"Put her on the bed, please, Hoby." Deckard's voice.

Heavy footsteps crossed the attic. Justin braved a peek from the edge of his hiding place. Hoby carried Chloe in his arms, though she was still covered by the white sheet, and laid her down on the bed.

Deckard Arcan stood near the door, blocking Justin's only hope of leaving the attic.

They've come home, Justin thought. *And they've brought Chloe with them.*

He eyed the covered body as it rested on the bed.

"We'll leave her up here for the time being," Deckard said. "We have more urgent matters to deal with now, and I need to have a word with our *guest*." Deckard spat the word with disgust.

He must mean Mr. Rand, Justin thought.

Hoby went to the other side of the bed and adjusted the blanket to make sure Chloe's body was completely covered. Then, a piece of glass crunched underneath his shoe.

Justin's breath caught.

Hoby froze and looked down, then followed the trail of shards to the broken window.

"What is it?" Deckard asked.

"The window is broken, sir."

Oh no.

But Deckard only waved his hand. "It must have been the girl. She's clever, so of course she tried to escape."

Libby... she was here.

"Please be sure to lock this door behind you. I have a feeling Chloe will be quite restless."

Deckard left, but Hoby remained behind for a moment. He scanned the attic, and Justin dipped back down behind the chest of drawers, lungs aching from holding his breath.

If he searches, he'll find me.

Then, after what felt like ages, Hoby crossed the room, his heavy footfalls pounding on the wooden floor. Justin heard the door close and lock.

He let out his breath, feeling like a drowning man that was finally able to resurface.

Once he calmed himself, he thought about what Deckard had said.

Mr. Rand is here. Libby is also here, or was. He said she tried to escape, which meant she was held here against her will.

Justin stood and went to the attic door, just to check. Sure enough, it was locked.

He had to find a way out of there. He had to help Mr. Rand—and Libby, if she was still in the house.

Justin heard a noise behind him. Old bedsprings squeaking.

No...

Impossible. It couldn't be. Mr. Rand had interrupted the ritual.

I have a feeling she'll be quite restless, Deckard had said.

Justin slowly looked over his shoulder.

The sheet-covered body sat upright.

And then Chloe turned her head directly toward him.

40

Chloe's body struggled to stand from the bed, moving like someone who did not have full control of her limbs.

When she was finally upright, the sheet slipped off and crumpled to the floor at her feet.

Chloe's eyes were empty and unseeing. The right was rolled upward, the left looking too far to the side. Her mouth was open, frozen agape.

Deckard's ritual worked, even if no one saw it.

The woman ambled toward him.

"C-Chloe—"

Her legs were rigid, toes pointed in, which made walking difficult. Still, she managed through the rigor mortis. And as she neared, she lifted a stiff arm, as if wanting to grab him.

She lurched forward, closing the remaining distance between them faster than Justin expected.

Justin dodged to the side just in time, and the dead hand barely missed him.

Chloe's wobbly corpse crashed into the door, bumping off it. Unaffected, she turned and staggered toward Justin once again.

Justin backed away, but his shoe caught on a loose floorboard and he fell, landing hard on his back.

Chloe's unsteady gait seemed to speed up, as if she had grown even more urgent to get her hands on him.

Justin didn't know what she would do when she did. But he knew he didn't want to find out.

He sat up and shuffled across the dusty floor until he backed into a wall. Nowhere else to go.

To his side was a wooden plank propped against the wall—likely a piece left over after completing construction.

Justin stood and grabbed the wood, holding it in both his hands like a baseball bat. "Chloe. Don't come any closer."

The woman did not hear him. She came forward.

So Justin drew the plank back as best he could and swung it as if he were going for a home run. The wood struck Chloe in the side of the face, and Justin heard a sickening crack of her skull. She went down hard, hitting the ground with a thud.

She lay motionless.

Justin looked down at her body for a while, plank ready in case she got back up again. But she did not stir.

What did you do to her, Deckard? he thought. She should've been buried and laid to rest, not resurrected into some half-dead monster.

If Deckard could do that to her, Justin shuddered to think what the pastor could do to Libby and Mr. Rand.

I have to get to them.

41

Hours passed while Rand was trapped in Deckard Arcan's study. He sat in the red chair, figuring that as long as his hands were bound behind his back, he might as well be comfortable.

Libby. I hope you found Simon and that you're okay.

The lock clicked, and then the man himself entered. Deckard Arcan. He still wore the same three-piece suit from earlier.

He closed the door and sauntered over to face Rand, studying him as if he were a disgusting rodent.

"Happy Sunday," Rand said.

"I bet you are thrilled with yourself," Deckard said, voice low and sinister.

"What were you doing with my daughter? Why was she here?"

Deckard only smirked. "She came willingly. She wanted to learn the secrets of Azora and begin her new life."

"Go to hell."

Deckard waved his hand. "Forget about the girl. This was never about her. It was only about you and me and Azora."

"There is no Azora. It's a demon mimicking an angel."

"Quiet!" Deckard snapped, his face twisting. As before, Rand saw that Deckard couldn't even bear considering the idea. "You do not understand the gravity of what you have done. You have intentionally interfered with the will of Azora. The resurrection this morning was a long time coming, something that Azora has been preparing me for. And because of you, no one witnessed it."

Does that mean it worked? Did he actually bring Chloe back to life?

Rand pushed the thought away and focused. "If Azora is all powerful, he could have told you I would show up."

"You think this is funny, don't you?"

"That you kidnapped my daughter and practice necromancy to convince people to join your cult? No, Pastor D, it's not funny at all. You are in a huge amount of danger, and if you let me, I will help you."

An involuntary chuckle escaped from Deckard's mouth. It was one of astonishment, as if he couldn't believe what he'd heard. "You think you can help me? The man who dabbles with evil spirits from hell?" He inched closer. "I am the one who tried to help *you*. I revealed your sin to you to give you an opportunity to redeem yourself. And what did you do? You interfered with the blessings of Azora. First Gerald Roberson, and now Chloe!"

"How powerful is Azora if a dumbass like me can undo his miracles?"

Deckard backhanded him and Rand's vision went

black around the edges. Deckard's unnatural strength left him feeling like he'd been hit with a brick.

"Your name and face have filled my prayers and visions lately," Deckard said. "The message from Azora is clear. You are a problem and you need to be removed."

Rand eyed Deckard, waiting.

"Tonight, at midnight, I will give you to Azora."

"Give me? Will he come pick me up? What does he drive?"

Deckard narrowed his eyes. "Give you to Azora's fire."

Flames erupted in the fireplace to Rand's left, a bright burst of yellow that sent waves of heat throughout the room. The light danced on the side of Deckard's face, casting the other half in shadow.

"Nice little parlor trick," Rand said, although he knew there was no timer or trigger. The man had the powers of the demonic entity that held sway over him.

Deckard pointed a finger at Rand. It was inches from his nose. "Midnight. Azora's chosen hour. If you have anything to say or pray about, I suggest you get started."

He left Rand alone in the study, closing and locking the door.

Rand stared into the fireplace. The fire burned intensely, although there was no wood or tinder underneath it, sustained by some kind of black magic.

He had no clue how much time he had, but he knew he had to free his hands and get out of there.

At midnight, Deckard planned to burn him alive.

42

Libby was alone in the old church, growing more anxious as the time ticked by.

Simon Cole had disappeared into the back room and had not come out since. She had to trust that his process was necessary before encountering a demonic entity.

That meant Simon Cole was a believer. Her dad didn't encounter many believers, but she should've figured that if there was one in town, Rand would have found a way to meet him.

She stepped outside for some air. The afternoon had grown chilly.

I hope Dad's all right...

Although it had only been a couple of hours, it felt like much longer since they'd been separated. There was no telling what horrible things could happen to him in that house.

Libby heard tires rolling up the dirt path that led to the old church.

She recognized the yellow, beat-up pickup truck coming around the curve. He drove slowly, as if the car couldn't handle the simple off-road terrain. He was probably right—Miller had had that car since before she was born.

She went to him as he parked and got out. He wore khaki pants and a blue plaid shirt, buttoned up. He had a duffle bag over his shoulder.

"You're going to chip in some gas money for that two-hour drive, right?" Miller asked.

She threw her arms around him and hugged him tight, surprising him. "Thanks for coming. Everything is so messed up. We have to get my dad back."

"We will," he said, patting her shoulder. "We always do."

"You need to meet Simon."

As they walked back inside, Miller surveyed the old church. His eyes were magnified by the thick prescription of his glasses—Libby had tried to convince him for years to try contacts.

"Who is Simon?" Miller asked.

"The pastor here. He's fought the demonic before and he can help us."

"Thank God. Does that mean I don't have to?"

They entered the dim sanctuary. Libby was startled when she saw a figure in the shadows, but then realized it was only Simon emerging from his back room.

"I heard a car," he said.

"This is my dad's friend Miller. Miller, this is Simon."

"Libby tells me you've had... experience in these unfortunate matters." Miller said.

Simon nodded. "I've been praying and preparing all afternoon."

Miller shook the duffle bag hanging from his shoulder. "And I've brought some gear. Crucifixes, Bibles, holy water, some sage."

"Did you find out anything?" Libby asked him. "From what I told you earlier."

Miller adjusted his glasses. His skin seemed to grow paler than it already was. "I believe you are dealing with a demon named Hazul."

"You were able to discover the name?" Simon asked. "How?"

"From what Libby described to me about his appearance, and from his behavior so far. He gains the trust of humans by giving them gifts in the form of healing and strength. Even allows them to bestow those gifts on other people. Sounds like what your preacher has gotten wrapped up in."

Simon's eyes drifted to the side as he paused to think.

"But there is always a price," Miller continued. "Lifelong servitude, and any attempt to break the contract results in death."

Simon took in a deep breath. "Right. Hazul..." He spoke the name with disgust.

"It's good that we know his name," Miller said. "That will give us an advantage." He paused. "Where's this guy holding Rando?"

"Inside his mansion on the other side of town."

"And I guess that's where we're going?" Miller's whole body was tense. Simon only nodded. Miller glanced between Simon and Libby. "Who's driving?"

43

Patrick Perryman stood in the mansion's foyer, eyes on the door of Deckard's study. Randolph Casey was inside, tied up and kept prisoner, and Pastor D was in there with him—they'd been talking for a while.

How long is he planning to be in there with him?

Already Deckard had spent more time speaking with their enemy than with Patrick that day. Every minute that passed, a hot anger boiled higher within him.

He'd returned to the mansion with Pastor D, certain that he had been bluffing to Rand.

But then, when they got home, Libby was not there. Hoby had released her, true to Pastor D's word.

Patrick knew he was always supposed to have faith in the man. But for the first time in a long while, he felt that resolve slipping.

Did Pastor D ever mean to allow me to marry her? Or did he plan to use her as bait all along?

The questions tumbled through his mind, and he could not stop them. But he also could not find a rational explanation for them.

Unbridled anger had been a big stumbling block for him before he'd met Pastor D, but ever since he'd dedicated himself to the church, it had not been an issue. Now it washed over him again, a familiar and unwelcome feeling, yet one completely out of his control.

What is happening? I don't want this.

But it felt so involuntary.

Images of him pummeling Pastor D's face flashed across his mind—he quickly forced them away, embarrassed and ashamed. And afraid, because Pastor D had the uncanny ability to see into his thoughts and soul.

The door to the study opened and Pastor D emerged. When he saw Patrick standing there, Deckard regarded Patrick with a cold, blank gaze, one that he was not used to seeing. Usually, the pastor's eyes were filled with warmth when they were together.

Without a word, Pastor D turned to walk down the dark corridor to the back of the house, apparently not intending to say anything.

"Pastor D," Patrick said, his voice weak and pathetic, even to his own ears.

Deckard tensed and faced Patrick. "What is it?"

Is he angry with me? Pastor D would have a good reason to be, especially if he could sense how upset Patrick was over Libby.

"It's just… I'm confused."

"When are you not, Patrick?"

The terse reply struck him like a blow to the face.

"What are you doing?" Patrick demanded. "Why are you spending so much time with him if he's so evil? And why did you let my bride go?"

He wished he could take the words back as soon as he'd said them. Pastor D gave him a look that made him feel tiny and afraid. It was the same glare he gave Randolph Casey, and Patrick inched backward.

"You are thinking much too small," Pastor D said, walking toward him. "How is it that all you can think about is your desire for a bride when that man in there has ruined everything Azora had planned for us?"

It was the first time Patrick had ever seen Pastor D lose his composure.

"There are far more important things at stake here. Surrendering the girl to have Randolph Casey in our custody is a trade I would do over and over again, no matter how much you lust after her."

"But—"

"You need to decide how dedicated you are to the will of Azora. I told you that a bride would blur your commitment. You swore it would not, but I knew it would. You are proving me correct. Get your head on straight. Remember all I have done for you and how Azora has changed your life. Because right now you are spitting over everything that has been given to you."

But... you promised. You broke that promise and that *is why I'm upset.*

He opened his mouth to say the words out loud, but his courage failed him. Pastor D had never spoken to him like that before.

"Head up to your room and pack your things," Pastor

D said. "Tonight, at midnight, we give Randolph Casey to the fires of Azora. Then we will leave Finnick."

"Fires? You mean... b-burn him alive?"

"There is nothing left for Azora here," Pastor D said, more gently now. "We must move on and start anew someplace where evil men such as Randolph Casey won't meddle with us." He then turned his back on Patrick.

When Patrick was a boy, his father used to sever the discussion in the exact same way. The conversation was over when Dad said it was, and that was that.

Patrick had no bride. His leader was angry with him—and perhaps had never respected him in the first place. Which meant he'd only kept Patrick around to use him.

And he will burn a man alive.

Patrick agreed that Rand was evil, but did they need to do that? Wasn't there redemption and grace?

And Libby. If we do this, she'll be gone from my life forever. Maybe she already is.

The thought of never seeing her again was too much, and tears quickly sprang to his eyes. He knew from his prayers and his gut she was meant to be his for the rest of their lives.

Now all of that was ruined.

There was one last chance to get it back. Pastor D would kill Patrick if he was discovered doing what he was about to do, but Patrick would go for it anyway. Years of obedience and subservience had earned him nothing, and it was time for his reward. Pastor D always took what he wanted, so why couldn't he?

Patrick went to his room and opened one of his drawers, taking out a ring dangling with several keys. A while ago, he'd secretly made copies of each key that Pastor D used: for the house, the car, and even the study where their prisoner was now being held. It was likely Pastor D knew Patrick had the keys, but if he did, he'd never brought it up.

He took the keys downstairs and headed for the locked door. He needed to have a word with Randolph Casey.

44

Miller drove Rand's Jeep to the mansion. Simon Cole rode up front while Libby was in the back.

Simon directed him down a dirt road off the main highway. Something caught Libby's eye. "Miller, stop!"

Miller slammed on the brakes, which sent her forward since she didn't have her seatbelt on.

"What's wrong?"

Libby peered through the window at the car parked along the road. *What the hell?*

"That's Justin's car!"

"Are you sure?" Miller asked.

"Yes! He's got the cross hanging from the rearview mirror."

"What's he doing here?" Miller asked.

"I don't know," Libby said, suddenly more nervous than she had been before.

"Is he in on it with them?"

Libby chewed her lip. She didn't think so, but maybe

he'd gone off the deep end, angry at her for not accepting his truth. Was he inside with Deckard, helping to keep her dad prisoner?

"Go." She tapped Miller's shoulder. "Let's hurry."

Miller stepped on the gas and drove up the dirt road, kicking up a cloud of dust behind them.

The mansion came into view ahead of them. The sight of it made Libby sick all over again. It felt like madness having escaped there only to come back. But this time, she had her team.

There were no lights coming from inside, and it seemed as if no one was home. But Libby knew better.

They parked and Miller crossed himself before leaving the car.

Simon said to Libby, "You should stay here and keep the car running. We may need to flee after we get your dad back. You should be ready."

"Getaway driver, huh? I can do that."

Simon climbed out of the car and Libby shuffled over the center console to sit behind the wheel.

"Hey," she said through the rolled-down window, and Simon looked at her. "Be careful. But please kick that guy's ass." He smirked.

Simon and Miller strode toward the mansion. One man was squat and overweight, the other elderly and limping. She would've thought that, by now, if her dad planned to keep engaging in life-threatening supernatural battles, he would've assembled a real team rather than a rag-tag band of misfits.

"Good evening, Simon," boomed a voice from above.

The columns on the front porch supported a balcony

on the second floor, and Deckard Arcan stood on it, looking down at them.

"Your friend Randolph has agreed to accept the will of Azora," Deckard continued. "You need to leave."

"We are not leaving without him."

Simon's voice boomed assertively. Libby reconsidered what she'd thought earlier. *Maybe these two aren't the misfits I thought they were...*

"You and your friends have caused me enough trouble already," Deckard said. "I'm finishing it tonight. I do not want to hurt you, but if you insist on pushing me, I will have no choice. Azora does not stand for being disobeyed."

"We aren't going anywhere," Simon shot back. "Let us in and we can talk about this."

"You know the time for talking is over," Deckard said.

"Come on, dudes," Libby whispered to herself. "All this rambling is useless."

Libby pushed her back against the seat and closed her eyes. She felt her heart pounding, and her breaths came in short gasps. "Come on, Dad," she whispered. "You can do it."

45

R and heard someone inserting a key in the study's lock.

Is it midnight already? No way...

But it wasn't Deckard Arcan who entered the room. It was Patrick Perryman.

The slight man closed the door behind him and walked over to the armchair where Rand sat.

He didn't lock the door, Rand realized.

He couldn't attempt an escape when Deckard opened the door earlier—the preacher was too strong. But Patrick was a different story...

The look on Patrick's face frightened him. It was a mix of desperation, fear, and uncertainty.

When he'd met the man on campus, he'd seemed nice enough, if a little in the clouds. Now Rand had to wonder just how deep into Deckard's dogma Patrick was.

Rand was just about to spring from the chair and make a break for the unlocked door when Patrick spoke.

"Why did you do that?" Patrick asked.

"Do what?"

"Ruin the miracle."

Rand licked his lips. "Do you believe resurrecting a dead person is a good thing?"

"Of course. It was the will of Azora finally coming to fruition. We have been waiting for this day for a long time."

"We? Do you mean you and Deckard? Or is it just Deckard? Because you sound a lot like him. Do you actually agree so strongly with him?"

"He has demonstrated his abilities over and over again."

"Has he?"

Patrick was silent. The way he spoke so far, Rand knew what was going on. The man's faith was fragile. He was doubting the things he had seen. Wondering how much of what he had experienced was true or just smoke and mirrors.

Rand had been through similar crises himself. Maybe that's why he recognized what was happening to Patrick in that moment.

Even with his hands tied, Rand knew he could overtake Patrick if the small man tried to stop him from escaping.

The unnatural fire that roared in the hearth had driven the heat in the room far past bearable levels. Rand was sweating through his clothes, and now Patrick's face was dripping.

"Libby was meant to be my bride."

He said it so resolutely, a statement of fact. The flames danced in the reflection of his glasses.

"What was that?" Rand asked, although he knew he'd

heard correctly. Anger flared within him.

"Azora told me in my prayers that she was supposed to be my wife. Pastor D was to marry us soon. Azora led her here to be with me."

So you were the one who lured her here. Sick bastard.

"Pastor D let her go. Traded her so he could have you. He should not have done that. After everything, I deserve her!"

That was too much. Rand leapt from the chair and head-butted Patrick in the face.

He yelped and collapsed immediately, glasses broken. His hands went to his broken nose, blood running through his fingers.

Rand gave him a swift kick in the stomach, which caused Patrick to cry out even more.

"I'd love to rough you up more, you little freak," Rand said, "but I have to deal with your preacher."

Rand went to the door and used his bound hands to open it, then entered the mansion's foyer. The cool air was a refreshing blast on his slick skin.

Patrick still rolled around on the floor behind him. Rand thought he heard the man crying.

I'm free, but I can't do anything here on my own, or with my hands tied.

The front door was to his left. He had to leave and reunite with Simon, and then return later.

But when Rand managed to get the door open, he saw Simon Cole and Miller Landingham standing in the mansion's yard. His Jeep was behind them, Libby in the driver's seat.

Libby's done it.

Simon and Miller spotted him at the same time.

"There he is!" Miller cried.

Miller jogged across to him as best as his pudgy body would allow. Simon Cole followed, wobbling with his cane.

"Deckard's upstairs," Simon said, once inside.

Miller patted the duffle bag that dangled over his shoulder. "I've brought supplies. Are you ready, Rando?"

Rand turned and showed Miller his bound wrists. "Can you help me out?"

"Oh." Miller dug into his khakis and pulled out a pocketknife. A moment later, the zip-tie fell away.

Miller dropped the duffle bag and unzipped it. Inside, Rand saw all the gear he'd need. "Will Libby be all right out there?"

"She's ready with the Jeep so we can make a quick escape," Miller told him.

Rand would've preferred her to be farther away, but he supposed a getaway driver was a useful thing to have.

"I've had just about enough of you."

Rand followed the voice. The staircase went up from the foyer and split off to the right and left. On the right side, Deckard Arcan glared down at them.

Patrick Perryman stumbled out from the study, holding his bleeding face. Deckard's eyes immediately snapped over to him.

"Patrick! You let him go!"

"No!" His voice was distorted from his injury.

"Of all people, *you* were the one who betrayed me."

"It wasn't me!"

"After everything I've done for you. How could you?"

Patrick started sobbing, seemingly growing smaller and smaller under Deckard's anger. Finally, when it was too much, he bolted. Rand watched as Patrick fled down the darkened corridor and toward the back of the house.

Deckard turned his attention back to Rand.

This is it, Rand thought. *Face to face again. A rematch. I won't go down easily this time.*

46

The chest of drawers was heavy, but once Justin got it sliding along the dusty floor, he was able to keep up the momentum.

He pushed the heavy furniture to the door that—although locked—seemed quite weak. Like a battering ram, it slammed into the door and the wood splintered. Justin fell atop the chest, waist driving painfully into the edge. A loud crash echoed through the attic.

I hope no one heard that, Justin thought as he rubbed his burning hip bones.

Regardless, he had to get out of that locked attic. He couldn't do anything if he was trapped inside, and spending more time with Chloe's corpse didn't appeal to him.

Justin pulled back the drawers and inspected his demolition work. He'd damaged the locked door pretty well.

He gave it a few solid kicks, and the wood around the

latch splintered and cracked, allowing the door to fly open.

There was a narrow hallway beyond, and on the other end of it, a flight of stairs that led him down.

Justin crept slowly, keeping an ear tuned for anyone approaching. Despite all the noise he'd made, it seemed he had gone unnoticed—for now.

Okay. Mr. Rand is in here somewhere. Maybe Libby too. I've got to find him.

Below the stairs was the mansion's second or third floor—Justin couldn't be sure. There was a hallway of rooms ahead of him, and he busied himself with checking each one.

Curiously, each room was empty, devoid of any furniture. He worked his way along, door by door, until he arrived at another set of stairs.

Then he heard a commotion from downstairs. And voices.

Justin crept to the staircase bannister and looked over.

From where he stood, he could see down to the first floor of the mansion. Justin was apparently on the third.

Mr. Rand was down there with two other men that Justin didn't recognize.

"DECKARD, please. We are only here to help you," Simon said.

"No! You are only here to defy Azora." Deckard spat back.

"Rand!" Miller shouted. "Behind you!"

Rand turned just in time to see Hoby charging at him.

The big man brought his fist back and swung, but Rand ducked out of the way.

Hoby rounded on him again. His chest and shoulders bulged in his tight t-shirt. His fists were clenched, popping the veins in his forearms.

Hoby grabbed Rand from behind, massive arms like a vise. Rand struggled and gasped as Hoby squeezed him tighter, like a boa constrictor, forcing the air out of his lungs.

"Nice work, Hoby," Deckard said. "Now tie him up again and we'll prepare to give him to Azora. I'll deal with these other two in the meantime."

Simon and Miller stood tense as they watched Rand struggle against Hoby's hold.

"Little help?" Rand barely managed the words through his breathlessness.

Simon yanked one of the crosses from Miller's bag and thrust it toward Deckard. "Hazul, in the name of the Lord, I command you to show yourself!"

Deckard recoiled from the cross as if struck by an invisible bullet.

Simon sure has priorities, Rand thought. He could no longer feel his arms.

"Hazul!" Simon shouted, voice loud and firm. "Leave the body of this man and show yourself!"

Deckard cried out. He clawed at his body like his insides were burning. Then his eyes glowed red, just as they had the first time Rand had fought with him. He lifted his head, opened his mouth, and vomited out a black, amorphous cloud. It streamed from his throat, Deckard screaming as the entity separated itself from him.

The dark cloud drifted to the top of the stairs. It hung there, then took shape. The arms and legs formed, then the body, and finally the head, punctuated by two blood-red eyes. Tendrils of black sprouted from the back of his head, resembling hair. He leaned on his front hands, like a silverback gorilla.

Rand felt himself released from Hoby's grip. His knees buckled and he fell to the side, landing hard on his hip. He quickly sucked in as much air as he could.

That's one way to free me, Rand thought as Hoby fled from the creature that had appeared. The large man burst through the door and was gone without looking back.

Miller rushed over to his side. "That's him, Rand. His name's Hazul."

"I'm fine, Miller, thanks." Rand pushed himself into a sitting position, arms and back still aching.

Hazul leapt from the top of the stairs and landed a few feet from Rand and Miller. Miller yelped and scurried away. Hazul kept his red, burning red eyes on Rand.

This one moves quick.

Rand shuffled away while trying to get back onto his feet.

"Hazul!" Simon was behind the demon, arm outstretched, gripping the cross. "In the name of—"

Hazul pivoted and swiped his shadowy arm, striking Simon in the chest, battering him backwards. His cane and cross spiraled across the room and he landed hard in a heap.

Rand scrambled around Hazul while the demon was distracted. The duffel bag lay on the floor.

Rand dug inside and pulled out the first things he grabbed—a cross and a bottle of holy water.

The hairs on his neck rose. He felt those red eyes on him.

"Rand!" Miller shouted. "Watch out!"

Behind Rand, Hazul's mouth gaped open, a black hole, and in the back of his throat a ball of fire formed. The heat blasted into Rand's face as if he were looking into a crater to the center of the earth.

The fires of Azora, Deckard had said.

Rand dodged out of the way just in time. A stream of fire erupted from Hazul's mouth like a flamethrower, engulfing the entire area where he'd been a moment before. The fire consumed the duffle bag, burning the crosses, the sage, and the Bibles.

All of their supplies were gone, except for what Rand held in his hand.

The flames, hot and powerful, spread throughout the room, filling it with unbearable heat.

Hazul rounded on Rand again, red eyes following him like magnets.

But Rand had his weapons now. He could finally fight back.

Rand raised the cross between them like a shield.

And then Hazul began to grow. His black body expanded—eight, maybe nine feet tall.

Rand craned his neck to look up, becoming smaller and more pathetic in Hazul's presence.

Oh, no...

A demon's power was relative to his size. Rand should have guessed Hazul had been hiding his true form—only an extremely powerful entity would be capable of perfect possession.

Rand's outstretched hand lowered against his will, as if

Hazul's dark presence pushed it down. The cross he gripped seemed so small and weak now.

This is too much, Rand thought. He'd underestimated his foe.

Behind Hazul, Miller had helped Simon to his feet and was inching him toward the exit.

Good, Rand thought. *You two get out while you still can.*

Your God has willed for you to die tonight. The voice was in his head, sharp and dark—Hazul communicating with him directly telepathically.

"No," Rand said, although he doubted.

You are God's plaything. A sacrifice. You think you are a fighting man, but your life is a joke to him.

The flames licked at the ceiling, growing wild and out of control. Smoke billowed throughout the room now, making it hard for Rand to breathe. He'd have to escape from the mansion soon.

But Hazul was not going to get out of his way, and had grown too large to simply run from.

Rand tried to ignore what Hazul said to him, but in his own heart, he felt the truth of it. He'd prepared for so long with Simon, and God had still been silent.

Miller and Simon made it to the door and stumbled through it. At least they would survive the fight.

Hazul opened his mouth again, the ball of fire forming once more.

Rand knew it was impossible to command demons when his faith was so low. But that didn't mean he had to stand there and be burned alive.

If not for God, then for everyone else, Rand thought, tightening his sweaty palm on the cross in his hand. *Libby. Miller. My future clients. They all need me.* He thought of Georgia and those he'd helped in the past, who all would have been so much worse off if he had given up on them.

Just because he felt God had abandoned him didn't mean he had to abandon himself.

The cross, Rand realized, looking down at what he held in his hand. Although it was small compared to Hazul, it still contained power.

Hazul had immediately left Deckard's body when Simon had used it to command him.

Deckard had slapped it out of Rand's hand the first time they'd fought.

At Gerald's house, Hazul had quickly fled, seeming terrified of it.

As powerful as Hazul was, he truly feared the symbol of the Lord.

Rand couldn't go around Hazul, so instead, he went under. Just before the torrent of flame swept over him, Rand charged, sprinting between Hazul's two arms that he leaned on. The demon's gorilla-like body had grown large enough that Rand could fit underneath it.

He thrust the cross over his head, and as soon as it touched Hazul, the demon let out an ear-splitting roar.

Rand dragged the top of the cross along Hazul's belly, a white line appearing where it traced, like a sword cutting into flesh.

He rolled through Hazul's legs just before the demon collapsed. Hazul shrieked in pain from the touch of the holy object.

Rand got back onto his feet and removed the top from the bottle of holy water he clutched in his other hand.

Hazul was trying to stand again, but Rand did not give

him the chance. He threw the water, a wide trail of liquid, and it burned Hazul like acid.

As the demon screamed in pain, his body began to dematerialize. The black form shrank, and then folded in on itself. Then it became a pillar of black smoke which sucked into the floor and vanished. Fleeing back to hell.

With lungs filling with smoke and unbearable heat nearly cooking him alive, Rand headed for the door to follow Miller and Simon back to freedom.

Sharp, blunt pain took him in the base of the skull. His vision blurred, and he stumbled and hit the floor.

His hand went to where he'd been hit. Warm blood met his fingers.

Rand rolled over onto his back. Deckard Arcan stood above him, pointing the barrel of his own gun at him.

47

Deckard was partly obscured by the billowing smoke.

Rand started to cough and the pain in the back of his skull throbbed. The only thing he could think of was getting out of the house before it came crashing down around him.

He started to drag himself away from Deckard.

"I said I'd give you to the fires of Azora, and I will," Deckard said.

"We need to get out." It took all of Rand's breath to speak. Hazul no longer possessed the man, so Deckard was as vulnerable to the fire as Rand was—whether he realized it or not.

"We are not going anywhere."

Rand's strength gave out, and he found he could not even slide away anymore. A coughing fit overtook him, the smoke burned his eyes, and the mansion had become an oven around him.

"In the name of Azora, I offer this sacrifice," Deckard intoned. "A sinner delivered to the fires of the angel."

No, Rand tried to call out, to plead, but there were no words left in his dry throat.

Movement out of the corner of Rand's eye. Someone else was there.

Who—

Deckard was too focused on Rand to notice. "May your blessings return to us as we give this evil man—"

Then Rand recognized him.

Justin Tidwell burst through a cloud of smoke, Simon Cole's discarded cane raised above his head. He brought it down—hard—on Deckard's outstretched arm, directly onto the elbow.

A shot fired, zipping to Rand's right and barely missing him. The gun dropped and Deckard went down, grabbing the crook of his arm.

Then someone tried to scoop Rand up from underneath his arms.

"I gotcha," Miller said. He tried to lift Rand, but he was too heavy.

Justin rushed to Miller's side and assisted the shorter man. Rand leaned on the strength of the two, nearly dead weight, as he was dragged from the burning mansion.

Rand coughed and sucked in the clean, cool air. The chills spiked his sweaty skin, and the relief from the heat made him feel as if he'd been delivered straight from hell.

"Dad!" He heard Libby's voice, but couldn't see through his watery vision. He felt her hands on his chest.

Rand's lungs burned, but he finally managed to stop coughing. He swiped at his teary eyes. Libby and Miller crouched down beside him, and Simon and Justin stood over Miller's shoulder.

"You all right, Rando?" Miller asked. "The preacher shot at you. Did he get you?"

I don't think so. Rand still didn't have the strength to speak.

"What the hell were you doing in there?" Libby rounded on Justin.

"Deckard's still inside," Simon said. "We need to—"

There was a loud crack and a crash—the roof of the mansion gave way and collapsed in on itself. Sparks and smoke rose high into the sky, lighting up the night.

The fires of Azora, Rand thought. *Seems suitable for you, Deckard.*

In a few more minutes, the entire mansion would be a pile of ashes.

Once Rand managed to get his breath back, he sat up. Everyone surrounded him now—Libby, Miller, Simon, and Justin. If any one of them hadn't come to his aid that night, he would not have survived.

Rand held out his hand. Miller clasped it and Rand pulled against him to get back to his feet. A wave of light-headedness came over him, but it passed after a momentary pause.

"Happy Sunday, y'all," Rand said. "Let's get out of here."

48

O'Conner's was the only cigar bar in the city, and Rand went there with his buddies about twice a year. The bill he racked up in the joint was always substantial, so he tried to limit himself.

It didn't surprise him, though, to learn that Charles Tidwell, Justin's father, frequented it at least once a week. When Rand had called Charles, he told Rand to come.

Inside, the sweet smell of cigars and oak blanketed him, and his mind began trying to convince him to pick out a nice cigar.

The lounge was small and intimate, with dim lighting and dark furniture. A group of three men in suits were lounging and smoking and sipping whiskey. Charles was among them, and when Rand walked in, Charles excused himself from his friends and went over to him.

"It was good to finally hear from you when you called. You had me worried."

"I've been hearing that a lot today," Rand said, thinking back to all he'd endured.

"What'd they say at the college?"

Rand had just come from there. He'd had a meeting with the dean. "The dean's a friend. I helped him out with a haunting before. That's how I got the job, actually. But a week was a bit too long, and it forced his hand. I'm on probation for a while."

Charles winced. "Sorry to hear that. I feel like it's my fault. I put you up to his, after all."

"Don't feel that way. Everything will be fine."

"Still." Charles took a drag on his cigar. "Can I get you a drink? As a token of gratitude."

"No, thank you."

"Really? Then why did you want to meet me here? I figured O'Conner's would be your kind of place."

"It is," Rand said. "I love it. But I only wanted to tell you that everything is done. You have nothing to worry about anymore."

Charles Tidwell scratched at his chin, cigar between his fingers, a trail of smoke drifting from the tip. His brow furrowed, and Rand knew he had something to say, or perhaps ask. He could already guess what it was.

"I've seen the news sites," he said, voice low. He glanced at the nearby bar. The young girl behind it was busy mixing a drink for one of Charles's friends. "About the fire. They're saying it was an accident. Maybe a suicide. Do I even want to know what happened down there?"

"No, you don't."

"Were you there?"

"It was almost me inside that burning house."

Charles winced. "And Justin? He got home very late that night, and wouldn't say where he'd been…"

"He was with me," Rand said. "Let's just say you should be very proud of your son."

That seemed to give Charles some comfort. A hint of a smile formed on his face.

But it was gone the next instant when something behind Rand caught Charles's eye. "Oh my God." Rand followed his gaze.

Justin Tidwell had come in and looked completely different. His long, disheveled hair was cut short and neatly styled to the side. His dark and baggy clothes had been replaced with well-fitted khakis and a tucked-in collared shirt.

"What do you think?" Justin asked his dad.

It took Charles a few moments to find his words. "Very nice and refined. Why did you..." He caught himself, probably thinking it was better to not even ask. "What are you doing here?"

"Mom said you were here." Then he acknowledged Rand for the first time. "Hey, Mr. Rand."

"Is everything all right?" Charles asked.

"Yeah. Just... wanted to hang out, is all. If that's okay with you." Justin looked down at the ground, embarrassed. "Maybe try a cigar. They're not supposed to let me in here, but I know you're friends with the owner, and—"

"We're sitting over there, son," Charles said, pointing to the corner of the lounge. "Of course you're welcome to join us." Now he had a full-blown smile on his face.

"I'll leave you to it," Rand said. "I hope y'all have a good evening."

"Oh, you're not staying?" Justin asked.

That surprised Rand. Despite everything they'd been

through, Rand never figured they'd be friends. "O'Conner's just isn't in the budget this month."

"And he refuses to accept a gift," Charles added.

"Can I talk to you before you go, Mr. Rand?" Justin asked.

"Sure," Rand said.

Charles nodded and returned to his friends to give the two of them some privacy.

"I wanted to thank you again," Justin said. "For showing me the truth of everything."

"I should be saying that to you," Rand told him. "Without you, I would be dead."

"I feel so dumb. How could I have bought into all that?"

"He was a convincing man. Don't beat yourself up too much."

But Justin didn't seem comforted. Rand was looking at a different kid, one who looked a bit older than he had the week before, a little wiser after going through what he had.

"What will you do now?" Rand asked. "Find another church?"

Justin shook his head. "I'm done with all that."

"Really?"

"I think my dad was right all along. Maybe it's best to invest in ourselves rather than wait for a make-believe guy in the sky to fix us."

Rand nodded. It was the reaction he would've expected anyone to have after learning the truth about Deckard Arcan.

"What about you?" Justin asked.

It was such a simple question, but for Rand, it ran deep.

"I'm still struggling with own my faith. Hopefully I'll find it one day."

Besides the demons and kidnappings and life-threatening situations, the most difficult aspect of the past week, for Rand, was the hollow sensation in his heart—a place where God should have been, but wasn't.

"I hope you do," Justin said.

"Go be with your dad," Rand told him. "He's missed you."

Justin nodded and started walking away, but stopped. "Oh, you won't be seeing me around anymore."

"What do you mean?"

"Just talk to Libby. I'm sure she'll tell you."

Justin joined his father and his friends. When he sat among them, he seemed to fit right in.

Rand frowned. For the first time over the past several months, he would've been okay with Justin dating his daughter. But he would be silly to expect a high school relationship to endure past what both Justin and Libby had been through.

He took one last deep breath of the sweet cigar smell and left O'Conner's.

"It is my prayer that we never forget Jesus Christ is the one true savior of mankind."

Rand had always known Simon Cole's voice was surprisingly strong for an elderly guy, but it was twice as powerful when he was preaching.

It was Sunday morning, and Rand and Libby sat in the pew closest to the door. They were squeezed in together —the sanctuary was crowded, and there were even a few people standing in the back of the room.

Rand wasn't surprised by the turnout. It was the first Sunday that Deckard Arcan's church was not available.

"The enemy will send many pretenders," Simon continued, making eye contact with everyone in his congregation. "Because it is the enemy's prerogative to deceive. But always remember: there is only one savior, and that is Jesus Christ. Only through him can we find redemption. No other is worth our devotion and praise."

When the sermon ended, Simon Cole stood outside the doors of the sanctuary and shook hands with every member of the congregation who filed out of his church. Rand lingered nearby and watched. It was a chilly morning even though the sun was shining. The storms had passed.

"He's great," Libby said.

"You coming back next week?"

"Eh. It's a long drive, don't you think?"

A man shook hands with Simon, and then buttoned his suit coat as he walked. He caught Rand's eye, and the two looked at each other for a few lingering moments. Rand recognized Sheriff Jones, who looked quite different out of uniform. Rand's stomach flopped with sudden nerves.

Jones only gave a short nod, expressionless, and turned his attention away.

I guess he knows now who the real enemy was.

After the congregation had dispersed, Simon made his way over to Rand.

"Good morning," Simon said. "I was glad to spot you in the back when I started my sermon."

"Wouldn't miss it," Rand said. "How are you?"

Simon had taken quite a wallop from Hazul. He'd already walked with a limp and cane, but now his gait was even slower and more lopsided than it had been before.

"I'll recover," he said, smiling. "The pain comes with the territory."

"I suppose." Rand remembered all the times in the past he'd been beaten, bruised, and knocked out by demonic entities.

"How's the town?" Rand asked. "Ever since…"

"This was the largest attendance I've seen in my church in years," Simon said. "Most of them are from Deckard's. They're seeking answers. They want to know what they saw that day with Chloe. And they want the truth about the man."

"Sounds like you have your work cut out for you."

Simon smirked. "And what about you, Rand? How are you?"

"Little banged up. In a bit of trouble at the university for missing a bunch of classes, but it could have been a lot worse."

"No," Simon said. "I asked how *you* are." He gave Rand a soft look.

Rand swallowed. He remembered Justin. And Georgia Collins. And all the people he'd helped in the past, all those who had nowhere else to turn, except toward him. He wondered how long he could take on all the burdens of others before he was finally crushed underneath it.

"I'll always be here if you need encouragement," Simon

said. "It's not an easy job. But you are clearly the one chosen for it."

"I wish there was a little more encouragement from God himself," Rand said.

"God must really trust you if he stays out of your way."

Rand smiled.

"I hope you join us here on Sundays in the future. Oh, and bring your friend, Miller. A bit of an oddball, but I like him."

———

ONCE THEY WERE on the road and heading back home, Libby reached over and put her hand on his arm. "I'm proud of you, Dad. Thanks for everything you do."

"Even if you get caught up in it?"

"I can take care of myself."

"I wish your mother felt the same."

"Now that everyone's okay, she'll get over it. Eventually."

Rand smiled. He knew that no matter how dark the road ahead, as long as he had family and good people with him by his side, he would get through it all.

———

Randolph Casey returns in The Black-Eyed Kids, the **third book** in the Randolph Casey Horror Thriller series. Visit Rockwell Scott's website to learn more and read a free sample.

www.rockwellscott.com/books

HEY THERE.

Thank you for spending your valuable time reading my book, and I hope you enjoyed it.

As you may know, reviews are one of the best ways readers can support their favorite authors. They help get the word out and convince potential readers to take a chance on me.

I would like to ask that you consider leaving a review wherever you purchased this book. I would be very grateful, and of course, it is always valuable to me to hear what my readers think of my work.

Thank you in advance to everyone who chooses to do so, and I hope to see you back in my pages soon.

Sincerely,

- Rockwell

ALSO BY ROCKWELL SCOTT

A Haunting in Rose Grove

A malevolent entity. A violent haunting. A house with a bloody history. Jake Nolan left it all behind, but now he must return.

Jake has it all — a new home, an amazing girlfriend, and nearing a promotion at work. Best of all, he feels he's finally moved on from the horrors of his traumatic past. But when he learns that his estranged brother, Trevor, has moved back into their haunted childhood home, Jake knows his past is not quite finished with him yet.

Jake rushes to the old house in Rose Grove — a small town with a tragic history — to pull his brother from that dangerous place.

But it's too late. There, he finds Trevor trying to make contact with the spirit that tormented them years ago.

And Trevor refuses to leave. He is determined to cleanse the house and remove the entity. But the supernatural activity becomes too much to handle, and Jake knows they are both unprepared for the fight. Worse, the entity targets Daniel, Jake's young nephew, and wants to bring him harm. And when the intelligent haunting shows signs of demonic infestation, Jake realizes they aren't dealing with a mere ghost.

Jake attributes the evil spirit for driving his parents to an early grave. Now it wants to claim the rest of the family, and the only way Jake and Trevor will survive is to send the entity back to hell.

A Haunting in Rose Grove is a supernatural horror novel for readers who love stories about haunted houses and battles with the demonic — the truest form of evil that exists in our world.

ALSO BY ROCKWELL SCOTT

The Gravewatcher

Every night at 3 AM, he visits the graveyard and speaks to someone who isn't there.

Eleanor has created an ideal life for herself in New York City with a career that keeps her too busy, just as she likes it. But when she receives an anonymous message that her estranged brother Dennis is dead, her fast-paced routine grinds to a halt. She rushes to Finnick, Louisiana — the small, backward town where her brother lived and temporarily settles into his creepy, turn-of-the-century house until she can figure out how he died.

But that night, Eleanor spots a young boy in the cemetery behind Dennis's house, speaking to the gravestones. When she approaches him, Eleanor's interruption of the boy's ritual sets off a chain reaction of horror she could have never prepared for. The footsteps, the voices, and the shadowy apparitions are only the beginning.

Eleanor learns that the boy, Walter, is being oppressed by a demonic entity that compels him to visit the graveyard every night. She suspects Dennis also discovered this nightly ritual and tried to stop it, and that is why he died. Because there are others in Finnick who know about Walter's involvement with the evil spirit and want it to continue, and they will do whatever it takes to stop Eleanor from ruining their carefully laid plans. Now Eleanor must finish what her brother started — to rescue the boy from the clutches of hell before he loses his soul forever.

The Gravewatcher is a supernatural horror novel for readers who love stories about haunted houses, creepy graveyards, and battles with the demonic - the truest form of evil that exists in our world.

ABOUT THE AUTHOR

Rockwell Scott is an author of supernatural horror fiction.

When not writing, he can be found working out, enjoying beer and whiskey with friends, and traveling internationally.

Feel free to get in touch!

Instagram
https://www.instagram.com/rockwellscottauthor/

Facebook
www.facebook.com/rockwellscottauthor

Twitter
@rockwell_scott

www.rockwellscott.com

rockwellscottauthor@gmail.com

Printed in Great Britain
by Amazon

56178379R00179